WHERE SE

LAND

This is the story of a young man's journey from the flatlands of Cambridgeshire to the New World. His life onboard the Neptune presented him with situations he had never known before. His life in the confines of a vessel carrying a cargo of goods and people opened his eyes to the differences that existed between those that have and those that don't.

Michael Cartwright lives in Boston, Lincolnshire with his wife. He has three children and two grandchildren. He has three passions in life: family, seventeenth centurty history and rugby union (watching not playing). He has a Bachelor of Arts degree in Heritage Studies and a Masters Degree in History. He is now retired and enjoys seeing his words appear on paper.

Where Seagulls Land

M D Cartwright

Published by M D Cartwright

This book is produced entirely in the UK, is available to order from most bookshops in the United Kingdom, and is globally available via UK based internet book retailers.

ISBN: 978-1-7398309-3-9

Dedication

To Oma who is sorely missed and to my children
Rachael, Victoria and Dominick

With continuing thanks to Brian Skinner and
Anna together with Bertie who have made this
journey a little easier.

To: SHIRLEY

With Love and Wishes

Michaels other books are:

The Yeomans Challenge, published by amazon.co.uk

ISBN: 979-8-5588133-8-8

Sleep Easy Brother, published by M D Cartwright in conjunction with WRITERSWORLD.

ISBN: 978-1-7398309-1-5

The Torment of Jamie Dower, published by M D Cartwright

ISBN: 978-1-7398309-2-2

Chapter 1

The journey had been hard and it was only the beginning. William Brook slid from the saddle of his horse and reached to get his saddle bags, he looked at his two travelling companions, they had covered many more miles than he had and did not seem to suffer from the aches and pains that he felt in his legs and back. The tallest of them called out,

'Come on young William this will be our last night on the road, tomorrow the city of Bristol will be our resting place before our journey really begins.' Alec's voice was one that held confidence and inspired those who listened to him.

The three men did not differ greatly in size, The tallest, the one who addressed William, stood almost six feet and was at least three or four inches above William and no more than an inch above the third man in the party.

'What say you, Robert?'

The third man turned as he tugged his bag from his horses back,

'Aye, we have a long way to go and it will not be as easy as travelling from Cambridge to Bristol.' It was the voice of a man who had seen the worst and best of life. Both the men had been friends of William's father during the turbulent times of the war of the three kingdoms, that was over and their lives had been turned around after misfortune and a great deal of misery.

William thought of the journey they had completed, the roads had not been that kind to them, their horses had been pushed to keep a steady pace and where they had slept had been enough to give them a night's sleep but comfort had been lacking. William had seen many sights for the first time, in his seventeen years he had not ventured far from his parent's farm. It had been his decision to seek a new life and adventure with the two men who he now followed.

The year was 1670, King Charles II was on the throne and the civil war that had ravaged the kingdom was over. The country seemed to have taken a breath and let out a sigh of relief as many of the restrictions imposed by the puritan parliament were lifted. William had no problem in getting permission to travel not just to Bristol but to venture across the ocean, he was full of expectation and excitement.

After making themselves known to the inn keeper they settled their horses for the night. The three horses they rode and the one pulling the baggage cart had done them proud and needed rest and food, as they did. They would eat then prepare themselves for the following day then sleep. William had heard the two men pray before they eventually slept which he found comforting in a way he had never felt before. After their meal Alec and Robert purchased a pipe each and sat in front of the fire which warmed the main room of the inn. Alec drew a breath of tobacco smoke and sighed, he would be with his family in no longer than eight weeks if all went well.

'I think we need to explain to William what he may expect to encounter on the voyage.' Alec looked at Robert and they both knew that what William was about to enter into would probably stay with him for the rest of his life. Alec got a little more comfortable in his seat. 'William when we set sail things may not be as pleasant as you are imagining at the moment. The voyage will be long and you may see things that will shock you. You must at all cost do as you are told, by the crew or by us, is that clear?'

Alec had not spoken to William in such a serious tone before which captured Williams full attention. 'There are many things that may prove very distasteful to your upbringing. There will be times

3

when the crew will do things, necessary things that you will find difficult to handle, you must, as I have said, do as you are told. William could not imagine what sort of things Alec was referring to and the look of innocence on his face made Robert reinforce what Alec had said.

'Life at sea is one of confinement, we will be living in each other's pockets, there will be times when hunger becomes a problem and thirst will cause many an argument. Disease will be a fact of life and death, Robert stressed his last words, again William felt uneasy with what he was being told. Alec then said,

'It is not too late for you to change your mind, I am sure that you could find your way back to Cambridge and I know that your family would welcome you back with open arms.'

William pondered on what he had been told, he tried to imagine what life would be like on board a ship, however, his excitement and hopes for the future washed out any doubts the two men may have created in his mind. 'I am prepared to obey any commands given and as for the things you have just told me I shall do my best to take hold of any distress that comes my way and deal with it.'

Alec and Robert looked at each other knowing that the boy could not visualise what lay before him and that it would take a great deal of guidance on their part to get William through the possible eight weeks at sea.

The morning sun shone through the early mist as the three men saddled their mounts and made the cart ready to go. They had a short distance to travel, as they drew closer to the City of Bristol William could see the houses multiplying on either side of the streets they ventured down. It was the smell that overcame his senses first, it was a sweet, sickly aroma of bodies mixed with the open drains he could see running down the centre of the passageways. William looked up at the houses they passed, the upper floors seem to hang over the edge of the street, it was Robert who cautioned him to be aware of any open windows as he may receive more than he bargained for if the contents of a chamber pot were thrown out by the occupant. William raised his eyes to the nearest window hoping that it would stay closed until he had passed.

It had taken them little time to reach the centre of Bristol but they were yet to get to the docks where Alec and Robert needed to conclude some business affairs with their agents. Alec reined his horse in and turned towards William,

'Robert will leave us soon as he needs to speak to agents dealing with our tobacco, and I will head for the docks and try to locate our ship, or at least where

5

it is due to birth. We may need to get rowed out or it is possible that the ship may be laid up if the tide is low. That means we will have to either wait or try to scramble aboard, I suggest we wait. It may be worth your while to come with me William to get a feel of the port and its sights and sounds. What do you think?'

Alec and Robert arranged to meet at the inn they had stayed in on their arrival from Virginia, it was clean and served decent food, it would only be for one night but they had agreed that they might as well try to get a little comfort before they enter the cramped confines of their ship.

William looked around, he could see many people going about their business, some with baskets others with handcarts they all seemed in a hurry.

'I think it would be good for me as I have never been in such a busy crowded place.'

'Good then follow me.'

Robert waved as he took a right turn making his way to the offices of the tobacco agents. Alec took hold of the reins of the horse pulling their cart and with William bringing up the rear led them towards the heart of the docks. William looked around fascinated by what he could see. There were men man handling bales onto carts, some going into warehouses others loading goods directly onto large wagons. It was noisy and the dust and dirt flew in all directions. At one point William could hardly breathe, something had caught in the back of his throat, it was a burning, gagging sensation, his eyes watered and he found himself gasping. Alec smiled as he saw the state that William was in,

'This area is where the trade in spices is made, there is a great deal of money in the sacks of precious peppers and the like that arrive from the east, if we were not in the tobacco market, I am sure that we would be handling the likes of cloves and nutmeg, mark my words there is a lot of money to be made from cargo arriving from the east.'

It was at this point that William could see some women standing along the side of the warehouses. They were talking to what seemed to be men from the ships, there was some laughter and William could see one man lifting a woman's skirt. She didn't seem to mind what he was doing. Alec followed William's gaze,

'That is another lesson you need to be taught. See the women,' Alec waved his had in the direction of some not so young women with gaudy faces and their teeth seemed to be either black or missing. William looked past the creatures and could see an inn with a sign depicting a mermaid swinging gently in the breeze, there were more men virtually queuing at the door and just over their heads he could see more women. He shook his head, he had little idea of what was going on, Alec drew up beside him,

'Beware of such places William, they can only do harm never good. There are those that take advantage of what is on offer but the risk they take is high.' He pointed to a man who seemed to be in a terrible state, he could hardly stand and when he looked up William saw that his face seemed to be eaten away with the flesh full of sores and puss. 'If you wish to spend any money you earn on the sort of women you see here then the chances of you catching one of many diseases is very high and if you do you will end up either mad or disfigured like that pathetic creature.' Alec raised his arm and pointed to a fellow in a state of collapse. 'Come we must get on, but don't forget what you have seen here and remember keep yourself clean and healthy by staying away from such places.

As they reached a point where they could easily see ships waiting either to unload their cargo or take on goods, Alec scanned the ships and stopped as he saw the 'Neptune.' It was a good-looking vessel, its masts stood tall and although its sails were furled it looked a good sturdy ship.

'You see the ship there' William followed where Alec was pointing, 'well that will be our home for several weeks.'

Looking across at the Neptune William was filled with dread and excitement together, it was a strange sensation but more than anything he wanted his journey to start.

'When will we sail?' He asked his voice gave away the emotion he was feeling.

'I need to speak to the captain to confirm when the tide will be right for our departure which I hope will be no longer than a day, so we have to make sure all our business is concluded quickly.'

Alec made for a building near to the church of St Nicholas, they crossed the bridge and turned left. Alec stopped and dismounted outside a building of some substance. Its frontage which overlooked the street was in good condition, the plaster was good and the timbers substantial. They were met by a young lad who asked who they were and who they wanted to see. Alec stretched his back then said to the boy,

'I am here to see John Dawlish.' The boy almost jumped when he heard the name.

'Yes, sir, wait a moment please and I will see if all is well and then I shall take care of your horses and cart.' He scampered away and was back within minutes. He took the horses reins and led them through the carriage entrance and then to the rear of the building.

They were taken into a building that showed wealth and prosperity. William noticed the doors were well made and carried some weight, the floors were polished and some had carpets with designs that William had not seen before. The boy led them through a hall then knocked on a door to the right. From within the room a firm voice told them to 'enter' the door was opened by the youngster who had guided them in. Alec went first and as William followed, he was impressed by what opened up before him. The window on the far wall threw light onto a large desk behind which sat a man who started to rise as they entered. He was a little shorter than Alec but broader in the beam. His face broke into a smile of greeting as the two men shook hands.

'Good to see you again Alec, how has your journey been, come sit and tell me your news.'

Before sitting in the chair proffered to him Alec turned to William,

'I have with me a young man who wishes to travel to the Americas and seek his fortune and future on the plantation.'

John Dawlish stood back a step and appraised William. He nodded with approval as his eyes travelled from William's head to his shoes.

'Well, there is something unexpected, I thought you would be with Robert not a new member of the company.' Alec smiled,

'Robert is seeking out our quarters for the night and discussing matters concerning our tobacco contract, we will meet later.'

Dawlish went to the long sideboard on which there were several decanters and glasses.

'You'll take a glass of something with me?' He looked at Alec who nodded, and what about our young friend here will he take a glass?'

William looked at Alec who raised his eyebrows as if to ask the question.

'Yes please.' William had not taken strong drink before and was a little anxious as to any affect it may have of him, but nothing ventured nothing gained. William looked at the ruby red liquid in the small glass he was offered and waited until the other two men raised their glasses.

'To fortune and good trade.' It was Dawlish who made the toast which was echoed by Alec and stutteringly William repeated the words. Dawlish continued,

'Now to business, I suppose you want to be brought up to date on the ship, its sailing etcetera.' Alec made himself a little more comfortable,

'Yes, I need to know the ships condition and any information you may have on the captain and crew as well as what cargo she will be carrying.'

Dawlish leaned forward and began to read from the papers he had before him.

'The ship, the Neptune, is one you have sailed on before I believe so you are presumably aware of the tonnage and layout of the vessel.' He looked from the paper to Alec who nodded, Alec could remember his voyage from Virginia although it had been not too difficult, if it had not been for a good captain and his mariners it could have been a lot worse. Dawlish continued,

'The captain will be the same but the crew may be a little different. The Neptune has been careened and her hull repaired, any leaks have been dealt with and the caulking has been successful. There has been a disease that spread through the area where the crew had been living and some I am afraid succumbed to the pox. However, there are many seamen in Bristol only too willing to crew a good ship with a good reputation. There is one piece of bad news and that is the Neptune will not be ready to sail for a further two days so you will have to seek accommodation until then,

'The delay presents little problem for us, I am sure my colleague, Robert, will be able to secure a couple of rooms for us until we depart.'

Alec turned to William,

'The captain is a man by the name of Carrick, he is a good man and although he stands no slacking or nonsense, he gets the job done, I am glad he will be with us.'

William listened as the two men talked through the cargo that the ship would be carrying. It ranged from cloth to cattle, how they would be carried by ship across the ocean mystified William.

The conversation between the two men went on for about another two hours and with a spinning head William followed Alec from Dawlish's office.

'We need to make sure that all the items in the cart are taken to the ship and secured properly and it will give you a better view of what life will be like for the next few weeks, so mount up and follow me.'

William again felt excitement rise through his body as he followed Alec towards the Neptune. It was approaching eleven and the ship would slowly drop and rest on the river bed until the tide turned. Alec had said that they would be leaving the following day with the tide so they needed to get all things sorted in the correct manner as quickly as possible.

The sight of the Neptune made William shudder as a thrill ran down his spine. She looked a massive beast in the untrained eyes of a farm boy from Cambridgeshire. The wooden hull of the ship could be seen, it looked solid and well-constructed, there were three masts which reached out as if wanting to be released.

'Well, what do you think?' Alec asked William,

'It seems massive, how many people will be travelling with us?' To William the ship looked big enough to hold all the people in a town let alone a village.' Alec looked at the ship and smiled,

'On this trip there will be fewer passengers than normal, the cargo is made of items that hold value and importance as well as livestock which is urgently needed in Virginia so the numbers will be no more than a hundred passengers with a crew of forty. The mariners will have their work cut out taking care of the animals and securing the cargo.' William thought for a moment,

'What sort of people will be with us?' William's curiosity continued. He thought what type of people they would be and how would he feel travelling in the confined space of a ship with those he had never met.

Alec could see that William had many more questions building up inside his head but they would have to wait. There were men working on the dockside moving bales and crates towards the ships, Alec approached a group and asked if they were dealing with the cargo for the Neptune.

'Yes.' The voice was thick with an accent that William found hard to understand. 'These are for the Neptune, why do you ask?'

'They are our goods, I see that they are in good condition and that you are preparing to load.'

'When the tide allows, we will start, is there anything you would like to see?'

'No, all is good and hopefully it will remain so until we reach the other side of the ocean.'

'Have no fear we will take good care of your cargo and see it onto the Neptune.'

With that Alec turned his horses head back towards the city and moved away from the quayside with William following in his wake.

Chapter 2

Alec and Robert had arranged to meet at the inn they had stayed in when they arrived, hopefully Robert would have secured them beds for the night but would have to do some negotiating to get a further night which was unexpected. Alec needed to find out from his friend what the news was on the price of tobacco, he had been informed of the profit that had been made on the shipment they had brought with them on their journey from Virginia and was highly satisfied. It had enabled him to invest the profit in the goods they would be taking back with them and leave them a handsome profit.

As they made their way to the inn William started to get a pain in his neck as he continued to look at the sights that they passed. There were so many different aspects of life to be seen, there were vendors of all sorts, butchers, fishmongers, costermongers and a whole host of individuals trying to make a living from those who frequented the port area. The smell hit William and he began to cough, he was not use to the variety of items on sale and definitely not use to the rich aroma that now assailed his nostrils. Eventually they left the tumble and noise of the market area, Alec turned his horse into the stable yard of a substantial building. Its half-timbered frame encased white plaster which shone in the sunlight. It was another busy place. Riders were arriving and departing, horses were being led from the stables and others were being brushed down, it was a hive of activity.

'Get down and we will try to locate Robert.' The two men let themselves down from their saddles and handed their horses over to the stable lads who took them away to be fed and watered. William followed Alec as he entered the inn, as he ducked his head and went through the half open door another smell hit him, this time it was one he recognised, it was the smell of ale and beer, that together with the what the horses had left with them seemed a lot more familiar to him than most experiences he had that day. The room was large and had a haze of smoke rising from those sitting at various tables. The men had long thin pipes the bowls of which were resting in their hand they all seemed to have a pewter tankard of ale either in front of them or being raised to their lips. Alec looked around the room and spotted Robert sitting on his own in front of a window which did not let in much light through the small grimy panes of glass, he called to his friend who turning raised his hand in recognition.

'How goes it?' It was Robert who spoke first.

'All is well so far.' Was Alec's reply.

'And how is our young friend faring in this city of sin?'

'He is doing well.'

Alec began with the bad news and explained to Robert how they now needed a further night's accommodation due to the delay in the Neptune sailing. Robert did not seem unduly perturbed by this he drew in a breath of tobacco smoke saying that the inn had plenty of room and that it would not be difficult to extend their stay.

'What news do you have for me?' Alec asked. Robert replied first having taken the pipe from his mouth, he broke off a rather soggy end and placed the shorter stem and the bowl of the pipe carefully into a pouch.

'We are in a good state of repair our goods and expenditure are in order and with a fair wind we shall continue to make good our investments.

Alec leaned back with a contented look on his face. William listened as the two men went through various financial transactions that had been made. With both Alec and Robert happy with their work it was decided to take a drink to celebrate in a small way. Robert found a serving girl and ordered good beer to be brought to the table.

The inn which they would be spending their last nights on shore was The Hatchet Inn, so called, it was said, after the axes or hatchets used by the local woodsmen in the nearby Clifton woods. It had been established for some time and had gained a reputation for the sporting events that took place both inside and to the rear of the building. There was a cockpit which was often in use and where many a sailor's hard-earned pennies were spent and lost. All this fired Williams imagination his mind was in a whirl, gambling and sometimes fighting were new to him, he gathered himself and turned to Robert,

'Where will we sleep, it seems very busy, do they have room for us?'

Robert smiled,

'There is room but only just, I have secured a room for the additional night but it means that we will have each other's close company over the next two nights and be aware that it may turn out to be a bit rowdy and sleep may not be easy to come by, however I am sure that with a glass or two of beer you may be able to get some shut eye.'

Alec then spoke directly to William,

'Strange things await you over the coming days and weeks, not only the ship but those who sail her. I have already told you the captain's name but I must explain that he is a little more than just a captain, he is a Master Mariner.' A puzzled look spread across William's face, he asked.

'What does that mean is he more than a captain?'

'Much more, he can master almost any ship and his skills are not to be questioned. If you are in need of the best man to sail a ship look for a Master Mariner and you will not go wrong.'

'What of the ship, The Neptune, where will we live, will we be able to eat and what will the food be like?' The questions flew thick and fast, both Alec and Robert smiled they knew that the young man in front of them was in for an experience that may change his life, not just on the ship but what awaited him on the other side of the ocean. They drank their beer and the two elder men tried to answer Williams questions. The time came for them to eat, Alec said that he would order for all three and that the choice would be, take what's on offer or go hungry. He called over the serving girl, who had a bright red face under her white cap,

'What have you got to eat this fine day?' She looked at Alec with a suggestion of a smile but the rushing around that she had been doing for the last few hours did not place her in the best of moods.

'We have a good kitchen, we have bread, mutton, beef, some chicken and we have sauces that you may have never tasted in your lives.'

Alec looked across at Robert who had tried some of the sauces when they stayed before, they were fiery and pungent they almost took the roof of your mouth off. He looked at Alec,

'Mutton, but without the sauce, just a good gravy for me and some good bread would go down well.'

'Good choice, but I think I shall have the beef as I am sure that it will be of the finest quality and it may be sometime before we get to taste it again and William what will you have?' William was not use to having a choice and after a moment's hesitation said.

'I will have the beef as well with a little sauce maybe, just to try it, would that be possible?' The girl smiled at the young man and said that she would see if she could arrange a little taste for him. Alec thought that her response may have been a little more than just about the food and smiled to himself, perhaps William might get more than he bargained for. They sat back and waited for their meals, Alec took the opportunity to explain about what and how they would eat on the Neptune. His description of how the food was prepared did not fill William with a great deal of confidence. The thought of fires being lit on a ship brought the sight of a burning vessel into William's mind but Alec assured him that any fire, be it the cooks or the passengers, would be tightly controlled and that no fires were lit until they had calm seas. Their food arrived and the smell drifting up from the pewter dishes made William's mouth water. He took up the bread which was still warm and broke a piece off. Carefully he dipped the bread into the sauce that was to the side of the ample slice of beef, he slowly opened his mouth and licked the bread taking only the smallest of drops of sauce. The explosion of heat and flavour rocked him back, never had he tasted such a thing. His first action was to wipe the sauce off his tongue with his sleeve but Robert stopped him and gave him a fresh piece of bread which William hurriedly put in his mouth. The heat and power of the sauce diminished as the bread lifted it from his tongue. He breathed a sigh of relief and coughing a little turned towards Robert,

'It's like eating fire without flames.'

'Take it easy and make sure you have a lot of bread with the meat and a little sauce and take your time.'

Alec and Robert were amused by the way William tried to get used to the new flavours he was experiencing. They watched as he gained confidence and eventually cleaned his plate.

The three men sat back appreciating the food and the warmth of the surroundings. William began with even more questions,

'Alec, you say you are eager to return to your family, do you have a wife and children? Alec drew a mouthful of tobacco smoke and let it drift from his mouth, he replied with a slight catch in his voice,

'I have a wife, a very good wife and two boys, one of eight and one of six. They are healthy and strong, at least they were when I last saw them.' William then turned to Robert,

'And you, Robert, have you children?'

Robert's face dropped and he stared into his beer,

'I had a wife, a beautiful partner who a man could not wish more of but she was taken from me by the fever and I have never sought to marry another.' William realised he had hit a sore point but continued,

'Do you have any children?' Robert straightened up but his face had a look of anguish about it,

'No children, but it is my good fortune that my good friend,' he patted Alec on the shoulder, 'asked me to be godfather to his sons and with that I feel that I have sons also.' A smile crept back over Robert's face as he patted Alec's shoulder again. What about you young William, do you intend to marry when you reach your new life?' William had not thought of anything like that, he was still too young and the adventure that lay before him held too much to allow him any thoughts of wives and children.

'No, my only thoughts are to reach a new country and create a life for myself, maybe that once I have achieved that I will consider marriage but that is a long way in the future.'

Alec stretched and looked out of the grimy window, he could see the light fading, they had been busy and needed to get a goodnight's rest as they would need to be alert to many things in the morning.

'We need sleep so my friends I suggest we make our way to our chamber.' The three men stood but before making their way to their room Alec paid for the meal and drink. As they walked through the

24

main room towards the stairs Alec took hold of a handful of Williams hair,

'This needs to come off and we shall seek the services of a surgeon barber and get you trimmed up so that the lice will have no place to hide.' William was a little scared of having his hair cut off, he had taken a pride in his looks when going to church or market but if that was what was needed then he knew his looks would have to suffer but his hair would grow back.

The room they had been allotted had enough room for one large bed in the centre of the room and a smaller one towards the far corner by a small window.

'We will share the large bed and William as you are smaller than the two of us you will have the privilege of having a bed of your own.' William was surprised but he soon found out that in the cold of the night two bodies were a lot warmer than one. Alex pulled out a bucket indicating to William to look under his bed,

'These are our piss pots, make use of them don't go pissing in your bed or on the floor otherwise we may have to pay extra.' William pulled a smaller bucket from beneath his bed and studied it, if he could fill that during the night it would be a surprise. After placing the bucket back under the bed, he lay down and was quickly told to get up by Robert who had removed a small book from his bag. Both Alec and Robert knelt and together spoke the words of the lord's prayer. William quickly dropped to his knees and joined in the prayer,

This was something that William thought he would need to get used to if it was going to be something that happened every night before sleeping. The three men made themselves ready for sleep and Robert snuffed out the candle, darkness filled the room and the only sound William could hear was the breathing of his two colleagues. He lay on his back thinking of all that had happened during the day and wondered what else he would find out during their final day before sailing.

Chapter 3

The new day hit them with sunshine which seemed to give all three men energy. After eating some cold meats and bread they made their way back to the offices of John Dawlish. They needed to finalise the disposal of anything they would not be taking with them that included the horses and the cart. William stood back from the conversation Alec and Robert had with Dawlish. At the end of their meeting all parties were satisfied with the arrangements and that left them time to explore the dock and make sure they knew where the Neptune was berthed. They could see the ship, it had been brought near to the dock, it gently moved with the flow of the tide, a lot of activity seemed to be taking place. William could see men carrying boxes and bundles onto small boats that were ferrying the goods out to the ship where they were taken aboard by rope pulley or by the men manhandling them.

'William, look over there.' Robert pointed to a group standing away from others. They appeared to be nervously talking and did not look too enthusiastic.

'Who are they?' William was curious the small group was made up of what appeared to be a man and wife with a son. The men's faces he could see under their hats but the women's were hidden under the cowls of their cloaks.

'They are passengers as we are, they will be travelling with us and no doubt we will see a great deal of them during the voyage.' William wondered what other passengers would be sharing their journey. Alec then grabbed him by the arm and turned him around,

'We have to visit someone who will improve your looks and make you ready for the voyage.' William had forgotten about the surgeon barber and with some reluctance followed Alec who led him to a doorway with what seemed like a red and white striped pole hanging outside the entrance.

'What's that.' William asked pointing to the pole.

'Blood and bandages.' Robert said through a smile. 'It's just to let you know that some surgeon barbers have been known to slip and well.....' William gulped,

'Is it really necessary, can I not just try to cut it myself, or even you could cut it for me.'

'No, it's better that a trained hand uses the scissors and razor.' William followed Alec through the door into what seemed to be a room set for torture but he did what he was told and as his locks fell to the floor he grimaced. After it was over, he looked around the room, there was a mirror of not particularly good quality hanging on the wall, William cautiously looked at his reflection and was horrified at what he saw, his head still had hair but not a great deal and his face seemed to be that of someone of lesser years. It was not a sight he relished.

Robert followed Alec into the chair and once they had been dealt with, they brushed themselves down and headed out back towards the Neptune. William looked around and could see the family still close together looking ill at ease, he thought of how they must feel without someone like Alec or Robert to guide them through the myriad of problems that any travellers may encounter. The Neptune had been brought alongside the dock. The three men walked to the gangway that was no more than four planks wide with a rope to steady anyone embarking. William slowly made his way over the water that was lapping against the side of the ship and the harbour wall stopping briefly he looked down and then back to the dockside was this the last time he would see land for several weeks or even longer.

Chapter 4

It was the middle of August 1670 when William took his first steps on the deck of the Neptune. He had the strangest of feelings he couldn't understand them it was a mixture of excitement and fear, was he leaving his world, one that he knew and trusted and entering a phase of his life that may lead to his fortune or possibly his death? He shook his head and stepped aside letting Alec and Robert pass with their bags,

'Come on William.' Roberts words jolted William back into reality. 'Follow us and don't get caught up in any ropes.' There were coils of ropes on the deck, what they were for he had no idea so he carefully stepped over them as he tried to keep pace with the others. Alec started to descend into the bowels of the ship, which from where William stood appeared to be dark and foreboding with a smell of its own. He followed on with Robert behind until Alec stopped and pushed through a door into what was a small room with very little light, in fact all that William could see was a grating in the ceiling where he heard the bustling and shouting of the men moving what appeared to be cargo and passengers.

'This is it, our home for the next six to eight weeks, what do you think William.' William's response was one of a total lack of understanding,

'Is this it, where do we sleep and eat is there no more room?' Alec reached over to him and put his arm around his shoulder.

'I told you it would be cramped so you had better get used to the space because that's all you're going to get.' Robert was placing their bags onto two bunks, he turned to William,

'This is luxury, the poor devils we saw on the quayside will have to do their best with what they have in the area we passed through, at least we have some privacy.'

'But where and how do the three of us sleep in here?'

'That's and easy question to answer, Alec and I have the bunks and you my young friend will have the hammock. William had not slept in a such a thing before and was terrified at the thought of what that would entail. Alec unfurled a roll of canvas which had ropes to either end.

'This is your bed.' He stretched out the hammock and Robert took one end and started to tie the ropes onto a hook which was embedded into a beam of the ship, Alec took the other end and finished fastening the ropes.

'There you are, ready-made for a goodnights sleep, come try it out you will be surprised how well it feels.' William carefully stepped towards the hammock, he pulled one side down and tried to place his leg into the canvas but it turned unexpectedly and he landed on his backside with a thump.

'Let's try that again and this time we'll give you a little more help.'

It took three more attempts before William got the hang of getting in and out of the hammock, with a sense of achievement he lay back with his hands behind his head and said with confidence, 'This will do nicely.'

No sooner had he won his fight with the hammock the three men were summoned on deck they made their way with the other passengers to an area on deck where the captain waited to address them. They stood on the wooden deck and looked up, Edward Carrick did not like passengers he preferred cargo and the sort of cargo that he could manhandle without complaint, passengers on the other hand would create more difficulties than he needed on a voyage of some four thousand miles. William could see the captain take a deep breath.

'My name is Edward Carrick and I am the master of this vessel. I will endeavour to transport you from Bristol to Virginia. The voyage will be long and arduous.' His clipped tones were sharp and to the point, he continued, 'You have been given your quarters and that is where you will spend the majority of your time. Food will be rationed out to you and along with anything you may have with you must sustain you until we reach our destination.' He paused and looked at the faces staring up at him they would have experiences they could not have dreamed of awaiting them over the next six to eight weeks. 'What you will treat like gold is water, we have a supply of both ale and water and we will collect rainwater when it appears but you will not use water for anything other than staying alive. If any person, be it man woman or child, is caught misusing water they will suffer severe punishment. If you have need to discuss anything regarding the ship you will first speak to a member of my crew who will then inform the Chief Mate, who if he thinks necessary will inform me. We have on board the following, a parson, a surgeon, a cook together with the carpenter they will see to the needs of those on board. You will see men working on the deck and you will keep out of their way for two reasons, one you will slow down their work and secondly you could injure yourself and although we have a surgeon on board, we do not have a facility to treat any serious injuries. Most of you will suffer some mal de mer you will NOT get in the way of the crew, you will be sick in the buckets provided and empty them over the side when told. You may come on deck when the weather allows, the crew will let you know when it is safe to do so.'

He turned to his right where a man of some thirty years stood upright, he had a trimmed beard and his hair was tied behind his neck with a black ribbon. 'This is Mister Dimmock, he is the Chief Mate and my deputy as I have said if you have anything to say it is to him that you will go to first.' With that Carrick took one last look at his cargo, turned and made his way back to his cabin.

Mister Dimmock then took over,

'You will go to your quarters whilst we make ready to sail, you will not come on deck until you are given the word by members of the crew.' That was all he said and as he started to give orders the passengers slowly made their way back to their allotted space.

William followed behind Alec and Robert as they climbed down to their cabin a voice from behind them called to Alec,

'Mr Sinclair.' Alec stopped and turned,

'Yes.' The captain wishes to see you in his cabin. Alec was a little perplexed but turned and followed the mariner to the upper deck. Robert and William continued to their quarters.

'Why should the captain wish to speak to Alec?' Robert turned and looked at William,

'We have a great deal tied up in this trip and I am sure that the captain is aware of Alec's connection with the owners of the cargo and the ship itself.' William in his ignorance did not fully appreciate Alec's position in the company of tobacco merchants he worked for. 'It is not only the goods on board now it is what is waiting for this ship when we reach Virginia. The latest crop of tobacco will be ready for shipment and it matters a great deal to the captain that his ship is fully employed.' William realised he had so much to learn.

'Are there any other cargo's than tobacco?' This was a delicate matter and Robert approached it with care.

'At this moment in time there is a great need of labour in the Americas. Plantations grow not only tobacco, they also have a large market for sugar cane, both are physically demanding, to achieve the amount that England requires large numbers of labourers are needed. This has resulted in manpower commanding high prices so there are some plantations who have bought high numbers of people from Africa.' William had seen the occasional black face in Bristol and at first, he had been very curious about them however he had just thought it another aspect of life that he needed to become accustomed to. Robert paused for a moment. 'There are many ships that deal only in what is known as 'black gold' that is the transportation of men women and children from the dark continent to the Americas. Captain Carrick is a strange man although he transports tobacco, which is the product of the slaves, he has not and will not be party to the transportation of human beings from the African coast. There are those with less scruples that are now shipping hundreds of these wretches from one side of the world to the other. Alec and I try to keep away from this business when we can. It is our belief that these men should be treated as such, men, we remember our days when we were prisoners after the battles of Dunbar and Worcester that we were seen by many as the lowest form of life. In those times it was known for many Scots to be sold into slavery and shipped to the new world you are probably unaware of Alec's journey to the Americas. William shook his head, Robert sighed and decided that it may be better for William to understand why they had a different attitude towards those that laboured for them.

'I will tell you a story which you may find hard to believe.' William sat on the bottom bunk and prepared himself to listen to Robert.

'Towards the end of the battle of Worcester many of the Royalist and Covenanter army were captured. They were herded like cattle in to fields close to the city centre, although Alec had tried his hardest to remain with your father, he was taken with several hundred others to an area where he and the rest of the men were told to sit down and stay where they were. If they tried to move, they would be taken down with the sword or shot. After several days with almost no food or water they were marched to the same place that we have just boarded the Neptune. Some four hundred men were crammed into a ship which set sail, on the first available tide, to the new world. The journey is best told by Alec but he has described it to me and the horrors that the men encountered were beyond hell. Sickness and disease took almost half the men who when they died were simply thrown overboard. The voyage took almost twelve weeks and towards the end there was almost no food or water. When the men arrived, they were in a terrible condition. It was then that they were given over to their 'owners'. Struggling to stay alive they were marched to various plantations where, finally they were given food and water. Their accommodation was no more than poorly constructed huts with no beds, the hard packed earth floor was where they lived and died. They worked in the fields from sunrise to sunset no mercy was shown by their overseers.

'I had a similar experience but, on another ship, and initially on a different plantation until I was sold to Alec's owner. We were thrown together which is where we met and had the good fortune, if you can call it that, to work together. We often spoke about your father and wondered if he had survived.'

Chapter 5

William was amazed by Robert's story, his father, or step father to be precise, had never told him what had happened in detail. He had been aware that his father had gone through an awful time before he managed to be sent to work for his family. William was aware that his real father had died when he was two years old and that the man, he called father had married his mother after a great many family problems had been resolved. Robert could see that William needed some time to fully appreciate what he and Alec had been through.

'We have told you our story and what happened to us before we had a chance to better ourselves so now you know all. What you must bear in mind that the treatment we received when working in the fields of the plantation was back breaking and that there was no let up for those harvesting the crops.' William again tried to understand what Robert was telling him but it was only those that had been through the agony who could truly understand what it had been like. Robert then told William something that he had not expected.

'You are aware of the number of passengers onboard, it's about a hundred, but what you probably do not know is that a great number of those are indentured to plantation owners.' William did not understand,

'The term indentured, what does that mean.' William dreaded even more horrendous tales involving these unfortunates. Robert cleared his throat,

'They are men, women and children who cannot raise enough to pay for their passage and so accept the offer of sailing to the new world and committing themselves for seven years or more to work for their new masters. It is slavery by another name and is something you will hear and see a great deal of in the months and years to come.' William thought of the family on the quayside and wondered if they were indentured, he would like to find out and would probably have time over the coming weeks.

While Robert was relating the story of their past to William, Alec had made his way to the captain's cabin. He knocked on the door and was greeted with a gruff 'Come in.' The low ceiling made him hesitate but after just missing a beam he managed to enter the cabin without doing himself any harm.

Edward Carrick sat behind a small desk, it fitted into the cabin easily and Alec could see the captain's bunk and another table where charts were spread out altogether it was not a largest of spaces but better that any other on board. Carrick did not rise from behind his desk he just looked up as Alec approached.

'Ah, Mr Sinclair, is it not?' Alec thought he could detect the faintest of smiles in Carrick's face but was probably mistaken.

'Yes, I am Sinclair.'

'I understand we have sailed together before, is that correct?' Alec told him that he had sailed on the Neptune from Virginia some nine months ago. 'I also believe that a great deal of the cargo belongs to you, or your company is that so?'

'Yes, I, that is to say my company have a large sum invested in the cargo you carry and would appreciate it if you and your crew would treat it as best you can.' Carrick now smiled,

'Yes, of course we will take every possible care of your goods but we cannot control the weather or the tides so you will have to bear with us.' Alec then broached a most difficult point.

'Are there any reports of raiders or pirates in the area we will be travelling?' Again, a smile appeared on the captain's face.

'I have heard nothing of the trouble you speak of and hope that we do not encounter any such rogues when we leave the safety of English waters.' With that he pulled a flat-bottomed decanter towards him and looked at Alec, 'Will you join me in a glass before we venture out into the ocean?'

'That would be most welcome.' Alec took the glass proffered to him and drank what tasted like fortified wine, it had a sweetness to it but Alec was aware of its strength. They drained their glasses and Carrick held out his hand which Alec shook, Carrick nodded as if to say that the meeting was over and Alec turned making his way out of the cabin and back to his two friends.

Robert and William were eager to hear what passed between Alec and the Captain, their questions came thick and fast.

'Please, let me draw breath.' Alec pleaded as he sat on the bottom bunk. 'We had a brief discussion nothing more than making ourselves known to one another. The captain is aware of our connection with the cargo and will try to make our journey as comfortable as he can.' Robert asked if he had found out anything about their fellow passengers which was something that Alec had not really spoken about.

'It was not uppermost in my mind, all I can say about them is that they appear to be a mixture of paying passengers, with a little more space and baggage, and those that are indentured who have very little and will have a rough time crossing the ocean.'

'How long will we be at sea?' William asked. He had no concept of time, his excitement and sense of adventure seemed to blot out everything other than his immediate surroundings. Alec could sense the young man's eager anticipation of what was to befall them.

'We will be on this ship for the next six to eight weeks, it may be longer but if we have good weather and favourable wind's we may reach Virginia sooner.' Alec had not discussed the length of journey with the captain but knew exactly the reply he would have received if he had asked the question. 'We need to organise ourselves and make sure we have enough provisions to last the voyage. Robert, will you see that the food we have is portioned out well, I would hate for any of us to go hungry.' He then looked at William. 'I think you may have a few surprises as regards food, the ship will survive mainly on salted beef or pork with some fish thrown in to vary the diet. There is a surprising amount of livestock on board which may

43

mean we get some fresh meat on occasion. Eggs, I hope, will be available from time to time, that is if the chickens lay. So, prepare yourself young man for a diet that may prove challenging.' William looked a little bemused, how would he survive on such things, he knew he had no other option and he was determined that the state of the food would not deter him from getting the most out of the journey. Alec continued,

'William your job, one of the most important, will be to keep our quarters clean and everything placed in order. You will, no doubt, see some of the others onboard who do not keep a good regime and who suffer for it. Neither Robert or I wish to be infested with fleas, ticks or other pests and if you discover any sign, you are to let us know straight away.' William did not relish the thought of being a cleaner however he knew that if Alec and Robert thought it necessary then it was.

A movement cut William's thoughts, they were moving, he could feel a gentle roll beneath his feet and then what felt like the ship had been released as they were pulled away from the quay.

'Are we allowed on deck?' William asked.

'No.' Was Alec's firm response, 'There will be a lot of activity and you will get in the way so bide your time, once we have cleared Bristol you will, I dare say, be allowed on deck.' William looked around their very small cabin, he was content that he had made the right decision but just hoped he could survive the voyage.

Chapter 6

It felt like an age until William was allowed to go on deck. It was a seaman, dressed in a woollen jacket, of indeterminate age and colour, baggy stained breeches topped off with a blue woven cap in a material that could have been anything, who William first set eyes on. The man was carrying a large coil of rope, he staggard as he passed. On the deck there were a few others, William spotted the family he had seen on the quayside before they boarded. He could see clearly now that the taller, older of the two men seemed to be the father with a slightly shorter version, who was most likely the son, and a lighter figure almost totally enveloped in a cape, who must be the wife or daughter. William tried to get a look at the face under the cowl but had no luck. He did not know how to approach any of his fellow travellers so he just went to the side rail and watched the waves. This proved to be the wrong thing to do as the motion of the ship and the rise and fall of the horizon made his stomach heave. He turned away from the side of the ship and made his unsteady way back to the cabin.

In their cabin, Alec sat with a sheet of paper resting on a board. He was noting how and when they had embarked, the date on the top of the page was 25th August 1670 he would note their progress and any problems that might befall them.

'How are you feeling now that we are underway?' William looked from Robert to Alec, they did not seem to be affected in the least by the movement of the ship.

'I am not sure if my stomach will take to the ships movement.' Robert reached into a bag on his bunk and took out a square thick biscuit, he broke it into four and gave a quarter to William.

'Eat this it will bind whatever you have in your stomach and hopefully ease the feeling of sickness.' William placed the hard biscuit into his mouth, it was solid and it took some time for his saliva to soften it. He started to chew, initially he gagged but eventually he managed to swallow an amount which made his stomach feel a little more settled. Robert said that it would only help in the short term and that most people onboard would suffer varying degrees of sickness during their journey. Alec turned to William,

'You will see many hardships during our time on the ocean so prepare yourself. We will try to guide you but you will have to face areas that you have never thought or dreamt of.' William pondered on what had been said, he would need to find out for himself what his two colleagues meant by hardship.

'Would it be safe to return to the deck, I feel in need of air.' Alec looked at Robert and nodded,

'Yes, it should be safe now that we have left Bristol behind.' William climbed the stairway passing through some of the passengers. He noticed that the family he had seen on the quay had some privacy. The young man and the girl were standing slightly apart from the man who William thought was the head of the family, it appeared that the boy was trying to encourage the girl to go on deck and was having some trouble. The father then seemed to lose patience. William waited for them to reach the point where he was standing. As they were passing the girl stumbled and William reached out a hand to steady her. She turned her head and for the first time William caught sight of her face, he was immediately surprised by the delicate features that stared up at him. The girl had a face that was oval in shape, her eyes were blue and shone through her fair lashes, he could see traces of her hair showing from under her cowl, it was fair, not blonde but a sort of mid brown with flecks of red. He found it difficult to take his eyes from her however reality returned to him when the young man with her thanked him for saving the girl from falling, his speech

48

was accented which made him a little unsure of where in the world they came from. William took the opportunity to find out a little more about them,

'There are three of you, is it your father that you travel with?' The young man took the girls hand to give her support.

'Yes, he is our father.' He seemed reluctant to speak more than that.

'Where do you come from, is it England or foreign lands?' The reply was curt,

'We are from any lands, it has taken my father years to get us in a position where we might be ourselves.' With that he turned back to the girl and made his way to the open hatch and the deck. William followed but realised that he would have great difficulty in pursuing any further conversation with them. On the deck the fresh air hit him in the face, it was refreshing after being in the cabin but as he walked onto the deck the motion of the ship triggered something unexpected. He staggered onto the planks of the deck, he reached out and managed to grasp a hatchway and prevent himself falling. Several of the crew saw him leave the hatch and laughed at his inability to walk unaided. William felt awkward and embarrassed he clutched hold of a rail and waited for the ship to right itself. He slowly managed to get to the side of the ship where he immediately felt whatever was in his stomach climb towards his throat, he managed to hold whatever it was and tried to take a breath. As he straightened himself, he could see the young man and his sister also feeling the effects of the rolling motion of the ship, they had now taken on a pallor that was not normal. The brother started to wretch and the girl followed him. They stood holding on the rail of the ship for dear life, a passing sailor smiled and said, 'Wait till it gets a little livelier.' Then passed on to his duties. William took one last gulp of air then made his way back to the cabin.

On his return he found Alec and Robert in deep discussion, they were planning what they would do when they arrived in Virginia. There was a lot to do. Alec listed the cargo and on what wagons they were to be loaded onto. Robert called out the names of the men who would be in charge of the various loads. William thought that this was a bit early to start thinking about what was to happen in the weeks to come.

'Why do you start to plan now, surely you have many weeks before you will have need of such information.' Alec looked up from the paper,

'You will learn that the better we plan the easier life is and it is never too early to start and it would be to your betterment if you were to take a look at what we are doing.' William sat on the bunk next to Alec and tried to follow what he was doing. The ledgers seemed to be full of figures and names not only of the goods but of those who they were to be delivered to and the men that would take them. Alec paid particular attention to the column containing the costs and charges, he pointed out to William that they needed to make a good profit to enable them to invest in the business and give them a good life. William could see how Alec reached his profit and thought of the money involved, it was much more than he had ever thought of.

The days on the ship fell into a routine, getting up after a poor night's sleep, hoping for something other than dried fish or salted meat to eat, praying that the weather would be good enough to allow them to get out of the confines of the cabin and onto the deck. William was in the habit of trying to exercise his body, he had seen some individuals that appeared to be in the same place every time he passed them bye. After getting a breath of air he would carry out his duties, emptying the buckets from the night before, cleaning the cabin as best he could, washing any clothes that had past the stage that they could be worn without spreading lice or something worse in sea water, which caused them to stiffen and rot at the seams. And so, life went on and he knew that it would be the same for weeks to come.

It was in the third week that trouble struck. The weather seemed to be fair and the ship was moving through the waves without causing too much sea sickness. William was on the deck and he saw the young woman and her brother, whose names he had discovered were Adele and Francois, he greeted them as best he could without tottering with the ships roll.

'Good morning, how are you today?' They were still not quite sure how to take William and he was unsure of how he stood in the eyes of the brother and sister who stood before him. Francois answered,

'We are well now that we seem to have become use to the movement of the ship.' William looked at Adele's face which had regained some colour but still lacked a smile. He tried to think of something else to say to possibly keep a conversation going for more than two or three sentences.

'I think we may be reaching the halfway point of our journey soon.' It was not the most original of statements but it was all he could think of. 'By my reckoning this is the fourteenth day that we have been at sea.' Adele looked at William,

'I don't think we are near halfway, perhaps a third that is all, we have many days to suffer still.' It was not the most enthusiastic response he could have wished for but at least she was talking to him.

They stood close to each other the conversation had almost dried up when from nowhere the sea swelled and the waves increased in power and height. The ship lurched violently throwing the three of them to the deck. Adele tried to stand but her dress and cloak wrapped around her so that all she could do was to cry out. William and Francois had both fallen, William was the first to regain his feet and he could see that Adele was being dragged towards the ships side. He managed to dive towards her had grab handfuls of her clothing but she still slipped perilously close to the side, William mustered all the strength he could and took hold of her cloak, he managed to keep her from getting any closer to the side of the ship, he knew if he let go now, she could be swept overboard. As he pulled her towards safety, he felt his leg give way and his whole body slid dangerously towards the crashing waves. William held on for all he was worth he could see that Adele's eyes were wide with fear, somehow, he managed to keep her from slipping any further, the pain in his leg shot through his body and caused him to cry out, Francois made his way towards them and with a supreme effort managed to pull them both to safety. The wave that had caused their dilemma had passed and in its wake the sea calmed down to a gentle swell. The three of them lay breathing heavily, Francois reached for his sister and raised her head, she was still conscious but her body was shaking. He cradled her in his arms trying to soothe her, he looked to where William lay, as he did there was movement on the deck, two seamen rushed forward to see how badly William was injured. The first man lifted William's head and was amazed to see that he appeared exhausted but none the worse for his efforts.

'Are you hurt?' The seaman looked down at William's leg which seemed to be at a strange angle. 'Your leg, how is your leg?' William could not feel any pain in his leg but as he tried to move it, he let out a yell. The seaman recognised William and was aware that he had a berth in a cabin. 'Let's get you to your cabin then we will be able to see what the trouble with your leg is.' Together the seamen helped William to stand on one leg then with one each side they carefully walked him to his cabin.

Alec heard noise outside of the cabin and opening the door found William propped up between two sailors.

'What on earth....' He moved to one side and William was brought into the cabin and laid on the bottom bunk. By this time William had begun to feel pain in his leg and he could feel it starting to swell.

'An accident happened when your young friend saved a girl from going over the side of the ship, he's a bit of a hero.' Alec looked at his young friend. 'His leg took a twist and might be broken.' The sailors voice showed concern as he rested William's head on a pillow. 'I think he will need the surgeon.' This piece of news alarmed Alec,

'Do you know where the surgeon can be found?' The sailor stood as upright as he could.

'Yes, he has a cabin close to the captain, I'll pass the message that he is needed here, it should not take long. The two sailors left Alec and Robert looking at a prostrate William who had taken on a pallor that did not seem too healthy.

'Just what have you been doing.' Robert asked the question looking down at William. You do go to some lengths to avoid your duties.' He noticed a faint smile appear on Williams lips. William tried to explain what had happened, how the wave had crashed into the side of the ship sending everything reeling, as he came to the end of his tale a face appeared at the door, it was a clean-shaven fine-featured face of no more than twenty-five the eyes were of a green shade that Alec had not encountered before.

'Is this where a broken leg is currently resting?' He moved towards William. 'This must be the casualty, what happened?' William told the story, the newcomer stood and leaned over William's body.

'I am Richard Hinds, surgeon on this ship, now let's see what can be done here.' He gently lifted the limb and started to manipulate William's foot who let out a cry as his foot was gently twisted. 'Hmmm, it appears that your leg is fractured, not badly but enough to cause you discomfort.' He carried on examining the leg he could find no other problems.

'There is swelling around the break and I shall have to wait until that subsides before doing anything else, so young man please stay where you are until the morning and I shall come back and see if we can make sure your leg is in the right position to go further, in the meantime don't even try to stand on the leg. I will be back as soon as the sun is over the horizon and you two men make sure he obeys my instructions.' With that Richard Hinds made his way back to his own part of the ship.

In the main hold Adele and Francois were being taken to task by their father,

'How could you let such a thing happen, you could have been killed.'

'But it was unexpected, we had no idea that the sea would throw up a wave that would rock the ship so violently.' Francois had not convinced his father that is was an accident, the thought of losing a child in the middle of the ocean made the older man shudder.

'And what about the young man who saved you?'
Adele was lost for words, she mumbled

'I don't know'.

'You need to find out, do you know of this
rescuer?' Francois answered his father,

'Yes, we know a little of him, he is English and
he is bound for Virginia but that is all.' His father said
that he should find out what happened as soon as
possible and if the young man sustained any injury.'

'I think he was injured, two sailors helped him
back to his quarters and it looked as if his leg had been
damaged.' His father grew red in the face,

'Do you know where his cabin is?'

'Err I think so.'

'Well, you will take me there now, and Adele
you will stay here, do not go on deck or anywhere else
until we return.' Adele shook her wet cloak and tried
to wring some of the water from it.

'Yes papa.'

Francois led the way as they neared William's
cabin they passed a well-dressed individual heading in
the opposite direction, they did not know him but had
seen him once or twice with the captain.

'This is the cabin papa.' He stood to one side to enable his father to enter. What the father saw was a fairly cramped area but far better than the accommodation he had.

'Excuse me gentlemen, is this the young man who saved my daughter?' Alec looked closely at the man who had just come into the cabin. He was in his mid to late forties with a neatly trimmed beard, his clothes were clean if not a little worn Alec could not assess his height as he stooped to enter the door. Alec noticed his speech was not what he considered to be totally English, his pronunciation was a little wrong but in a charming way.

'This is William, who we understand played a part in preventing anything happening to a young lady on deck.' At this point William raised himself onto one arm and looked at the stranger,

'How is your daughter, I hope she suffered no injury.' The stranger saw the film of sweat that covered William's face.

'She is well, her only problem is how she will get her clothes dry.' The man looked again at William his eyes travelled from his head and then followed the line of his body to his feet. As he looked at Williams leg's he could see something was not quite right.

'Have you damaged your leg?' William moved a little to try to make himself more comfortable.

'Yes, the leg may be fractured, the surgeon will see me tomorrow and then decide what to do.' William could see the man went into deep thought and then surprisingly said that he may be able to assist and did they know when the surgeon would visit next.

'He said it would be at dawn.' There was a brief pause then the visitor said,

'Good, good I shall be here when he visits.' This puzzled William,

'Why do you want to see the surgeon?

'I may be able to assist, I am an apothecary, and I have some knowledge of broken limbs and how to treat them it may be that the surgeon could use my skills.' William looked at the man he could see his offer of help was genuine.

'Sir, what is your name, I know you are the father of Francois and Adele but I do not know you.'

'My name is Martin Saurin. I am originally from France and I, with my son and daughter are hoping to make a new life for ourselves in the new world.' He looked again at Williams leg. 'Keep your leg raised it will keep the pressure off and you will feel

59

more at ease.' Martin Saurin turned and left the cabin feeling in his own mind that he could and would help the young man who saved his daughters life. When he arrived back at the area, they had been calling theirs, Martin spoke first to his daughter,

'You were very fortunate, it could have been very bad for you if that young man had not been able to prevent you from being swept overboard.' Although his first language was French, he would only speak English to his children and although they knew a great deal of French, he insisted that they spoke English. His wife had taught the children French from an early age and they spoke it well but they were headed for a land where English was the main language and he wanted his children to be confident when they spoke. Looking at Adele, he told her that she should offer to help the young man and his friends in any way she could as a gesture of thanks, he would ask in what way she could assist when he went back the following morning. Adele did not like the idea of her services being offered, what could she do, she could clean and wash for them but on a ship that was difficult she told her father that she would do whatever he agreed. Martin then turned to his son,

'Help me gather some of the herbs and mixtures so that I can offer them when I go back, I think pain relief may be the thing that would be of most help, so make up the draught that we discussed yesterday but be careful I have very little in the way of ingredients and those that remain I must use to cultivate plants when we reach our new home.' Francois carefully opened a large sack, it had various pockets and in each pocket were dried seeds. His father had become somewhat of an expert in the rejuvenation of seeds and bringing on good quality plants that he required to carry out his work. Then the father together with his children sat and tried to eat some of the dried meat and fish. They had been able to light a small fire on a bed of sand and with a little of the precious water managed to soak some of the meat. The salt was becoming too much for them to bear but Martin knew that to survive they must eat.

As the sun rose over the ocean Richard Hinds collected together various items from his store. He would need a splint of some description and bandages to hold the lad's leg in position. When he was satisfied, he made his way back to William's cabin. He was met by the taller of the two young man's companions,

'How is the casualty this morning?' Alec liked the look of the surgeon, he had a manner that showed confidence, he approached William with an air that put those he spoke to at ease.

'Let's have a look at this leg of yours,' he rolled the blanket from William's leg and started to examine it, as he did there was a knock on the door and Martin Saurin stood holding his precious herbs.

'I am the father of the girl this young man rescued yesterday. I understand he has a damaged leg.' The surgeon looked at him not really knowing what to make of the man.

'Yes, his leg may be broken, have you any knowledge of such things?'

'I am an apothecary, but I also have knowledge of bones and how to set them.' This was good news as far as the surgeon was concerned. The setting of bones was a skill he had some idea of but by no means was he an expert.

'I need to have a look to see if I can ascertain which bone is fractured and how bad it may be.' With that he started again to gently feel William's leg starting with the ankle. As he pressed William let out a yelp, the pain was sudden but the surgeon released the pressure he had used. Hmmm he looked up at Martin,

'I think your services may be required but I think it is a minor fracture of the smaller of the two lower leg bones.' With that he stood and made way for Martin to examine the leg.

'I would agree with you, I think that it will be easy to align and that it is a break that should heal well.' William had listened to the two discussing his leg as if he wasn't there. The surgeon nodded,

'Can you set it now?' Martin nodded, yes but it may cause a little discomfort to the patient, but he is young, healthy and brave so it should be a simple task.' William was unsure of what he meant by discomfort, yes, he was brave but not stupid.

'How much pain will there be?' His voice showed some reluctance to participate in anything that would hurt.

'I am sure your friends and the surgeon will get you through it without you suffering too much.'

The apothecary positioned himself as close as he could, he ran his hands over the broken limb. He could feel where the bone had suffered trauma. It was not a bad fracture and would heal fairly quickly. Taking the leg in his hands he pulled with his right and felt with his left the bone met with relative ease. William had felt an initial surge of pain as his leg was pulled into position, the world seemed to spin out of control. It didn't last for more than a minute, the surgeon took a slatted wooden splint, carefully rolled it around William's leg and pulled tight on the straps that would hold it in position. He then made sure that

Williams boot was securely fastened and the ankle was secure. The surgeon and the bone setter stood back and admired their work, Richard Hinds looked at Martin Saurin and nodded.

'It will take a few weeks but all should be well.' He said with a satisfied look on his face. The bone setter agreed.

'It is a good join and he will be back on both legs in no time.' The two men looked down at William, the surgeon asked,

'How do you feel?' William's reply was a little shaky,

'A little sick and my leg is throbbing.' The surgeon smiled,

'That will pass but if you feel more pain and sickness call for me but I am confident that you will heal quickly. He looked at Saurin,

'Yes, I concur with the surgeon you will heal well.'

The surgeon stood, 'Well I must be about my duties, I am sure there are others who require my services.' As he made his way to the door he turned to Saurin,

'I must say mister bone setter we did well and if I have any further need of you may I send for you?' Saurin collected his bag of herbs,

'Yes, I am at your service.' With that Richard Hinds left the rather crowded cabin and returned to his own quarters.

Before Martin Saurin left the cabin, he produced from his bag a small sachet which he gave to Alec,

'If the young man experiences pain soak this in water and let him drink as much as he can, it will ease the pain and help him rest.' Alec thanked him and watched him pass out into the morning.

'Well, we better get our arrangements sorted now that we have an invalid amongst us.' Robert said smiling at William. I am sure getting our hands dirty will not present a challenge to us.' He looked across at Alec, 'I think that I may be better off in the hammock as I have a little more flexibility than you.' Alec raised an eyebrow, they were both of a similar age and he resented the fact that Robert thought he was more agile than him. He agreed and then tried to imagine how William would fare with his leg in a splint.

'Robert, do we know where the carpenter can be found?' Robert shook his head,

'I don't know but I am sure I can find out from the crew, why?' Alec looked at William's leg,

'He will need some assistance in getting around so a crutch or stick may be needed.' Robert agreed,

'The carpenter should be easily found, I will seek him out and see what he can do.' With that he straightened himself and left the cabin.

'Now young William what are we going to do with you?'

It was on the second day after the accident that there was a gentle knock on the cabin door. Alec opened it the apothecary stood with his bag of magic and beside him was a young woman who Alec thought must be his daughter.

'Good morning to you.' Alec said with a little surprise in his voice. The apothecary bowed his head,

'I have come to see if there is any more I can do for your friend.' Alec invited them into the restricted space of the cabin.

'I think what you did yesterday was more than we could have hoped for.' The apothecary went on.

'My daughter wishes to thank the young man for saving her and she would like to help in any way

66

she can.' With that Martin stood to one side allowing his daughter to see inside the space that William occupied. She was amazed that three men could fit into the space but realised that two bunks and a small table was like a mansion compared with how she was forced to live. Adele pulled the cowl of her cloak away from her face, Alec drew a breath, the girl had an elegance about her. He could see that through her youthfulness there was a beauty trying to emerge. William propped himself up on one elbow,

'Adele, how are you, have you recovered from our battle with the sea?' The girl blushed a little which in William's eyes made her all the more attractive.

'I am well.' She said in her accented English. At that point her father said to Alec that if his daughter could assist in any way with the care for William she would be at their service. Alec looked from Robert to William then back to Adele, 'I cannot think of anything at this moment.' He said but if she could visit William to help him regain his strength that would be good.

'Very well, I shall send Adele to you each morning and if you have any duties for her to perform then that is what she will do.'

As they were about to leave William asked if Adele could talk with him, it would make a change from listening to his two friends. Alec and Robert took on an expression of hurt but then smiled. Adele agreed that she would return the following morning. William was pleased that he had been able to encourage her to visit, what they would talk about was yet to be decided, he had no idea how their talks would begin, what he could say would be limited to his life on the farm and little else, but at least it was a start.

Chapter 7

It was three days after the incident where William injured his leg, Adele had visited each morning and although their conversation was stilted when they began it had taken on a more relaxed feeling. He had asked Adele to tell him about herself and her family she had said that their story was long and quite complicated.

'We have many more days in this floating prison.' William was not enamoured by what he had been told of the conditions onboard. Adele spoke plainly and described what was going on sometimes in graphic detail.

'It smells, it is the passengers, when the weather is poor, they cannot use the place in the head of the ship, they use wherever they can. That could be the area where they live or if they can get to it the hold in the ship where the ballast is. We have been at sea for three weeks and still have far to go, if we have much more bad weather, I fear that we shall all be stricken with disease.'

From his bunk William had heard his friends speak of how the life onboard had deteriorated and that the food had become monotonous as well as lacking in any goodness. He looked at Adele, even though she was annoyed by the conditions on the ship William thought that her face still held something special. He enjoyed watching her and listening to her voice, he found that he could face his confinement all the better after he had spoken to her.

On the morning of the third day Adele had just finished explaining how her grandfather had travelled through France when there was a knock on the cabin door and Richard Hinds, the surgeon, asked if he could see the patient.

'Please come in.' William was pleased to see the surgeon and hoped he would see an improvement in his leg. As he entered Adele made ready to leave, they passed closely and as they did William saw the look on the surgeon's face, he seemed to stop in his tracks and coughing he tried to clear his throat,

'Excuse me.' He said trying to make room for Adele to pass. She looked up at him and for a moment lost her footing, stumbling she stretched out her hand which was caught by the surgeon. 'Steady, we don't want two broken limbs in one place.' William could see a flush appearing on Adele's cheeks, she let her hand linger slightly longer than was necessary, her reply was soft tinged with a little embarrassment,

'Thank you, sir.' She reached up and pulled her cowl down to cover her face and then left the cabin hurriedly. Richard Hinds followed the figure of the girl with his eyes as she made her way out of the small space of the cabin.

'Who was that?' He looked at William for an answer.

'That is Adele the daughter of the man who set my bone alongside you.'

'Really, you mean that lovely girl is Saurin's daughter.'

'Yes, she visits me daily and we talk of our lives, it is something she agreed to try to assist my recovery.' The surgeon stopped for a moment, his thoughts were taken by the girl he had just met, he was a single man, in his life, he had not been so instantly captivated by any female. He shook himself then turned back to William.

'How is the leg, have you had much pain?' William adjusted his position on the bunk,

'No pain just boredom, except of course when Adele visits.' The surgeon smiled he could understand that the girl would add a little sun into anyone's life. 'Let's have a look.' He lifted William's leg and inspected his foot then above the knee, replacing the leg he looked at William and nodded, 'Its healing well but it needs several weeks to fully knit, so I am afraid you will be stuck here for some time.' William's face dropped,

'Alec has had the carpenter make me a crutch, is there any way I can use that to get out of this cabin, its driving me to distraction, the only time I feel I am in the land of the living is when Adele visits.' William pointed to the crutch in the corner of the cabin. Richard Hinds took the crutch in two hands, it seemed sturdy enough and had a grip that William could steady himself by.

'There is no time like the present.' The surgeon said as he brought the crutch to the side of the bunk. 'Let's see how you do, there is not much of a swell so you should have a good chance of remaining upright.' He helped William into a sitting position then after he had swung his legs out of the bunk, he handed him the crutch. William tried to lever himself up but found it difficult so the surgeon took an arm and started to lift. William slowly became upright he found his balance shot to pieces but eventually managed to stand on one leg supporting himself with the crutch. Richard Hinds was pleased with what he saw,

'There you are, you can at least get up from the bunk, as to how far you will be able to walk is another matter.'

'This is all I ask at the moment.' William was pleased just being upright filled him with a sense of achievement.

'Don't try to go far, that leg of yours is not badly broken but if you were to fall again it may not be as easy to repair.' Richard Hinds was pleased with his visit and not only for seeing William's progress but also for meeting the astonishingly captivating daughter of the Apothecary.

As he made his way back through the ship to his own quarters Richard Hinds could not get the image of the young woman from his mind. She was, he thought a very attractive individual and one that he hoped to see more of. He had not long settled himself behind his small desk when a seaman came crashing through the door,

'Please come quickly, there is need of you.' The sailor appeared breathless and out of sorts.

'What is it man.' He asked as the sailor steadied himself.

'There is need of you in the main deck, the Chief Mate sent me to fetch you, can you please come with all haste.' Richard got up from his desk,

'Lead on I will follow.' The sailor turned and quickly made his way back to the Chief Mate. Richard asked what the urgency was, the sailor replied that a woman was giving birth and that she was in great difficulty.

'Were there no other women to help with the birth.' Richard thought how he was rarely needed at births as other women would have far greater knowledge of what to do than him. They reached the deck and at the far end there was a group of women clustered around what Richard thought could only be the woman giving birth. Those standing close by made way to allow Richard to reach the troubled woman. He could see that she was in pain, her face showed her agony. He took the woman's hand and gently told her he was going to examine her, she let out a scream that echoed through the deck. Richard did not have to lift her skirts and the women attending her had tried to see what was causing the difficulty. Richard felt the woman's lower abdomen and could feel that the child was in a difficult position. He looked up at the nearest helper,

'We have to try to reposition the child, help me.' The women knelt by his side and between them

74

they tried to rectify the situation. They tried several times but whatever they did they could not get the baby into a good position. The mother was now screaming in pain, one of the helpers cradled her head and tried to comfort her. Richard could see that the only way would be to cut the baby free but he was not sure of how to carry out the procedure. He tried again to realign the baby but failed, the mother screamed again this time it was a sound that the women standing close by knew of old and that this was the end of the woman and possibly her unborn child. Richard drew back as the woman exhaled, her body went limp, it was the end of her life, he then tried to see if he could find any sign of life in the baby but his efforts were fruitless. Both mother and child had died in his hands. He felt utterly useless, his hands trembled as he rearranged the woman's clothing. The Chief Mate placed a hand on Richard's shoulder,

'You tried your best.' Richard looked up,

'Yes, but it was not good enough, I should have saved them both.'

Richard was nearly knocked onto his back as a man of about thirty years burst through the surrounding onlookers.

'My Mary, what have you done to my Mary?' He knelt beside the woman lifting her head and kissing her face. The Chief Mate took hold of the man and tried to pull him away, he would not let go of the woman and spun around to look at the person who was trying to separate him from his wife. 'I will not leave her, and my child, what have you done to my child?' The man then realised that both were dead, his head dropped and his shoulders heaved and fell, he buried his face into the breast of his wife, his hands clutched her clothing. The Chief Mate tried again to move the man but had no success. Richard and the Chief Mate moved back from the body, the Chief Mate motioned to one of the women,

'You know this man and his wife?'

'Yes, they are from the same town as us.'

'Will you stay with him until he has regained control and then send a member of the crew to fetch me.'

'Yes, I will.'

Richard picked himself up and with the Chief Mate walked away from the scene. As he made his way back to his cabin, he met the apothecary who, seeing the look on Richard's face, asked what the problem was. Richard explained as best he could but found that describing what had just taken place difficult to put into words. Martin Saurin looked at the surgeon with empathy, he had seen many deaths due to complications not only those involved in birth but also those resulting from minor injury where he thought he had cured the ailment. Martin followed the surgeon back to his cabin and sat while he poured a glass of brandy and with an unsteady hand took a sip from his glass.

'There is so much more that I should be able to do, not just for women in labour but for those who should be destined for a long life not a sudden death.'

Martin watched the surgeon take another sip of the brandy,

'You did all you could in the circumstances, you tried there is nothing more that could be asked of you.'

Richard shook his head. 'You did not see the look of anguish on the woman's face or that of her husband when he saw her dead body still with his child inside her.' Martin felt that all he could do was to listen to Richard for as long as he wanted to speak about the woman's death.

The following day William woke to the ship moving a little more than he had experienced in the previous days. Some of the items in the cabin were moving on their own accord, he tried to get out of the bunk but could not move his good leg sufficiently to gain a relatively stable position. Alec could see him struggling and moved to take his arm,

'Do you think you should be trying to stand when it feels as if the ship is heading towards bad weather?' William could see that his friend was having a little trouble standing steady.

'I would like to try,' William said as he reached out for a helping hand. He managed to stand but as he took his first step he fell back, fortunately it was not on his injured leg. He sat on the side of the bunk,

'I suppose that this is as far as I shall be able to get until the weather calms down.' He said almost to himself. Alec tapped him on the shoulder,

'It may not be long before you are able to get up, rough seas seem to come and go quite quickly and hopefully you will have the company of Adele to take your mind off of your confinement.' William conjured up a vision of Adele in his mind and smiled to himself, yes, he would enjoy her company and forget his predicament for a while. Before Adele arrived, Richard Hinds visited to check on the patient. William thought it strange that the surgeon should call so soon after his previous visit, he listened to what the surgeon had to say and he became a little agitated as he knew that Adele would be visiting shortly. The surgeon seemed satisfied, he told them of the tragedy of the woman and her baby which did not lift their spirits. Adele arrived in a slightly flustered state the roll of the ship had caused her to reel from side to side as she tried to make her way through the ship and its passengers. She had heard from her father of the tragedy that Richard had attended. She looked almost pitifully at the surgeon and placed her hand on his sleeve, without thinking he placed his hand on top of hers, it was a very quick movement as she snatched her hand away but the gesture had been made which William had seen and immediately felt a sense of loss.

'I shall need to speak to your father this morning.' Richard said in a rather softer than usual voice. Adele looked at him with widened eyes,

'I shall tell him, do you wish him to come to your cabin?'

'Yes, we have an increasing number of passengers starting to suffer from various complaints and I need to consult him to establish the best treatment for them.' Adele nodded and bobbed in a form of curtsey and stumbled as she did which caused a flush of red to creep into her cheeks. She steadied herself by leaning on William's shoulder, this time he placed his hand over hers. She regained her balance quickly removing her hand she said that she would speak to her father. Richard left the cabin still carrying the thought of Adele in his mind, he had never felt this way before, not in his early youth and had been too involved in his studies to even think about the opposite sex when he attended the Royal College of Physicians. His life had been all consumed by anatomy, chemistry and natural history and gaining the knowledge and experience to enable him to make diagnosis and give some idea of how problems with the body would eventually heal itself with the help of medicines and physical treatment. This young vision that had presented itself before him had caused him some alarm and he needed to be able to concentrate on the matters in hand rather than drifting into a dream world.

Adele sat unsteadily on a chair next to William's bunk,

'What shall we discuss today?' Her voice was a little strained, William thought that this was due to the condition of the ship but in reality, she was also a little perturbed by the closeness of the surgeon and the effect it had on her.

'You did say that you would tell me how your family came to be in England and how you are now on your way to a new world.' Adele adjusted her cloak and after making herself as comfortable as she could began.

'My family are originally from the South of France close to the city of Grenoble and were deeply religious. My great grandfather suffered during the wars of religion. As a follower of Baron des Ardrets he considered himself to be a Huguenot and followed their belief that conflicted with the church of Rome. My family suffered the swords of the French royalty who sought to eradicated any form of Protestantism from their kingdom. The followers of Calvin were particularly persecuted as they were considered threat not only to the crown of France but to the established ruling classes. The years that my great grandfather lived through did not see the end of the religious conflict. Many families left the area taking with them the knowledge of trades and skills which made the area around Grenoble prosperous. My family travelled through France trying to find a place where they were free to worship and live a life of relative peace.' William tried to imagine a family forced to leave their homes, what would that be like in England? He then remembered his mother and father telling him of their fight to live the way they wanted to, how his father had left his home to fight for a cause and never returned. He wanted to know more but Adele told him that they had plenty of time until they reached their destination, she said she would continue on the morrow.

*

Martin Saurin had watched his fellow passengers carefully. He had seen a gradually deterioration in their condition. He knew that the food that they had to eat was causing problems, there was no fresh produce and the heavily salted meat and fish did not help matters. It was a blessed relief when the crew were able to try to catch fresh fish, there had been success and failure, some of the catches were of a size that would feed many and others days nothing at all. The apothecary had seen, during his travels, a great emphasis placed on the consuming of fresh produce, fruit and vegetables, which did not exist onboard the ship. He had spoken to some of the crew, particularly the bosun, who had explained to him that it was becoming normal for ships to take onboard such things as preserved fruit and a form of pickled vegetable that gave some help in fighting scurvy,

'It is not just the fact that during a long voyage food suffers, it's also the vermin onboard. As much as we try to get rid of rats and other rodents it's a never-ending task. We do have several barrels of apples which have been carefully stored but they will not last the trip.' He looked a little crestfallen when Martin mentioned one of the most common problems onboard, scurvy.

'How do you cope with that.' Martin knew that without fresh water and decent food scurvy could affect a large proportion of the crew. Although he had very little experience of the disease, he had seen its affects during his travels. The bosun stroked his chin,

'I try to get the crew to take care of themselves, but how do you do that in such a confined space with only the rations onboard.'

'Do the apples help?' Martin wanted to find out what could help controlling this debilitating disease.

'I think they do but we only have a limited amount and as for the passengers I am afraid they have to fend for themselves.' Martin was disheartened by what he heard, he knew of the symptoms, the tiredness, the aching limbs, the swollen gums and spots on the legs. Scurvy was not a pleasant sight to see. He had been told that although deaths were common, with care it could be managed. He had been aware of what the ships leaving the ports in the south of France carried with them. The carrying of dried fruits, nuts and fresh lemons was not uncommon, but trying to get such things in England to take on a voyage to the new world was almost impossible. He had managed to secure some lemons which he had sliced and put into several large jars. He would make sure that his children ate at least one slice a day and he would see how they fared. Martin enjoyed speaking to the ship's crew, he found he could get some down to earth information from them and they were not afraid of speaking their minds.

Edward Carrick sat at his desk and opened the ships log, he kept meticulous details of the voyage. His entries were clear and concise, the ships position, the conditions, the state of the victuals how, the cargo fared and the passengers, who had died, an entry that gave him the most difficulty. As he sat, he opened the passenger list and ran his finger down the long column of names until he reached the name of the family that had just lost the woman and child. The captain had managed to get the husband to tell him his name and that of his wife,

Name	Age	Occupation	Place of birth	Bound for
Stephenson	27	Carpenter	Gloucester	Virginia
Wife Ellen				

He drew a line through the name of the wife and entered in the last column of the log,

Died on this day in childbirth

He closed the log knowing that it would not be the last entry of a death during this voyage.

The bosun had another duty which was not a pleasant one. The dead woman had' to be seen to. He had detailed two of the crew to get a section of sail

84

cloth, enough to wrap the corpse in, he then had to prise the husband way from the body, which was difficult. The ships parson had been of great help. He spoke in gentle terms to the husband trying to assure him that both his wife and child would enter the kingdom of heaven. When the bodies were encased in the sail cloth the last stitch was administered then the bundle was lifted on to the side of the ship awaiting the final words from the parson. There were a number of people on deck to attend to burial at sea, Richard Hinds stood close to the husband in case he should fall, Martin looked on and wished he could have done more. The captain stood alongside the parson and looked over those that were also paying their last respects, he was very aware that this would not be the last burial he would attend on this voyage. Already the water had taken on a bad flavour and the ale together with the beer would only just see them to the end of their journey.

Martin Saurin could only think of his loss, his wife had succumbed to shipboard disease when they crossed from France to England. He had thought it was not possible to contract anything in such a short space of time. His wife was full of life when they had set out. She was a picture of health, her cheeks were rosy red and her eyes sparkled. It was when the ship they were on was blown of course that the problems began. It was not just the sea sickness that affected her it was the closeness of the other passengers. There must have been upwards of three hundred. They had been crammed into a space that should hold no more than two hundred. Those that travelled were from all over the continent, some from The Netherlands, Spain, France and the German states and of course they brought with them all the pain and suffering that went with a population fleeing from their home land. Martin saw his wife quickly appear drawn and lifeless, her whole being seemed to slow down and become laboured. He tried everything he knew to help her but with the two children to care for it was not easy. His wife had begged him to take care of the children first and leave her to the fate that God had given her. Martin's love for his wife was absolute, although he cared deeply for his children his wife held his heart. As much as he tried, he could not stop the fever from taking his wife. It was three days of agony and torment until she took her final breath and he was able to close her eyes for the last time. There had been no formal burial, a parson read from the bible, it was not in her native tongue and not the passages she had been raised with. Her body had been given to the sea and his life crashed into a horror that was only made good by his children. Although they were only ten and eleven years of age their care and comfort were something that enabled him to regain his sanity. He promised his wife as she entered the sea that he would do everything to make his children's life one that she would be proud of. It was this episode that focused his mind on trying to find cures for any ship board diseases.

Shortly after the woman and child were consigned to the deep Captain Carrick called for the surgeon to meet him in his cabin, thinking that this could only be linked to the health onboard the ship Richard Hinds asked Martin Saurin to accompany him. The two men met at the captain's cabin door just as the ships bell rang out three sets of two indicating the forenoon watch. It had fascinated Richard how the ship was run, watches were not common amongst the crew and the captain, first mate and surgeon were probably the only people onboard to carry one, they were expensive items, out of reach of the common man's pocket. Knocking on the cabin door the two men straightened themselves, the call for them to enter came in a firm voice, when they had opened the door, they saw that there were already two others as well as the captain waiting for them.

'Gentlemen, come in.' It was an almost friendly greeting. With the Captain were the Chief Mate and Bosun. It was a tight fit but they managed sit around a central table.

'I trust you know each other?' There was a murmur of acknowledgement then the captain continued. 'We are reaching the mid-point of our journey and I need to know from you your thoughts on how we fare.' The four men looked at each other with a little surprise the captain would usually ask individuals for any information he needed. This meeting was a little out of the ordinary but all four men could see the logic in it.

'Mister Dimmock, what can you tell us of how the ship is and are there any areas that concern you?' The chief mate looked at those around the table,

'The ship is in good condition, we are fortunate that we have not encountered severe weather so far. My only concern is that the passengers are now beginning to suffer from their confinement when there is a swell and together with the food starting to taint, we may experience problems in that area. The livestock we have are surviving on the fodder we give them. All is well but as you say we are only half way through our voyage.' The captain nodded he had been making notes and as he dropped his quill, he looked at the bosun.

'How are rations, do we have sufficient to see us through?' The bosun, a man used to the sea and dealing with both crew and passengers.

'We have sufficient for our needs, the salt beef, pork and fish are enough for us to feed all onboard for at least twenty-five to thirty days. The water is my concern the levels have dropped and we need rain to capture and top up the barrels. I am told by the cook that we have preserved cabbage and other dried pulses such as peas that we can use but there is nothing fresh left so we are limited to what we give the men.' There was a short silence as the seriousness of the situation sank in.

'Now, Mr Hinds, how are the passengers and crew, is there a great deal of sickness, have you seen signs of scurvy or other diseases?' The surgeon cleared his throat,

'As far as I can tell we have not had any break out of a serious complaint, however, if we travel without fresh rations, I have no doubt that some will suffer and that the weaker of those onboard may suffer badly.' The captain rested his head on his hand,

'Is there anything that you may have experienced that may help us?' Richard Hinds chose his words carefully.

'It may help to get the passengers on deck to get fresh air and some sun on their faces, the conditions on the deck where most are living is becoming a breeding place for disease and lice and that together with increase in rodents makes me anticipate more serious outbreaks in the near future.'

The captain's prime objective was to get the cargo and ship to Virginia in the best possible condition. He turned to Martin Saurin,

'And you Mister Apothecary, what do you say?' Martin cleared his throat,

'It is as the surgeon has said those onboard need fresh air and fresh food to avoid an outbreak of something serious, however, I know that this is not possible. It would be of help if those passengers that are able to be put to use cleaning the areas that they occupy. If they could be tasked to scrub the deck on which they live and get rid of the filth that is now accumulating, that would help prevent some diseases.' The captain thought that his was something that could be done as long as it did not interfere with the running of the ship. He turned to the Chief Mate,

'What do you say Mister Dimmock, could we get those passengers cleaning without causing problems?' Dimmock had a smile on his face, getting the passengers working would be a good idea and the crew, he was sure, would like to see the 'cargo' working.

'I believe that this could be arranged, and if the weather permits, after they have cleaned, they can be allowed on deck in say parties of twenty at a time.' The captain looked at the men before him, he had not known some of them very long but he prided himself in being a good judge of character and had faith in that judgement.

'I think gentlemen, that we will follow the recommendations of the surgeon and apothecary. If I could leave it in your hands to organise Mr Dimmock, and Bosun stay in contact with the surgeon regarding the state of the victuals and Mr Saurin will you please keep in close contact with the surgeon regarding any deterioration in those who share the space near you. I think that is all for the time being, I will call for you to attend here in five days when we can assess our progress or otherwise.' With that they stood and made their way towards the cabin door,

'Mr Dimmock, please if you will, a moment more of your time.' The captain needed to make sure that the chief mate was aware of how far they would go to put what was discussed into operation. The bosun, surgeon and apothecary left and made their way back to their places of work.

The conversation between the chief mate and the captain centred on how to get the passengers to keep their areas clear and clean.

'Do we have any individuals who stand out as possible leaders and if we do how willing would they be to encourage their fellows to work.' The captain's voice did not hold much confidence in his experience those onboard were mainly concerned with keeping alive, they did not lend themselves to the hard work that was required to keep the ship clean and anyway that was the job of the crew, wasn't it? The chief mate struggled to come up with any names,

'You know of the apothecary and there are a couple of god-fearing sorts who may be able to preach that cleanliness is next to godliness, but not many others.' Edward Carrick had been the master of several ships and had experienced larger numbers than he had aboard the Neptune, his aim would be to get the more agreeable individuals to work alongside the crew.

'I think we will start with the apothecary and then we can also speak to the three men who seem to be well versed in handling others.'

'I don't know if you are aware that one of those men, the youngest, broke a bone when he prevented the apothecary's daughter from being swept overboard. He has been treated by the surgeon and is doing well but will be of no use in cleaning or managing others until he is fully recovered.'

'The other two, Alec Sinclair and his associate who's name I can never recall, they are used to handling people, I think. Sinclair has a role on one of the major plantations so if anyone can get the cargo working it would be him. Have a conversation with them and see if you can arrange for them to advise all concerned.' The chief mate replied,

'I will speak with them this day and hopefully set things in motion.' He turned to leave, his work would now be not only seeing to the crew but to the passengers as well. The bosun, his mate, the cook and the deck hands would all be involved, he knew that squabbles would almost certainly arise but he had the experience and the strength get things going.

Chapter 8

Alec Sinclair had been dealing with the labour on the plantation for several years. He had seen the changes in the types of humanity that arrived from all parts of the world. There were those from his native Scotland, some from Ireland and Wales and many from England. They were mainly indentured souls whose passage had been paid for by the plantation owners. They would be indentured to the plantation for a minimum of seven years. Their dream would be to serve their time then claim some land and make a life for themselves. Those dreams, Alec knew, would only be fulfilled by very few. For the indentured workers it would be hard work, long hours and poor food, their survival rate would be low. The new world held more dangers than they could imagine. The climate was not too dissimilar to the one they had known but disease, starvation, native tribes and physical dangers of cropping tobacco would count for a high number of their deaths.

It came as a surprise when the chief mate approached him and started to talk about getting those onboard to work. He was aware of the mixture of individuals that made up the passengers. Most of those that he had seen and spoken to were terrified of dying at sea and losing their souls to the devil. His first thought was to get the parson to speak to those and encourage them to help themselves through cleanliness and godliness. Alec told the chief mate that he had seen that faith could not only move mountains, but also keep a ship clean.

'Would you be willing to speak to the parson with me.' Alec was not sure but if it made life onboard any easier then he would. His colleague, Robert, had heard the parson preach and his view was that the man had some substance however he did lack the charisma needed to truly bring his flock together.

'I will try to help in whatever way I can, it may be easier if we could demonstrate how their lives would be better served in a clean ship rather that one filled with vermin and disease.' The chief mate agreed, they would seek out the parson that day with a view to getting him involved with their plan.

The parson, a God-fearing man, had little knowledge of the world. He had been sheltered by his family, particularly his mother, who had high hopes for him. Unfortunately, things did not develop the way they expected. His progress in to the ministry was hampered by his family's background. His father had been a staunch protestant and as such had stood firmly against the monarch. The restoration of Charles II had left the parson's family in limbo, what were they to do? It had been his father, after ingratiating himself with certain members of the country gentry, saw his son enter the church but the parson knew he was not a preacher. He would have liked to have continued with his studies and become a teacher, but he was a loyal son and followed his father's wishes. The first post he obtained was that of a curate in a fairly large church in the diocese of Lincoln. He learnt quickly but still felt that he was not a true man of the people. After several years he felt that he needed to get away from his father's constant badgering about his career and how he should aim for the higher positions in the diocese. It was a parishioner who spoke to him about the new world and how a person could start afresh without ties to his homeland. 'Did he have the courage' he asked himself, 'Could he travel across the ocean in search of a better life?' And what was a better life, he had no idea.

It was after a great deal of soul searching that he finally made up his mind to go. His family were shocked, why would he want to leave the comfort of Lincoln to try to make a life for himself in a strange and dangerous land? It was with some difficulty that he eventually persuaded his father to give him his blessing. The parson had travelled on two ships before setting out on his long voyage. He had taken a ship from Boston, Lincolnshire, to Newcastle. The journey was short but the seas were rough. Once he had got over his initial sickness, he found that the small close-knit crew and the passengers seemed to suit him. He had preached to those that wanted to listen and found that he could speak to them a lot easier than those parishioners in Lincoln. When he arranged his passage to Virginia, he was not sure what he was doing, however, it would be a new start, a fresh beginning, a new world.

'Ah parson.' The chief mate had not taken to this man who wore the robes of the churchman. 'We are in need of your advice and assistance.'

'What can I do for you?' His voice was full of curiosity.

'The ship is in need of some work to make it a more liveable place and your position may help us achieve our goals.' The parson looked from the chief mate to the surgeon and then to Martin Saurin. 'Are you aware of these gentlemen?' The parson coughed, he had been introduced to the surgeon but the other man he was not aware of.

'I know Mr Hinds but I do not know the other gentleman.'

'This is Mr Saurin, he is an apothecary and is assisting Mr Hinds.' He turned towards Martin Saurin, 'This is our parson, Mr Peters.' The two men eyed each other Martin took in the almost delicate frame of the parson, his pale complexion and fair hair made him almost translucent. At the same time Geoffry Peters could see that the apothecary was a confident individual with a sense of purpose exuding from every pore. They shook hands, Martin was a little surprised with the strength in the parson's handshake which gave him a little hope that he was not the weak individual he first appeared. Richard Hinds explained to the parson exactly what they wanted from him,

'We need you to preach cleanliness to the passengers, we have a situation that we cannot let get out of hand, we all will suffer less if we can show all onboard how crucial it is to keep their areas free from dirt and waste.' The parson nodded.

'I couldn't agree more, I have seen the situation slowly become hazardous, there are those in the area where they sleep, in the same clothes as when they boarded the ship and although I understand that's all they may have at present, lice will certainly become a serious problem in the very near future.' Richard and Martin were pleased to hear the parson's comments. The chief mate then spoke to the three men.

'We need to assess exactly what the condition of the ship is, I suggest we visit the deck where the passengers keep themselves and it may be that Mr Saurin could lead us through the area.' Martin agreed.

'When would you like to see the area?' The chief mate looked at the three men in front of him.

'There is no time like the present, so gentlemen if you can spare the time, I suggest we follow Mr Saurin to see what the challenge we have set ourselves is.' It was at this point that Alec Sinclair appeared, as he approached the group of men the chief mate spoke,

'This is a man that has a great deal of experience in dealing with men and organising labour. He will be giving us the benefit of his advice in the days to come'. Alec looked at the other men and could see that they had an air of determination about them.

'Gentlemen I will assist wherever I can.'

The four men picked up a lamp each then followed Martin as he led them into the deck where he and his family slept.

'This is my domain, as you can see my son is making sure that all is in its rightful place, we have three bunks for sleeping, we have raised them from the deck and our clothing set upon them, this keeps them as dry as we can.' Richard looked around the Apothecary's sleeping arrangements, it was primitive but workable. Martin continued, 'There are others who had no money to secure a space who are reduced to living as best they can on the deck with few clothes and straw for warmth and comfort, come I will show

99

you.' As they walked through the families and individual's they could see signs of disease starting to take hold. There were children with poor clothing and some with bound legs and feet indicating that they had suffered some injury. Martin held a lamp out in front of them as they reached the darkest part of the deck. In a corner there seemed to be a bundle of clothing, Martin asked a woman nearby what it was.

'It's the old couple, they are not really old but just seemed to sleep all the time.' Martin walked over to the heap of dark material, he prodded it with his foot,

'Hello, are you suffering?' There was no reply. He took a short pole from the side of the deck and pressed it home against the pile. Almost immediately there was movement but not what was expected. The four men jumped back as two rats ran from the dark pile, they scuttled off into the black recesses of the ship. The chief mate shook his head, turning to those nearby shouted in a voice that needed to be answered,

'You people, did you know this, this pair of human beings?' He looked at the faces in the dim light of the lamps,

'They were always together and very quiet.' It was a woman standing next to her children, her face could just about be seen. Her face belied her age she had to be over forty years, the chief mate thought. Alec was alarmed at the lack of concern,

'Did nobody speak to them, did you not think something was amiss?' There was a shuffling of feet but no answer. While Alec was speaking, Richard and Martin tried to see exactly what had happened. The two bodies were intertwined it looked as if they had died in their sleep holding each other. Perhaps, Richard thought, their last moment on this earth was spent in an embrace that would last forever.

'They have past the state of rigor so they must have been in this condition for almost two days.' Martin knelt beside the surgeon, he could see what Richard had said was correct. The stench was almost unbearable as they lifted the blankets from the bodies. The parson gagged as the corrupt smell of death filled his nostrils, he turned his head not knowing what to do or say.

'We will need to get these bodies out of here as quickly as possible, if you could remain here, I will get some help to remove the corpses.' Richard nodded, he tried to see details of the dead couple but the light did not show everything. Martin walked around the couple and removed more of the bedding they were using, it was a pitiful sight it looked as though they had been together in life and death. He could not believe that he or his family had not known of what was happening on the same deck that they had their quarters but the deck was a dark place and those in the far corners were difficult to see and as for the smell, the animals below made a stink that overpowered everything else.

The chief mate returned followed by four of the crew. They had with them a sheet of canvas which they spread alongside the dead couple.

'As quick as you can lads, let's get this over and done with.' The four sailors initially held their hand over their mouth and nose then they started to move the bodies. They were surprisingly light and they were moved onto the canvas quickly. It was at this time that there was a murmur amongst the passengers, they had seen the captain enter the deck and make his way towards the place where the bodies were being handled. Edward Carrick was no stranger to death and the dying but even he had to catch his breath as he approached the scene, he looked at his chief mate,

'What is the situation?' The chief mate explained how the two had been found and that they had been dead for over twenty-four hours. 'This is unacceptable, why did not any of the other passengers know about this?' The chief mate explained how the two dead people were man and wife and that they did not speak to the other passengers.

'But surely somebody would have noticed what was happening.' He shook his head in disbelief. 'How long before this is cleared?' His question was directed at the chief mate,

'We are starting to remove the bodies, we should be done very shortly.'

'And you parson, you will have to say your words speedily because these poor creatures will be consigned to the deep with all possible haste.' Geoffry Peters had regained his composure,

'As you wish captain I will follow the bodies on deck, my service will be brief.'

'Thank you, Mr Peters. Mr Dimmock, let me know as soon as all is in order and I need to know the names of the unfortunates as quick as you can.'

'Aye, Aye captain.' The chief mate turned to the crewmen and watched as they quickly encased both bodies in the one cloth, they would be buried as they died, together in each other's arms. The sailcloth was quickly stitched and weights were placed against the bodies. The passengers parted as the bodies were brought to the deck opening, heads dropped in a form of respect. On deck the parson was waiting, the sailors paused as he said the lord's prayer and as the last words fell from his lips the two bodies were tossed into the sea.

The chief mate had a great deal of difficulty in finding the names of the dead couple, those nearby seemed not to have had any communication with them, just when he was about to report his lack of success to the captain a woman came to him and said that she had been with them before they sailed.

'There name was Goodchild, I remember it because I thought it a pretty name. The chief mate sighed with relief. He thanked the woman and made his way to the captain's cabin. He knocked and waited until he was beckoned in. He found Edward Carrick studying charts that were spread on his desk, the chief mate reported the names of the deceased couple, with that the captain moved away from the charts and took out the passenger list. The name Goodchild was in the middle of the second page, Edward read along the entry,

Name	Age	Occupation	Place of Birth	Bound for
Goodchild	58	Servant	Salisbury	Virginia
Wife Jane				

He then drew a line threw the entry and wrote in the last column, died this day of melancholy. Satisfied with the entry he closed the log and returned to his chart. He then looked up at his chief mate, thank you Mr Dimmock, please let me know of any other occurrences. The chief mate turned away from his captain and made his way back to the middle deck.

Richard Hinds looked around the scene that had held the dead couple. There was still a smell that lingered, it was something that he hoped he would not experience too often. The four men stepped back surveying the area the chief mate drew himself up to his full height and in his powerful voice spoke to all on the deck.

'This is the result of the filth that you live in. Your existence depends on whether you want to finish this voyage or die where you sleep.' All those that could hear knew exactly what he was saying, he continued, 'You have a choice, you can either live in this hell and wait to die or you can help yourselves by following the instructions you will be given. It will mean that you will be required to work and work hard, or you can join those two poor unfortunates we have just cast into the sea.' Richard and Martin looked at each other and realised that the chief mate had seized the opportunity to put what they had discussed into operation. Richard looked at the man with a certain amount of admiration it was a clever move and one that would remain with the passengers for some time to come.

Alec had not spoken much, he had been looking at the conditions that passengers were living

105

in, he had seen and suffered worse himself. He knew that the fact that these creatures could not see the sky for most of the time, would have lowered their morale. The parson was on deck with the burial party leaving the other four to discuss their next move. Alec spoke first.

'I appreciate the dangers of disease and injury, but if these people are to remain in darkness, without sun or fresh air we will have a struggle to get them working. He looked at the chief mate, 'Is there any way that we could get them on deck, not necessarily all at once but at least give them a sight of the sky once a week or even once a day?' Richard Hinds agreed with Alec, it was a similar suggestion to that which he made earlier, however the chief mate could not see a way to allow the passengers on deck when his men were trying to keep the ship on course. He tried to take in the conditions that the passengers were living in but the bad light made it difficult, it was the smell of corruption that confirmed to him that things needed to improve or deaths would become a common occurrence.

'I will arrange that at least twenty of these souls will be allowed on deck during each watch, but no more otherwise the crew may be hampered in their duties.' Alec thought that it was a start, just getting a few into the fresh air would be of benefit.

The day had been one of event and tragedy, William had been unaware of the deaths. He thought the commotion he heard, he thought, was just the daily comings and goings of the crew. He had been visited by Adele and she had continued with the story of how her family ended up on board a ship bound for the Americas. He looked at her face and was still entranced by her features, she smiled,

'I have told you of the fight my grandparents had in the time of the holy wars. I shall now tell you of the journey they travelled to gain freedom.' William sat on the bunk and listened intently, Adele continued. 'Their life was hard and all-around families were being taken from their land, some even had their children taken from them if they were thought to be heretics. All those who were seen to be enemies of the Church of Rome were abused and maltreated. So it was with heavy heart that my family kept moving. My grandfather had one hope that was to educate his children to a level that would enable them to raise themselves in any society. My father was born in the year 1630 and my grandfather began teaching him Latin as soon as he could speak, he had only three books which he treasured they were, the bible, Bibliotheca anatomica and Magia Naturalis. His love of science and the study of the human body were uppermost in his thoughts when educating his children.' William stopped her,

'You say children, how many children did they have?' Adele looked down for a second,

'There was another child, another son, but alas he died at the age of six years. He was the youngest of the two and his death affected both of my grandparents in a way that left them distraught. They would never have another child so their attention was fully focused on my father.' William nodded with an understanding look on his face, Adele continued. 'Their travels through France were filled with fear and pain, my father had told me of how his parents had found surviving almost impossible, they had to find work to live so they did anything they could. It was a blessing when my father sought out Calvinist meetings and through them obtained some work and food. His Huguenot upbringing gave him strength of will and a certain belief and determination to carry on. It took them over three years to work their way through France as they had to avoid Louis XIV's dragoons knowing that if they fell into their hands their lives would be short.' Adele stopped and looking at Williams eager face told him that he would have to wait to learn how her family managed to get out of France. She stood and made ready to leave, as she did William felt her presence and did not want her to go but he knew there was no way he could detain her any longer and there was tomorrow.

'Will you return in the morning.' He asked, 'There is so much more I would like to know of your family.'

'I shall but as soon as your leg is better there may be no need to keep you entertained, however I will carry out my duties that I promised my father.' William did not want that day to arrive, he lay back in the bunk and watched her make her way out of the cabin. It was a short time after Adele had left the cabin that Robert appeared, he was eager to get in touch with Alec,

'Have you seen Alec?' William snapped out of his dream which was difficult as the main character in his imagination was always Adele,

'Sorry, he left some time ago, I believe he was meeting the chief mate and the surgeon.'

'Did he say where this meeting was to take place?'

'I am sorry he didn't say.'

'If he should return, please tell him I need to see him urgently.'

'Is there something wrong?'

'No, it's our cargo, I think we may have a problem in the way it's been stored.' With that he turned and made a quick exit from the cabin. William was alone, he lifted his leg which seemed to be healing, he felt no pain and had been able to get around with the use of his crutch when the weather permitted. He stood on one leg and managed to get the crutch under one arm, carefully he made his way to the door. He had little idea of what he was about to do but the boredom of life on one leg, stuck in a small cabin with little to do made him wish for a something to happen. Somehow William got himself to the entrance to the main deck, he hobbled along eventually reaching the open air. He breathed in the salty tang and for the first time in days felt refreshed. There was little activity, the crew were securing ropes, some were adjusting sails others were cleaning areas that had seen better days. He could see one of the sailors resting against the hatchway, William made his way towards the man,

'Good day to you, the weather appears good and the ship is making good headway.' The sailor looked a little bored with Williams opening remarks, he had no time for passengers but just as William turned to speak again, he stumbled as the ship rolled. The sailor caught him by the arm and manoeuvred him close to a hatch cover where William could sit. The sailor looked at Williams leg,

'What have you done, is it broken?' William adjusted his leg resting it on the lip of the hatch.

'Yes, it is not a bad injury, or so I am told, I should be well before we reach our destination.' The sailor looked again at the leg bound in a splint that the surgeon had used to immobilise the limb.

'You will need both legs where we are headed.' William looked at the man, his age was indeterminable, he could have been thirty or fifty or even older.

'What do you know of Virginia?' William watched the tanned face break into a grin.

'I know many things, some good, some very bad, you are in a cabin so you must have money which means you will not suffer as some do.'

'How do you mean?' The sailor shook his head,

'You will find out when we arrive, if we arrive, we still have twenty days or more depending on the wind and tide before we get close to the Americas.'

'How can we tell if we are close to our destination?' Again, a smile appeared on the sailor's face,

'When we reach a place where the seagulls land that is when you will know.' William looked out across the enormity of the ocean and tried to imagine what awaited him. His time with Alec and Robert had

111

given him some idea of what he could look forward to, some good and some things that might challenge him, this was the life he had chosen and he was determined to make a good life for himself in the new world.

Chapter 9

Richard Hinds did not think that communicating with the passengers would be as difficult as it turned out to be. The number of different dialects was totally unexpected, those from the south could not understand those from the north and it was the same east to west and it went further there was a sort of hierarchy. The indentured servants were at the bottom followed by those with skills and then there were those who travelled in some comfort not dissimilar to Alec and Robert who had an investment in the cargo or servants. Richard asked the chief mate why the majority of passengers were classed as servants when it was clear that they had no masters at sea.

'Their passages have been paid for and they are indentured for periods of five or seven years. They have been entered on the lists as what they are purported to be however, all those that travel the seas know that they are slaves by any other name and they will be treated as such when they arrive at their destination. Some of those onboard are members of the same family and will be employed on the same plantation, the owners of that plantation have paid for their passage and that payment has purchased each one of them. They are no longer freemen or women they have forfeited their freedom in the hope of a better life but I can assure you that it will not be the case. They will be worked until they can do no more, some will die of disease others will just die before their time. There will be dangers that they have never dreamed of.' Richard had some idea of the life in the new world but raised an eyebrow,

'What dangers are you referring too?' The chief mate stroked his chin,

'Everything from restless natives to starvation, some plantations are in areas that remain almost wilderness, there are many animals that feed on the weak who may fall, there are the native tribes that may seem to be friendly but you can never trust them.' Richard became very interested,

'How do you know of this, you're a ships chief mate, what do you know of plantations?' The chief mate stretched his arms,

'You see that man, the one known as Alec Sinclair.' Richard looked in the direction that the chief mate was pointing. 'He's a man to ask about life on plantations, he was once a slave now look at him, he is a well-respected member of the community. I have seen him change over the years, I was on the ship that brought him from England many years ago, he was a prisoner, captured after one of the last battles of Cromwell's war.' Richard tried to imagine what that would have been like,

'How did those men survive?' It was a question that was asked before thinking, of course those that were prisoners were nothing more than any other form of beast of burden.

'That man was fortunate, as was his friend. The story is that they both saved the plantation owners family from burning to death in a fire, they were rewarded by being taken into the household of the owners. Their story is one in a million and I have never heard of anything like it since.' Richard pondered a moment then came back to the present with a jolt. The man they had just been discussing was explaining how they needed to arrange for the passengers to work in teams that needed to be made up of those who understood each other. Richard agreed, he thanked the chief mate for the story he had told him then looked across the dark deck and those souls waiting for something to happen.

Alec started by trying to get families together, once he had a party of ten, he then tried to explain what he wanted them to do. At first the going was tough and making himself understood proved to be a task and a half. The chief mate had arranged for brushes and rags to be brought to the deck. Richard and Martin were to try to show how they wanted the areas washed down, only sea water could be used which would not show to those that were cleaning much kindness.

Slowly but surely, they somehow managed to get the groups cleaning. It was a surprise when the first twenty were told that they could go on deck, it was not just to take the air, whilst they were on deck they were to clean buckets and scrub the area around the holes in the prow that were called heads, they were the only designated places to use for pissing and shitting. They held no privacy and the filth was sickening, the only thing to wipe their arses on was a tow rag that dangled into the sea which they would drop back into the ocean to clean. Buckets of sea water were dragged up and thrown over the heads until the majority of faeces were removed. What was used in time of bad weather was ten times as worse, passengers would make their way to the hold and do whatever was needed onto the ballast where it accumulated and stank. Once the cleaning had started the passengers although not in the best of condition seemed to gain a sense of purpose. A routine began and the cleanliness improved.

Edward Carrick had taken ships across the Atlantic on many occasions, he had seen how the sanitary conditions had deteriorated onboard and how that affected both crew and passengers so he was pleased to see a change in how the passengers reacted to the arrangements put in place by the group of men he had discussed the problem with earlier. The weather had been calm although they still had a reasonable breeze to keep them moving. Carrick wanted to get the voyage over with, he had business to transact when they arrived. He had been granted land to the west of the settlement of Jamestown, it was enough for him to establish himself within the community. He had seen how others had managed to thrive through the horrors of crop failures and attacks by the native tribes. Through sheer determination they had created a sizable town and it was growing fast, every ship brought new life and trade.

Carrick's aim was to eventually become a member of the house of burgesses and establish himself in the world of politics and he could only do this by becoming a pillar of the establishment so this was to be his final trip. He would hand over the ship to whoever the owners selected then he would devote his life to advancing his position in business and the development of his property. Life for him had been one of many ups and downs he had experienced times when life seemed to be against him and his future very uncertain but now, he had made the decision to follow a chosen path he would devote himself to gaining wealth and position in the new world.

As he worked out the course to be taken there was a knock on his door,

'Yes.' He did not like to be disturbed when studying the charts. The door opened and Mr Dimmock, his chief mate ducked under a beam and walked towards Carrick's desk.

'What is it Mr Dimmock?' The chief mate needed to update his captain on the progress he and his fellow organisers had made. It had been two days since he together with the surgeon, the apothecary, the parson and Alec Sinclair had started the passengers removing the filth from their area, they had achieved a lot. The passengers had got over their initial objections to cleaning, when it had been pointed out that it could mean the difference between landing on the shore of the Americas or ending their time at the bottom of the ocean.

'We have made progress with the passengers and thank God, their deck is in far better order.' Carrick looked up from his chart,

'More importantly Mr Dimmock, how are the crew, how are they taking to the passengers being allowed on deck?' The chief mate moved a little closer to the captain's desk,

'They are learning to cope with the intrusion and it is likely that they may even see the benefits of having the passengers cleaning some of the areas that they had been responsible for.' The captain leaned back in his chair,

'A good compromise and as long as it lasts to the benefit of all.' He lay down his compasses and pointed to the chair in front of his desk. 'Take a seat Mr Dimmock.' As the chief mate took his seat Carrick reached for a decanter on a side table. 'You will join me in a glass of port Mr Dimmock?' The chief mate was a little surprised but gladly accepted the offer. Carrick poured two glasses, handing one to his chief mate.

'Are you aware that this will be my last trip in the Neptune?' Dimmock had heard that this was the case but he had no confirmation.

'I had heard such gossip but until I heard it from you, I put it to the back of my mind.'

'Well Mr Dimmock it is true and I shall be joining the other poor souls on the land around Jamestown.' The chief mate took a sip of port,

'Have you any idea of what is to become of the Neptune?'

'She will carry on, there are many more voyages left in her wooden keel, but as for who will be taking her after I depart is another matter. Would you like to take on the role?' Dimmock was surprised by the question, although he had been on ships all his life, he had not become a Master Mariner, true he was qualified as a mariner but he was a man who preferred to be second in command rather than at the helm.

'I think that I serve my masters as a chief mate well, my heart says that it would be a role I would cherish but my head tells me that I am better suited to my present role far more than skipper.' Carrick looked at the man before him, he had been a first-class chief mate and they had worked well together, he thought it sad to see him spend the rest of his career as he was but if that was his wish then good luck to him.

'If that is your wish then I am sure you will have many more years ahead of you on the Neptune.' He raised his glass. 'To the Neptune.' The chief mate echoed the toast and both men emptied their glasses. Dimmock rose from his chair and thanked his captain,

'I hope that my future captains will be as skilful with ship and men as you captain.' He made his way back to the main deck with a sense of loss after what he had been told but also with a view to the future and what that held for him.

On the main deck the chief mate could see that the ocean was beginning to become a little more active. He had the experience that told him to anticipate some lively weather. The bosun walked towards him,

'We may be in for some troublesome seas in the coming hours.' The chief mate looked again at the clouds building in the distance.

'I think you are right bosun, so we had better prepare those below for what could be rough times ahead.' The bosun turned and made his way toward the stern, he caught site of some passengers just arriving on deck, he turned them around and was met with some disgruntled moans and groans but having told them that a storm was brewing they followed his orders and went back to their deck.

As expected by those that knew the sea, the sky darkened as the clouds became heavy with rain. An almost peaceful period fell upon the ship. The waters calmed and the wind subsided.

William had made his way back to the cabin and to his surprise he found Robert at the small table, he was looking intently at the ledgers he and Alec had brought with them.

'Is there a problem?' William asked. He noticed the frowned look on Robert's face.

'No, at least I don't think so.' He turned a page and ran his finger down a column of figures. 'I thought we had miscalculated but after checking it appears that all is well.' He pointed again to the column and William looked down at the ledger. 'It was not clear if these items had been correctly entered, you see here,' he pointed to the entry marked 'Agricultural Goods.' It was amongst these items that I found what I had been looking for they should have been entered separately but it is of no consequence, everything is accounted for.' He sat back and William could see the tension leave his shoulders. 'What have you been doing on deck, is there anything I should know?' William looked around the cabin,

'I have been told that Alec is now helping to organise the passengers, after the incident of the old couple who died without any of the others noticing.' Robert scratched his head,

'That is a thankless task and whatever he may have done may be undone when the expected bad weather reaches us.'

'What bad weather, it is very still on deck, it may be a little dark but at present there is not a breath of wind.' William's innocence at sea was clear, Robert thought that his young friend had so much to learn.

'It is the calm before the storm, I suggest you stay here for the next few hours, during that time you will see how things change. The ship will hopefully ride out any bad weather but prepare yourself for some dangerous times. I must find Alec, he will need all the help he can get if the passengers start to become afraid of the storm.' With that he patted William on the head and left to find Alec. William sat and waited, he thought of what Robert had said and wondered if Adele would be able to continue with her visits, her family's story had awakened his imagination, the life that her grandparents and parents had lived through conjured up all sorts of images in his mind.

Robert found Alec along with the surgeon, apothecary and parson, they were busy trying to make sure that the jobs that they had allocated were understood and carried out correctly. It was the young men who posed the biggest problem, they did not see the need for all the tasks that had been set and as the ship appeared to be stable with hardly any movement, they did not take easily to being told what to do. Robert took hold of Alec's sleeve and pulled him to one side,

'There is a storm approaching, it could be with us within the hour, I would suggest that these people are made aware of what may befall them.' Alec turned and looked at those in the gloom of the deck. He raised his voice,

'I have just been informed that there is a storm approaching and that you need to make sure you and your possessions are secure.' As he spoke the chief mate came into sight.

'You are correct Mr Sinclair, there is a storm on the horizon and it will be with us before not very long. You people are not to go on deck, if you do the crew will deal with you without mercy. Every sailor will have his duty and if you deter him from his role then you will suffer is that clear?' There was a mumbled response, those who had been making the deck fit to live in wanted to know how the storm would affect them, the chief mate stood forward.

'The ship will change from what it is now to a place where you will not want to be. You will not light fires, you will not go on deck, you will carry out any orders you may be given and with god's grace we will survive the storm.' What the chief mate had said did not sink into the minds of those who had never experienced bad weather at sea, some had travelled from France or the Netherlands to England during those voyages some had met foul weather and survived. It was those individuals who spoke about the troubles they had seen and felt. Even the testament of those who had sailed before did not convince some of the more stubborn passengers.

'You will find yourselves at the mercy of those who sail this ship and woe betide any man, woman or child who does not listen to what they are told.' The chief mate finished what he had to say and shaking his head turned and made his way on deck to speak to the bosun. On deck he joined the bosun and they both looked at the way the sea was beginning to rise and fall. Mr Dimmock instructed the bosun to prepared the ship for the oncoming storm and he left to inform the captain of the change in the weather. The captain stood from his desk when the chief mate knocked on his door,

'Come.' He could feel the ships movements start to increase, he had seen through his porthole the waves increasing in power and height.

'Captain, the weather is changing and the glass indicates a storm ahead.'

'Yes, I can feel it, have you seen the coxswain?'

'He is already at the helm and awaits your instructions.'

'Good.' He grabbed his jacket making his way towards the door. 'I shall be with Mr Leigh at the helm if you require me and I fear I shall be busy for the next few hours.' He smiled at his chief mate as he passed him. When he arrived on the upper deck, he could see the crew making safe all that they could, the coxswain was at the helm with another and together they held the ship on course.

'Mr Leigh you know what we should do.'

'Aye, captain, steer into the wind and hope for the best.' Edward Carrick saw his coxswain clutching the whipstaff moving it to try to position the ship into the wind. The crew had secured what they could and were now trying to make sure they did not fall victim to the heavy seas that loomed up before them. The first waves lifted the Neptune partially out of the water and then dropped it with a deafening crash, the coxswain held tight with his captain by his side.

'I think we will have a fine dance with this sea.' He said as the rain started to fall.

On the passenger deck there was a shocked silence when the ship was struck by the first large wave. Some fell others staggered to gain their balance and some lay where they slept. Faces showed fear with eyes wide open as they waited for what was to come next. It was moments until the next surge took the ship high, there were screams not only from the women as the passengers were tossed across the deck.

Those brave young men who complained about the work given to them now cowered like frightened dogs, shaking as the ship treated them like sacks of flour. They were nothing now just another member of the terrified crowd that tried to fight against the upheaval they found themselves in. Martin Saurin together with his son and daughter held each other, they climbed into one of their bunks trying to keep their position as the rest of the passengers were thrown around the deck. There were screams and shouts as people crashed into the sides of the ship and into one another. Martin hoped that this would be a storm that was short lived, he watched as the chaos increased amongst his fellow passengers.

William was taken totally by surprise, he had climbed into his bunk but was nearly thrown out by the movement of the ship. Alec and Robert burst through the door,

'Better make yourself as safe as you can, this tempest may last for several days if we are unlucky.' It was Alec who spoke he was not his usual calm self, he had experienced storms on board ship before and knew that they were in the hands of the gods whether or not they would survive. Robert pushed William to one side and jumped into the bunk with him.

'If I try to stay upright, I will be thrown around like a feather in the wind.' William moved over to accommodate Robert.

'How long will this last, William asked, Alec coughed and cleared his throat,

'It may be a day it may be a week, nobody can tell, just pray that the ship can ride it out.'

Martin and his family held each other as they watched others trying to reach a safe place. All were affected, men women and children. The children were beyond comforting and after crying they seemed to fall into a stupor, their eyes glazed, staring ahead without feeling of any kind. The rolling of the ship carried on, as the waves grew in height that of the ship also increased. The fall and crash resulted in screams that only came with the fear of death. The hours passed but the storm remained, throwing the ship around as if it were a toy. Sickness started and whatever was left in stomachs was brought up and the smell began to lay heavily on the sweating, screaming mess of humanity that was strewn around the deck.

Edward Carrick, with his coxswain, held the ship into the wind. They fought with all their might against natures strength, the world was against them they had little to help them fight the wind, rain and fearful waves. If the ship were to be lost both men knew that all those who travelled with them would have little chance of surviving. The sea would not prey on the weak or the strong it would take all, none would be spared. The chief mate looked through the driving rain and could just see the waves crashing onto the deck, it would not take much more to capsize the Neptune, his thoughts for a moment turned to those he knew on shore, there were those who he counted as friends, those who were of his blood and those he did business with, not many. His life had been at sea, he raised his head feeling the full force of the rain sting the flesh of his face, if he were to die, he wanted it to be at sea. If he were to join all those who had gone before him to the depths he would be satisfied. He, like most could not swim, he laughed to himself, what good would swimming be in a sea such as this. There was a sudden rush of waves which brought him back to the present, he knew his duty, he turned and clung onto the doorway leading to the deck below where the passengers were now in a state of total panic. As he entered the main hold the scene was one that he expected, people were either screaming of praying, some doing both.

As the crew fought to stay alive those below deck did not know if they were on earth or in purgatory, for many it was their first time at sea and they had never dreamt that they would be so close to death. While the storm raged William, Robert and

Alec held onto their bunks for dear life. Talking was hard to do, they would shout to each other but could understand little. Food was of little importance, anything just to keep them alive was good enough and as for rest or sleep that would only be for the dead or dying.

No passenger would come away from this scene of hell without some damage, it could be physical or mental but they would carry the scars with them for the rest of their lives. Martin Saurin reached for his children, they were old enough to take care of themselves, but they were his children, his life, he would do all in his power to ensure their safety. The three hugged each other their bond became stronger as the storm grew louder. Martin could see that the work that had been carried out had now been undone, he could see vomit and blood making trails across the deck as the ship rolled and heaved. How long would this storm last? He asked himself, it had to end soon surely, but the ship kept being thrown by the waves and those it carried continued to ask their god for forgiveness.

Chapter 10

It took three days for the storm to leave them, it had quietened down during the second day however they were told by the crew to remain below. In the gloom of their deck those that could tried to stand, the floor was awash with sea water, sickness and blood. As the storm eased Edward Carrick sent for the chief mate, Carrick had stayed with the coxswain for the majority of the time that the storm raged, they, with the rest of the crew fought the storm and won a reprieve. The men on the deck felt the wind ease on the second day and on the third it was almost gone. There was a lot to do, Carrick called his chief mate and bosun to try to get some idea of any damage that they might have sustained.

'I think we have been very lucky.' The bosun said as he climbed the stairs to the upper deck. Carrick surveyed the scene, they had taken every precaution before the storm hit them so he could see that their masts and rigging were intact.

'I have checked below and the bulkheads seem to have held, there is water but we can get that out when the ship is more stable.' The captain was pleased.

'Gentlemen, the crew have done well and I will ensure that they receive not only my thanks but also a penny or two extra.' There was a cheer from those who were close by. 'Now, Mr Dimmock, I need to know how our passengers fared, could you find our surgeon and anyone else who might be of assistance and look to see those that have been injured, I shall be in my cabin, I need to try to check our position but get word to me if there are any major problems.' The chief mate touched the tip of his cap and turning made his way below. He met the surgeon who was also keen to assess any damage that may have been caused by the storm. They entered the area where the passengers had been during the storm. It stank and there were bodies everywhere. Richard Hinds looked at the state of those that were nearest to the deck entrance, he looked around to see if he could spot Saurin and his family. He saw them climbing from their bunk, they did not look too bad, perhaps dishevelled and disorientated but other than that unhurt.

'Are you injured?' Richard's question was directed at Martin Saurin,

'We are together with little damage but I fear many others did not survive the storm without harm.' The chief mate glanced around at the hundred plus passengers, many were huddled together others stood holding onto whatever they could not daring to let go for fear of falling. It was fear that Richard Hinds could see, he could almost smell it. There were bruises and minor cuts which would need to be kept clean, but how that could be achieved he had no idea. There was little water and what remained was so precious it had to be used sparingly. Very few of the people on this deck had dry, clean clothes it would be a nightmare to try to attend to all those that needed help. There was only salt water but that would have to do, Martin looked around there were few serious wounds, thank God, and as long as the ship did not suffer another tempest they may survive.

It took no more than a day to get the ship back into some semblance of order, the crew raised the sails and with a gentler wind the ship steadied itself and they continued on their course. William sat on his bunk and watched his two colleagues discuss what damage could have been done to their cargo. Alec stood and faced the other two,

'It may be that there is a lot of cleaning up to do, I may be called upon to help, so in my absence can you,' he looked from Robert to William, 'make sure that the cargo has not sustained too much damage. William, while I am assisting others Robert will start to tell you of what to expect when we reach landfall, we have another fourteen days or so before we reach our destination and we need you to understand exactly what is required of you when we reach Virginia.' This came as a slight surprise to William, he knew that he had a lot to learn before they reached the new world, he wondered exactly what Robert would teach him and would he be able to spend time with Adele, what would the coming days hold for him.

The days following the storm were filled with anxiety. Those on the deck below still got down on their knees to ask God for a safe journey. Those that suffered cuts and bruises seemed to recover quickly the thing uppermost in their minds at this stage was food and water. The ship had passed the halfway stage of its voyage across the Atlantic, the water had become even more precious and as for the food, William watched as Robert took hold of a ships biscuit and knocked it against the side of the table as he did a shower of small maggot like things fell to the floor.

'Don't want to eat too many of them.' He said as he inspected the hardtack for any other creatures that may have hidden beneath the surface. Eating such a delight was very difficult especially if a person's teeth had become loose over the week's they had been onboard, but it was food and if it helped fill a belly then it would be eaten. Robert smashed the biscuit hard down on the table top, it fractured but not into small enough pieces for them to easily consume. He smashed it again, this time small pieces scattered over the table top, he picked a few and handed them to William who tried to moisten them with his saliva. It was hard going, it took him an age to get to a stage where he could swallow,

'Is there no beer or ale that we could use to soften this?' He was looking at the hard tack with disdain,

'It may help, let me see it there is anything we could use other than sea water.' Robert left making his way to the galley hoping that there might be something to help digest the solid mass of the hardtack. He came across the ships cook who was in deep conversation with the bosun, without a quartermaster onboard it fell to them to manage the victuals. They both turned to face Robert as he approached,

'What can we do for you.' The question came from the thin face of the cook, there was no way that he had been eating more than his own rations he was as thin as a broom handle. Robert knew that anything to do with rations needed to be treated with diplomacy,

'Pray tell me is there anything that could help us with the biscuit we have?' The two men looked at each other they were aware of the difficulties that existed with the rations, they also knew that things would get worse not better in the days to come. The cook shook his head,

'We have beer and you can have your allotment it may help but beware the taste may not be to your liking.' Robert would take anything if it would help.

'My friends and I would be forever grateful if we could get anything to help eat what we have been given.' The cook took a large jug and disappeared returning shortly with the sound of liquid swirling around inside it.

'Here, take this hopefully it will make your rations a little easier to eat.' Robert took the jug and carefully headed back to the cabin. He had not spilt a drop and as he entered the cabin William together with Alec looked up expectantly.

'I see you have something, at last we may be able to soak these lumps of stone into something that we can eat.' They each placed a biscuit in a bowl and poured the beer onto the hard surface. They sat and watched, waiting for a sign that would suggest the biscuit was soft enough to eat. Alec looked up,

'Leave them it will take some time for them to soften, while we wait tell me of what you have been doing whilst my time has been taken with our fellow passengers.' Robert explained that he had been checking their cargo and all seemed well, he also told Alec that he and William had started to look at the ledgers together and that although there was a long way to go, William seemed to understand what was involved with their business.

'What about the young woman who has been visiting you.' Alec noticed the colour creep up Williams face and smiled,

'With the storm and the problems with passengers I have not seen Adele for several days.' He looked into his bowl where the biscuit was still in one solid piece. 'I would hope that she continues her visits, her account of her family's troublesome past is one of great intrigue and I want to know more.' Alec looked at Robert they could tell that the boy was smitten with the young beauty.

'Perhaps I will be seeing her father in the coming hours and maybe I could ask if she intended to visit you.' Alec could see William's face redden even more.

'If you could I would be more than grateful, I promise I will learn whatever you want me to, I am a good scholar and I will prove worthy of you.'

'I will try to speak on your behalf.' Alec turned to Robert. 'We need to start preparing for land irrespective of what weather we may encounter. It may be best if we take William into our confidence, he needs to be aware of what may be required of him when we reach land.' Robert looked at William.

'Well, now you need to study hard, we may be able to spare you while you talk to the apothecary's daughter but the rest of the time you will spend studying what we give to you, is that understood?' William raised himself from the bunk and with the aid of his crutch stood,

'I hope I will do your faith in me justice and as for this.' He tapped the crutch against the splint holding his leg in place, 'I should be rid of this shortly and hopefully be able to carry out any duties you require of me.' Alec looked at Williams leg,

'Let's not be too hasty, I would rather see you on two good legs if that takes a little longer. We have another twenty-five days or so, the storm may have delayed us, so do not do anything foolish, wait until you can stand without any discomfort.' William was slightly annoyed at Alec's comments but in his heart, he knew Alec was right.

*

The following morning William raised himself, his night had been one of trying to sleep with a leg in a splint, thoughts of what he would be taught by Robert and Alec together with dreams of Adele.

138

After shaking the night from his body and clothes he waited for Robert to start his education. Robert was not that eager, he would have to explain almost everything that happened on the plantation which would present a problem in holding William's attention particularly if his mind wandered to his relationship with Adele. There would not be any way that William could take notes as paper and ink were in short supply so Robert would have to ensure that the salient points were planted deeply into William's mind. He looked at the young man who seemed to develop by the day, his features were more pronounced, a strong chin, high cheek bones and steady eyes.

'We have to start from the beginning with the land.' Robert shuffled in the chair making himself as comfortable as he could. 'We need good land, land that has not had crops grown on it before. The majority of the land we use has been selected carefully, it would have been covered with vegetation which would need to be cleared then what remained burnt following that the area needed hoeing so you can imagine that to achieve this it would require men and many men were hard to come by initially.' William watched Robert as he tensed a little,

'Where did the men come from, were they settlers or natives?'

'They were settlers, not the first, many of those that set foot on the shores of the new world did not survive, this was the next wave of adventurers from England, The Netherlands, Scotland and some from France.' Robert hoped that William would not have too many questions. 'Crops were tried and many failed however success with one particular seed gave hope to many, that was the seed of the tobacco plant. I will not go into the history of who, where and why that crop survived and flourished needless to say it did.' Robert did not realise that teaching William would be as difficult as this but one thing led to another and he had to cut out what was not necessary. 'The plantations grew in size as the need for tobacco increased particularly in England. This meant that more labour was required so many were promised the earth if they were to sign their lives away and become indentured for many years to the plantation owners. Even this was not enough so it was decided to buy as many bodies as they could and many of those came from the aftermath of Cromwell's war such as your father, Alec and me.' He paused and seemed to lapse into thoughts of another time, he snapped out of his dream.

'How do we grow this plant.' Robert's voice changed it became one of a master teaching a scholar. 'Preparation of the seed beds begins in January or February the sites of the land to be sown is carefully selected the beds are raked and covered with pine to protect the young plants. There is a need to make sure that the young plants had every possible chance of developing so they are about one every four inches.' Robert paused again and studied William's face, it looked as if what he was telling him was being absorbed so he continued. 'We have many problems like any farmer there are pests and weather to contend with it is normal practice to transplant the tobacco to other fields in May. The earth would be raised to about two feet in the shape of small hills and with a great deal of care the plants would be moved.' Robert could see that William had another question for him.

'How was this done?' Robert stretched his shoulders, he was not a teacher, Alec would be better at this he thought.

'This would take many men and would be back breaking work and even when this had been completed the crop master may decide that the crop needed to be moved again. The plants at this time need a great deal of care, it is vital to keep the crop clear of weeds and pests hopefully with the grace of God the plants would develop.' At this point Robert felt that he had given William enough to go on with, he did not want to discourage the lad and at the same time wanted to keep his own enthusiasm for the task. 'I think that will be all for your first lesson and we will continue tomorrow.' Robert was aware that Alec would have wanted him to get further with William but he thought it would be better to break things into small parts to let them sink into William's mind and then move on. As luck would have it, they heard a small knocking on the cabin door, Robert reached up and pulled the door open revealing the figure of William's dream. Adele stood in the door way as she stepped into the cabin, she removed her cowl revealing the features that William had been longing to see.

'Adele, please come in.' William's voice was full of excitement. Robert moved from his seat to allow Adele to take her place at the table.

'I am going in search of something for us to eat and possibly drink, I may be some considerable time.' He turned to William. 'Remember what we have discussed I shall ask you to repeat it tomorrow.' William lifted his hand and smiled then turned towards Adele,

'It is so good to see you, how did you fend in the storm, tell me all that has happened to you.'

Adele sat and began to go through the events that she had been involved with during the storm. Her description of the way her fellow passengers had acted was not what William expected. She told him of the way people had been thrown across the deck, bouncing when the waves took hold of the ship.

'Were there many injured?' He asked.

'Not as many as I or my father expected, yes there were bruises and cuts but nothing serious. What I found hardest to come to terms with was the amount of vomit and waste, it just swilled around the deck and stank. The smell was almost too much to bear, we were not allowed on deck, no fresh air only dampness, hunger and fear.' William tried to conjure up the scene, he knew the area that she spoke of but he found it difficult to imagine the piss and shit that would have been floating around their feet.

'What did you do?' She realised that he was having difficulty in imagining the state of the passenger's area.

'We tried to keep off of the deck, my father, brother and me huddled together in one bunk and just prayed that the storm would pass, it still remains a stinking hell hole but we have no option but to clean what we can and make the best of what we have.' William shifted his position moving his leg to one side,

'Now that the storm is over are you willing to take up the story of your family?' She looked at his face, he really had no idea of what she and her family had been through, not during the storm or during their existence before boarding the ship.

'I will tell you of my family's journey and hope that you can imagine the trials that they had to endure.' William sat back slightly and Adele began to relate to him how her father had been taken across northern France and into The Netherlands. While William listened, Robert had made his way to the galley where the cook was preparing something for the crew. The aroma that came from the large cooking vessel was not appetising, what was in the pot remained a mystery, it must have been some of the salted meat that the cook was trying to make edible. Beneath the cooking pot was a fire that had been lit on a hearth of bricks which protected against fire, the cook looked at Robert with curiosity,

'What do you want?' Robert looked around the cook's domain,

'Is there anything I can take to feed myself and two friends?'

'You can have what everybody has, salt beef, pork and peas with maybe a little pickled cabbage.' Robert did not relish the thought of yet another day of eating meat that was so heavy with salt that it would probably kill him rather than satisfy his hunger. The cook took a portion of the salted meat with two scoops of dried peas,

'Make with this what you will.' The cook did not say this with a smile, he looked as if he could do without people entering the galley, he had a meal to make and he did not like strangers taking his time away from his duty. Robert took what the cook held out,

'Thank you, is there any beer or ale?' The cook looked even more annoyed,

'What do you want, blood?' The look on the cook's face did not encourage Robert to take the conversation any further. The cook grunted. 'See the bosun he may be able to give you something to drink.' Robert knew that this was the end of the conversation and that he would have to take what he had been given and be thankful for that. As he made his way back to the cabin, he passed the surgeon who asked after William,

'How is he now that the storm is over?' Robert looked at the surgeon, how he looked so fresh faced was a puzzle to him then he realized it was his hairless chin all the others on the ship carried a beard and hair that had taken on a life of its own due to the amount of lice that could be found.

'He is well, I left him in the safe hands of the young daughter of Mr Saurin.' At this Robert could see the surgeons body tense.

'Is she still with him?'

'I would think not she has probably returned to her father by now.' The surgeon stopped and as Robert left him, he turned and made his way to the passenger deck. Richard Hinds looked around the passengers, he saw Martin Saurin with his children they seemed to be in deep conversation. As he approached, they stopped and turned to greet him. Martin Saurin spoke first,

'I am pleased to see you, there may be work for you and I to do.' This was not what the surgeon wanted.

'What sort of employment had you in mind?' Saurin spoke briefly to his son,

'Francois is worried that there may be a young boy that needs our help.' Saurin made a space for his son to stand in front of the surgeon. Francios began to tell of a young boy who had a serious problem, he had seen the boy in a terrible state, he had been covered in sweat and could not stand.

'Where is this unfortunate?'

'He is to the rear of the passenger's quarters, his mother is with him she has tried to comfort him but with little success.' The surgeon looked at Saurin,

'Shall we look at this boy?' Saurin nodded,

'Francois, take us to him.' With that Francois made his way to the rear of the area where the passengers slept mainly on the floor.   As they approached a woman in distress came to them,

'It's my son, it's Daniel, he only had a grazed knee we told him not to be such a child, he never complained and now this, he is ill, very ill. Please can you cure him?' As soon as Saurin set eyes on the boy, he knew that it may be too late for them to do anything. Richard Hinds placed a hand on the boy's forehead it was hot and the drops of perspiration covered the boy's brow.

'There is poison in his blood and I fear that nothing we can do will help him.' Martin Saurin had seen this before in both children and adults it would normally be a case of trying to get the humours back into balance, however what he saw had gone too far and even if they were in time, they had nothing to treat the problem. As they crouched over the boy, they could see he was near to drawing his final breath. His eyes were closed his mouth open there was no speech and then he gasped his last breath and the body slumped back into his mother's arms. The wail that came from the mother's lips echoed around the deck it sent a shudder down the spine of all those that heard it. Richard stood,

'I shall have to inform the captain.' Martin nodded and turned his attention to the mother. He tried to comfort her but had little effect on her state. He asked gently,

'Where is your husband, can I fetch him?' She shook her head,

'He is waiting for us, we are to start a new life, he has made good and we were to live well and our son was to grow strong and prosperous, now all we have is his body, what can I tell his father, what will we do? She cried out to her god but no relief came to her, in her arms lay a dead boy who held her dreams for the future.

Martin took hold of Francois arm. 'Find the parson quickly and bring him here.' Francois stood and hurried off in search of Mr Peters. When Richard reached the captain's cabin, he heard several voices from within, he knocked and waited until he was beckoned in.

'Yes.' It was a voice that had a little irritation in it. Richard opened the door and entered. 'Ah Mr Hinds what can I do for you, I hope you are not the bearer of bad tidings?' Richard's face told the captain that it was not good news.

'I am afraid we have another death among the passengers.' The captain looked up from his desk where he had charts spread out.

'Who has died, is it a passenger?'

'Yes, it is a young boy of about seven or eight years of age.'

'This is sad news indeed, how did he pass?' The captain together with the chief mate and coxswain looked steadily at the surgeon.

'The boy had poisoned blood from a cut to his knee, it appears that it was not deemed serious by his mother and therefore she thought nothing of it until poison had gained entry to the boy's blood, after that it took little time for the body to start deteriorating.

'Mr Dimmock will you please make the necessary arrangements.' The chief mate stood and left the cabin he would need to arrange for the bosun to take care of the body and the parson would need to be told so that a service could be conducted.

'Mr Hinds is this an isolated incident or is there something contagious in this poor unfortunate's death?'

'No, captain, this is something that the boy contracted following a fall and then getting something from the deck into the wound.'

'That is a small mercy, we have enough problems without an outbreak of something onboard.'

'Captain, I do think that we should continue with getting people into the fresh air as much as possible and get them to clean as best they can.' The captain looked at the coxswain who had made it clear that he did not agree with the passengers inhibiting the crew from their duties.

'Mr Leigh, we have discussed that the weather has eased and that we may be in for a period of calm so please make it known that the passengers will be allowed on deck on the understanding that if one of them should interfere with any of the crew carrying out their duties, they will all be confined below.' The coxswain was satisfied with the captains ruling as was Richard Hinds.

The boy's body was wrapped in sail cloth and then brought to a central place on the main deck. The parson read from the good book and then finished with the lord's prayer. The service was short, throughout the prayers the boy's mother looked on with a stone face, her expression did not change, there was anger in her eyes, what would she do now? What would she

150

tell her husband who awaited her in the new world?' She clenched her fists and struck the hatch cover nearest to her, a woman of about the same age tried to comfort her but was shrugged off so she stood alone with her grief. The wrapped body was held over the side of the ship and then released into the waves, it sank slowly then disappeared from sight. The mother turned with her head down and made her way back to the area where she and her son had spent the last days of his life.

Chapter 11

Dawn broke on the day after the boy's death to reveal a cloudless sky its blue joined the green of the sea there were a few waves but nothing that posed any difficulty. It was the chief mate who approached Edward Carrick with a request that he hoped the captain would agree to.

'The sea is calm and our victuals are in need of some replenishment, can I give the order for the tender to be made ready and for members of the crew to see what the ocean holds for us.' The captain looked at the sky, the horizon seemed to be an eternity away,

'Perhaps it may do the men good they may even enjoy the sport of trying to catch something to eat other than salt beef.' Turning back to the chief mate he answered in a clear voice, 'Yes, an excellent idea, one that may to be of benefit to all onboard.' The chief mate wasted no time, he called for men to man the tender, there were plenty of volunteers.

'Mr Truscott, please make the tender ready. You will take six men with you, I believe there is a net in the tender together with some line, as quick as you please. Make sure you do not return empty handed as fresh fish will be expected on the captain's table very soon.' The bosun selected the six he would take and together with other members of the crew they prepared to drop the tender alongside the ship. The passengers on deck watched the antics of the crew as they manhandled the tender into position. The bosun stood in the boat as it was lowered and steadied it as it rested on the gentle swell.

'Come on you men, we have work to do and fish to catch.' The six selected men climbed down the ropes from the deck with practised ease. When the bosun felt all was well he called for the men to position their oars and with this achieved he called out a rhythm for the men to follow as they pulled against the sea. The bosun stood in the stern of the tender steering it away from the ship. As he looked across the water, he knew that there should be a catch waiting for them but only time would tell. At the rail of the Neptune both crew and passengers watched as the tender grew smaller as the crew pulled away from the ship, the chief mate ushered the passengers back to what they were doing telling them that there would be nothing to see for some time if at all so they would be well advised to get on with any tasks they may have been allotted.

The commotion on deck filtered down to the passengers and Adele asked her father if she could try to discover what was happening. Martin Saurin looked at the innocence on his daughters face with a father's love that made him unaware of just how tough and resilient Adele was.

'Yes, if you find out anything please be sure and let me know, I shall be with Francois he has lapsed in his Latin and now that the ship is on an even keel, we need to get on with his education.' Adele pitied her brother, she knew that her father had nothing but good intentions however she was aware that her brother may be more suited to something other than becoming a student. He had, in confidence, told her that he would rather be active than restricted to the life of an apothecary, his dream was to seek adventure in the new world, help clear the land, build a life for himself and one day marry and have his own family. Francois realised that before he could break the bond that existed between him and his father he would need to comply with his father's wishes, so Latin it would be.

Adele made her way towards the upper deck and as she did so a figure appeared in her path, she could not make out who it was until the figure was almost on top of her.

'Excuse me.' She was slightly shocked to hear Richard Hind's voice, she had not seen him during the storm although she found herself thinking of him more than was good for her and she couldn't understand why. His polite tone sent a little shiver down her spine, she looked up at him and tried to focus on his features. He reached out to move past her and as he did, he touched her arm it was a gentle brush against her flesh, she felt her heart beat a little faster as they moved past one another.

'Are you going on deck?' he asked.

'Yes, I heard noise and wanted to find out what was happening.'

'The crew are making ready to launch the tender with a hope of catching some fresh fish.'

'Will they be able to do that, they are sailors not fishermen.'

'Most of them have spent their lives at sea not only as sailors they have fished many waters and have a good eye for a catch.' Richard grasped the opportunity. 'If you will permit me, I will escort you onto the deck.' His words did not come out the way he wanted and he thought he must have sounded like a teenage boy lacking in confidence. Adele held out a hand,

'Please, that would be very gracious of you.' He took hold of her arm and gently supported it. As they climbed the stairs to the upper deck, they both felt a sense of something strange, their bodies tensed a little and then relaxed. Richard looked at the young woman next to him, he felt that whatever happened on this voyage he would do everything in his power to capture this beautiful creature's heart.

As they reached the deck, they could see the crew swinging out the tender and lowering it into the sea. The bosun was standing in the boat with one arm holding on to the ropes, he continued to look from the side of the ship to those who were in control. The tender swung out and then descended to the surface as it hit the sea the bosun released the lines that held the boat then he grasped the rope ladder that had been thrown over the side and pulled it taught. The selected six men climbed over the side in turn and with ease made their way down to the tender, once all were safely down the final line was released and the tender drew away from the side of the ship. Those that were watching waved as the sailors pulled away. The sea was still calm very little wind could be felt, the sky stretched out to the end of the world, nothing could be seen but the sun filled blue of the sky and the gentle waves of the sea. Richard and Adele watched as the men pulled on the oars, they grew smaller with each stroke and in what seemed only minutes they were just a speck in the enormity that was the ocean.

In their cabin William was listening to Robert who was trying to explain to him the cultivation process involved in growing tobacco.

'The plants need to be replanted and then when they had reached a certain height the leaves growing closest to the ground had to be removed, this was called by the crop master 'priming' and at the same time the plants would have the small bunch of leaves at the top removed which resulted in the plant not expending its energy developing flowers and seeds. This process of removing leaves as the plant grew continued whilst it developed. There were many more things that needed to be done to the crop, that would be better explained when they arrived at the plantation.' One area Robert would touch upon was, pests. 'Like all farmers we suffer from the destruction caused by many bugs and grubs. One of the more prevalent was the horn worm which could attack in their hundreds and destroy a crop in less than a week. This, William, is yet another task that requires many hands as these worms and other beasts needed to be removed from the plants and destroyed. If the crop succeeded to grow without being ravaged by pests, drought and disease there were still many obstacles to be overcome before anything approaching harvest could be considered. Think on what I have told you and try to understand that the growing of a tobacco crop is not for the faint hearted and if you wish to become a member of the those that run the plantation you need to know a great deal more.' Robert stretched, he hoped that Alec would take over from him as his mind was beginning to cloud over when talking to William and he wanted him to be better prepared than he could make him when they eventually reached the plantation.

The crew returned to their routine although in the calm weather that they now found themselves there was not a great deal to do. Some men passed the time in splicing ropes others took out bones and began to carve scenes of ships, mermaids and sea creatures. Some gave themselves up to other members of the crew who with a needle tried to pick out a pattern or name on their fellow sailor's arms, backs, and in some cases, faces. Those passengers on deck were full of curiosity and stood watching the men who felt nothing towards them.

'What will you do when we reach Virginia?' The question brought Richard up short.

'I hope that I will be able to establish myself as a physician, I have the skills not only of a surgeon, I have also knowledge of the body, its ailments and many of the remedies to cure a great many problems.' Adele looked up at his clean features, his eyes were full of confidence, she knew that he was a man that would prosper in anything he set his mind to.

'And what of you, what does life have installed for you?'

'I don't know, I will go with my father and care for him and my brother, where they lead, I shall follow.'

'You are worthy of more than just being a follower, surely there is something you would like to do other that being a housekeeper?'

'What can a woman do?' Her voice dropped, she had known that her life would revolve around her father and whatever he decided she would have to follow. 'I am a bearer of children, a chatelaine nothing more. My father will choose a husband for me and that will be the end of it. My prayer is that whoever that maybe he will treat me with respect, as a partner not as a slave.' Richard listened to Adele with a certain amount of horror, at that moment he made a promise to himself that he would move heaven and earth to ensure that the woman by his side would stay by his side. Adele turned away from Richard she had not spoken like that to anyone before, she felt a tear creep down her cheek, she wiped it away quickly, for some unknown reason she grasped Richard's arm and looking up at him said,

'We do not know what is in store for us, perhaps we will die before we reach our destination, perhaps when we arrive there will be nothing for us, perhaps disease and starvation will take us.' She let his arm go and turning held her hand to her face and made her way from the deck. Richard stood and watched her back disappear, what was he to do? They had possibly another twenty days at sea, maybe less, he needed to think long and hard about his future, he looked out to sea there was nothing just ocean, his nights would be full of questions, he could not afford to dream, he needed reality.

Chapter 12

The first venture taken by the bosun in the tender was not very successful. There had been fish, clearly seen by the crew but not in the numbers the bosun wanted to see. He steered the boat back to the ship, the men pulled hard on the oars and they made good time getting back. As the tender was lifted from the water the faces on deck look disappointed there was no great joy from the sailors or the passengers.

'It was not a good day.' The bosun said as he climbed over the ships rail. 'We will try again tomorrow and hope for better luck.' The fish that had been caught were taken to the galley where the cook, like the crew, was disappointed.

'Is this all there is?' He said as he lifted the largest of the fish. 'This will do for the captain but others will have to wait.'

'There is enough for the crew to have a piece, isn't there?' The cook lifted what was on his bench and looked at what he considered to be a poor specimen.

'I can only try, did I hear you say you will try again?' The cook looked at the bosuns weary face,

'Yes, If the weather remains fair, we will cast the net again and hope that the gods are with us.' The bosun left the cook to conjure up what he could, the captain would eat reasonably well and the crew would get what remained others would have to wait until the bosun had better luck.

Those on deck slowly made their way below to try to make good of the dried and salted rations that they had, perhaps they could soak the peas in beer anything to keep them from starving. Amongst those leaving the deck William made his way the best he could alongside Alec and Robert,

'Do you think the bosun will have better fortune tomorrow?' Alec looked at William,

'I hope so, we could do with something to fill our stomachs other than salt beef and salt pork.' William then asked the question that every person onboard the ship wanted to know,

'How many days before we reach Virginia and can we survive on what is in the hold?' It was Robert who answered,

'If we are not able to catch a wind or even a breeze we may be stuck here for some time and that would mean any food that is on the ship will become gold, so eat what you are given and pray that the bosun has better luck tomorrow.' When they reached their cabin Alec took out what food they had kept by and divided it up between them. They ate what was before them, swallowing was hard and their stomachs rebelled.

Richard Hinds had other duties apart from that of trying to tend to the injured, he had perfected the art of shaving and hair cutting. In his trunk he had a set of superb razors which he used himself and those who could afford to pay him. As the ship lay almost motionless, he made his way to the captain's cabin, it was an ideal time to remove the growth of several days, he knocked on the captain's door,

'Yes.' It was not the usual sharp voice that he expected.

'It's the surgeon.' He waited,

'Mr Hinds, come in please.' Richard entered with his box of razors in hand.

'I thought this may be an opportunity to take off the growth that has appeared on your chin.' The captain stretched his arms watching as Richard walked in with his box of tricks.

'No time like the present, I am not required on deck and the course has been set so do your best.' Richard opened his box and took out a razor, he also unrolled a leather strop and began to sharpen the razor until it had an edge that he was satisfied with. There was no good means of softening the whiskers on the captain's face, sea water would have to do although the sharpness of the razor should remove any stubble that the captain had. As he started to shave Edward Carrick he asked if they would reach Virgina within two weeks or would it be longer,

'If the wind remains as it is we may not reach our destination in our lifetime but if it gains some life then we may make up time and distance, if that is the case then we may be only one week later than anticipated.' Richard expertly moved the razor across the captains face then down the line of his jaw to his throat.

'What will you do when we reach Virginia? The captain asked,

'I have letters of introduction from my father and hope to secure a position as surgeon physician in the town. I have relatives that are aware of my plans and they agreed to find a small house I could rent from where I could practice my calling.'

'And what about the man who has been assisting you?'

'You mean Mr Saurin, the apothecary?'

'Yes, the man with the potions.'

'I am not aware of any plans he may have, I know he has to find somewhere for his family to live and that he needs to earn enough to keep them.' The captain turned his head slightly,

'He may struggle to survive if he has no one to help him.' There was a moments silence as Richard thought of Saurin and his family,

'I am sure he will find a way he seems to be resourceful and full of determination especially where his children are concerned.' Richard wiped the captain's face and as he drew the cloth away the captain ran his fingers across his chin, it felt smooth and without blemish.

'Thank you, Mr Hinds, once again you have made me feel as if I can cope with the worries that await me.' Richard left the captain's cabin, as he walked back towards his own bunk he started to think about Saurin and his son and daughter, particularly about his daughter.

William listened to Alec and Robert as they went through the process of raising a tobacco crop.

He tried to take in all that was said but did not have the interest or the will to follow what was being said, he thought that maybe it would make better sense when they got to the plantation. His mind tended to wander, he thought of Adele and how much he liked her. During their last few meetings, he detected a change in her she seemed not to be as attentive as she once was. He asked her,

'Have you something on your mind?' It was a foolish question, all those onboard the Neptune had things on their mind, the ship was becalmed and the lack of progress brought many thoughts to many people.

'I am thinking of what is to become of us in the months and years ahead. What will we be faced with, we have no idea about the land, the people, the hazards oh, it seems that we are entering a place that could be the finish of us.' This was the first time that William heard her speak in such a manner.

'I am sure we all will make good, there will be trials for all of us to get over and no doubt there will be casualties ahead but we can and must make good of what we have.' She looked at him, his words of encouragement pleased her, he was a fine man and would make some girl a good and faithful husband one day.'

The day that followed was again clear with the sun shining down on those milling around the deck. The tender was lowered into the sea and the six men plus the bosun pulled away. Those watching from the deck hoped and prayed that they would have better luck than yesterday. The bosun sat in the stern with a hand on the rudder of the boat, his eyes scanned the horizon for any signs that may indicate fish. They had been rowing for less time than the previous day when the bosun saw sea birds diving into the sea, not just one or two but many. He encouraged the men to pull hard and steered towards the mayhem that the birds were creating. In no time at all they reached the area, the men at the oars could see fish, hundreds of them, as the boat slowed, they made the net ready and with a heave cast it over the side. They circled around pulling the net in an arch, the fish were being trapped their silver scales shone like stars as they struggled for freedom. The bosun could see that together with what appeared to be a mass of herring, a larger fish was using its strength to break free. He had seen such fish before, they had made good eating but were difficult to land. All six men were bringing the net to the side of the boat, it was a good catch and they would eat well that day. The herring danced around their feet and the huge silver and blue beast of a fish took all their strength to get into the tender. They dipped their oars and made their way back to the ship in triumph.

Those standing closest to the rail of the ship watched as the bosun guided the tender alongside, they could see the catch, it was manner from heaven. It took time and effort to get the boat and the fish back onboard those on deck crowded around and had to be sent away so that the crew could deal with the catch. The passengers' eyes widened as they saw what was probably going to fill their stomachs that day, the herring still danced and the sea birds up above cried and darted down trying to capture any escaping fish.

The cook and the crew set about dealing with the catch, there was gutting to be done, what could be eaten was saved, which was most of the fish head included, fins and guts were thrown over the side which is where the birds fought for whatever they could see. The large blue and silver beast that had been trapped in the net was a different matter. It was still alive, the cook despatched it quickly with a heavy marlin spike, its carcass was taken to the galley the cook had work to do the fish would make a fine table for the captain and his inner circle. Amongst the herring were various other varieties some larger others smaller. The catch was sorted, the best for the captain, then for the crew the better of the herring and tastier other morsels that left the remainder for the passengers. There was sufficient for all but the cook knew it would not last long, the longer this quiet weather held the more days that their rations would

168

need to last. The hundred plus passengers together with the crew ate well, the cook prepared the large fish, which one of the crew called a tuna, he would slice it thickly into steaks and cook it quickly, he would make do with the dried peas and some corn to accompany it, he was sure that the captain would be pleased.

Small fires were lit on top of a sand base just enough to cook the fish and it wasn't long before all those onboard were prising off the flesh of the herring and stuffing it into their mouths. In the captain's cabin Edward Carrick sat with his chief mate, coxswain and bosun they looked at the meal in front of them, their mouths watered and stomachs rumbled. The fish together with a glass of the captain's wine lifted their mood.

'Gentlemen, let us hope for a change in the weather and a speedy trip to the new world.' They raised their glasses and toasted the weather.

It was the cooks voice that could be heard giving instructions to the crew,

'We need them gutted and ready for pickling or drying.' The smell of the gutted herring was almost overbearing but the crew had been dealing with fish most of their lives so the effect on them was minimal.

The cook watched as the herrings were handed to those men charged with hanging them to dry,

'Careful now, we need every one of those silver darlings.' The men continued, it was not something they would do on shore as that was a woman's job but on board it was every one's job. The chief mate approached the cook,

'Can we save many?' he asked looking at the many hands holding knives that flashed as they sliced open the bellies of the fish.

'We shall have a goodly few but how long they will keep for is a mystery, how long before landfall?'

'It may be ten days it may be fourteen, you know as well as me that it is what is up there that dictates the length of our voyage.' The chief mate was looking up at the sunlit sky without a cloud to be seen.

'Maybe we will have enough fish together with the salted pork and beef to see us through but we will have to use our skill and knowledge to eek out the water or anything else that is drinkable.' The cooks worried look only confirmed what the chief mate was thinking.

The herring had been a success with William, Alec and Robert, they had eaten well the fish had been a welcome change. They sat in their cabin, William lifted his leg onto the bunk, it still worried him as he did not want anything to jeopardise his entry into the world of tobacco. Alec and Robert continued with his education they went over again the problems that could damage the crop. There were strange terms used that William needed to become familiar with such as topping and sucker shoots, how long the crop could be left before harvesting, how it could be assessed by the colour of its leaves and the texture, it was so difficult for William to imagine the feel of the tobacco leaf. Then Alec tried to explain what happened to the leaves once they had been harvested and how tobacco barns were used. Alec went on to speak about sweating and sorting, it was getting a little too much for William to take in, he tried his best but he felt overwhelmed by the information that came from his two colleagues. Alec could see that William had come to the end of his ability to take in any further details concerning the harvesting of tobacco so he paused and looking at Robert said,

'I think that's enough, our young friend needs something other than tobacco to fill his time, perhaps a visit into the fresh air would do him good.' Robert smiled,

'He still has so much to learn, at present he may find a conversation with another more acceptable than being lectured by us.' Robert moved out of the way allowing William room to get to the door.

'Be careful with that leg I know it has been a hinderance to you but without it you would be lost.'

'I will take care but I do need to see the sky.' William lifted himself off of the bunk, took hold of his crutch and awkwardly headed for the deck. As he left Alec glanced at Robert,

'What do you think of our young apprentice?' Robert raised an eyebrow,

'He will need a great deal of our help if he is going to be of any use on the plantation. I think it may prove easier when we arrive but I fear that the conditions may defeat him if he is not suitably warned so for the rest of the time aboard we should hammer home to him the pitfalls of living in Virginia. He, like many of the passengers, has a vision of the promised land when they will be entering somewhere that lacks a great deal of what was common in England.' Alec sighed,

'We can only do our best and as for those other poor souls they will no doubt find out as soon as we arrive that it is not a land of milk and honey.'

They had both seen the posters and leaflets in taverns and many shops offering free voyage to the

172

new world for those who were willing to indenture themselves for a period of time. Many of those on the passenger deck had committed themselves without fully knowing what would be awaiting them when they reached Virginia.

*

William found his way to the open deck, the smell of gutted fish greeted him. After retching he gained control of his stomach and tried to take in the sight. The crew were gutting and cleaning fish, some were dealing with ropes and tackle others inspecting the sails with the bosun. He thought he heard Adele's voice and looked into the gloom of the opening to the deck that held the passengers. He could see that she was talking to the surgeon, her voice was low and gentle and he could see that she was looking up at his face as she spoke. William's heart almost froze, what could she be talking to the surgeon about and why did she speak in such a way? As Adele turned to move away from the surgeon he bowed and gently guided her by holding her arm, William took a breath and held it, what was happening, was Adele being courted by the surgeon? He did not want to contemplate such a thing. He moved away towards the ships rail and waited for Adele to climb the steps to the open deck,

'Hello, what are you doing out of your cabin?' Her voice was clear but had lost its gentle tones that he had heard when she spoke to the surgeon.

'I need some air.' He looked out at the ocean and for a moment wanted to be alone.

'I fear that the air is tainted by the smell of gutted fish.' She kept her eyes on the young man who she had spent many hours with, to her he was not his normal self. 'Are you unwell, is your leg troubling you?'

'No, my leg is getting stronger with every passing day I just yearn for the sight of land and an end to this.' He waved his arm in an arch tracing the horizon. 'Alec and Robert are very good friends but their company can become a little too much at times.'

'Why do you say such a thing, they are your benefactors are they not?'

'I am with them because I chose to be, I shall work for them and no doubt pay them back with my labour for all they have done for me.' His mood was dark primarily due to Adele's apparent fondness of the surgeon.

'Do you want me to continue with the tale of my family's journey?' There was a look of expectancy on her face,

'If you don't mind, I would like to be with my thoughts, please don't think badly of me I really need to get my priorities in some order.' Adele stood back and gave William some space, she had not seen him in this frame of mind before, every person on board the Neptune would be taking stock of what would be their fate when they reached the shore so she smiled at him and retraced her steps back to her father and Francois. William watched her go, the sinking feeling in his stomach was not due to the ships motion he felt that he had lost something precious although he could not bring himself to believe that his feelings for Adele would never be returned.

There was chatter on the deck, various members of the crew looked up at the sails, a gentle breeze began to fill some of the canvas.

'Everyone below, there is work to be done.' The bosun's voice left no one in doubt that all should go below and keep out of the way. As the passengers left the deck, they could hear the commands of the bosun and the men running to get the sails ready for the wind. Edward Carrick had felt the change in movement of the ship and he knew instinctively that the wind was picking up. He made his way from his cabin and as he reached the quarter deck the chief mate approached him,

'If this develops, we could make good the lost time we suffered during the doldrums.' The captain looked across the vast seascape, he could see that the waves were slowly gaining power and the ship in turn started to cut its way through the ever-changing ocean.

'I sincerely hope so Mr Dimmock, we need the sea to be with us now.' They both stood and watched as the crew started to get the sails ready to be hoisted.

Richard Hinds had reached his small cabin with the thought of Adele still on his mind, she had something that almost bewitched him, was he imagining things, was the sea having some effect on him? He sat at the small desk where he kept his diary and entered his thought for the day, he knew that the time was drawing close to when he would need all his faculties to enable him to get his life in Virginia started. He had several strings to his bow, yes, he was a surgeon and yes, he could cope with most things, he also possessed the skills of a physician which may take him to a higher echelon in society. He hoped that a house would be waiting for him and that he would be able to set up a base from which he could do business. He needed something else, he needed someone to help him. Adele came back into his mind, he tried desperately to focus on the life he would try to build, his thoughts then went to the events that he had experienced during the voyage. The deaths of several passengers he could have done nothing to prevent, even with the aid of Saurin. He thought of how together they had managed to get the passengers to clean their area and how the young man, William, had broken his leg and with their aid he would recover. His mind raced, could he take on the apothecary as someone to assist him, would he be able to pay him or would he leave him to provide cures and remedies himself? He looked out of the small window, he could see the waves breaking gently and the white crests folding over on themselves, he would speak to Saurin, yes, he would speak to him and hopefully he would be able to make progress.

The sails filled with the wind and the ship lurched forward the chief mate stood and looked out over the gradually changing surface of the ocean. It had turned from a still blue to a rolling green-grey, the white plumes grew steadily bolder as the ship picked up speed.

'Mr Dimmock, Mr Dimmock.' The call of his name brought him back to reality.

'What is it?' It was a younger member of the crew who called to him, the boy caught his breath.

'There is a fight and several have been injured.'

'Where?'

'On the passenger deck, there is blood, a lot of blood.'

'Lead on, show me the place.' The boy ran and the chief mate puffed as he tried to keep pace. The boy ran into the darkness of the passenger deck, in the light of the small lamps that hung by the bunks and sleeping areas Dimmock could see three or four men being held apart by others he could just make out the blood on their faces and on their shirts.

'What is this?' His voice was one of authority, those involved looked up at him. One of those holding back a fighter spoke,

'It has been over a woman.' That's all the chief mate needed, a dispute over a woman.

'Which woman?'

'Her.' The man pointed to a figure being held a few paces from the fighting men. The chief mate recognised the woman even in the gloom, she was the mother of the boy who had died from poison of the blood.

'Your name?' Dimmock asked the woman bluntly, he had no answer. He asked again,

'What is your name?' Still the woman was silent. The chief mate took a step closer to the silent woman, he lifted her head so that he could see her face a little more clearly. 'I need your name, now answer me.' Still the woman remained silent, he turned from her to the men who had been fighting he could make out that they had held no punches back and on the side of one man's head saw that part of his ear had been bitten off. 'You.' He pointed to the first man who was stemming the stream of blood coming from his nose. 'What is this woman's name?' He coughed away a mouth full of blood.

'Rose, her name is Rose.' The chief mate looked from one of the fighters to the other then spoke to the young lad who had first told him of the fight.

'Get the surgeon and ask him to bring bandages and some thread and make it quick.' The boy turned on his heel and sped off in the direction of the surgeon's cabin. 'Now you brave fighters what have you to say for yourselves?' The one with the chewed ear started to say something when the one with the bloody nose interrupted. The chief mate held up his hand,

'You first.' He gestured to the one holding what was left of his ear.

'She wanted me, I know she did.' The chief mate turned to the woman called Rose,

'Is this true, did you and this brave fellow lie together in agreement?' There was no response from

Rose, her face told nothing, her eyes were glazed over her face was pale and drawn the chief mate could see no emotion, no pain, no guilt. 'Answer me woman what happened here.' Dimmock's voice no longer held sympathy he had enough of this, he turned to the bloody nose. 'What about you, how did you and this man come to blows?'

'Look what he has done to my ear.'

'Never mind your ear answer my question.'

'It was her, she led me on she wanted me to be with her.' This did not ring true the woman still remained silent with no sign of understanding showing on her face. The chief mate was getting nowhere he looked around for someone else who could throw some light on what had happened. He pointed to a woman who stood close to Rose,

'What about you, can you tell me what went on here?' The woman clutched her apron and then after looking from fighter to fighter she said'

'Rose did not agree to be with either of them, it was that one that started it first.' She pointed to the one holding what was left of his ear. 'He could see that Rose was not in a good state of mind and he tried to lay her and lift her skirts.'

'Then what.' The chief mate thought at last he was getting somewhere.

'Then that one, the one with the bloody nose tried to pull the other away and then take his place.'

'What was Rose doing when this was taking place?'

'Nothing, she just lay there in her usual state.'

'And what is her usual state?'

'She hardly speaks and moves only to eat a morsel nothing more.'

The chief mate heard the surgeon's voice.

'What have we here Mr Dimmock.' It was almost a cheery manor that the surgeon had as he looked at the damaged men.

'They may be in need of a few stitches especially that one.' He pointed to the man with the bitten ear.

Richard Hinds had brought with him a bag it contained basic things that should be able to address any injury caused by a brawl. The boy who had been sent to fetch him had told of the blood and damage to a nose. He quickly took hold of the head of the man with the bloody nose and held it back and placing a folded piece of linen against the nostrils told the man to hold firm, he then looked at the bitten ear. While the surgeon was assessing the damage Mr Dimmock was still listening to what he was being told by those close by. Another woman stepped forward,

'They,' she pointed to the two men. 'Have been trying to get between any woman's legs for days now, they are like alley cats on the prowl.' Another voice then chipped in. 'They tried it with me but soon felt the back of my hand and the fist of my man.' There was a murmur of agreement from the women looking on. The chief mate looked at the two culprits.

'You are nothing but scum if you have tried to take this poor woman, Once the surgeon has done with you, I know of a place where you can work off your energy.' He looked at Richard Hinds,

'Mr Hinds, can these men work are they fit to scrub?' Richard looked up from bandaging the severed ear,

'Yes, I think they would benefit from some strenuous exercise.'

'Good, then you men come with me.' The two men stood both looking justifiably guilty and keeping at arm's length followed the chief mate.

Although the captain was the maintainer of the law aboard ship the chief mate took it upon himself to deal with this particular incident, he would inform the captain of his actions later. On the deck Mr Dimmock summoned a member of the crew,

'Joseph, what are you about?' The sailor came to a halt,

'I am going to the heads to see what state they are in.' The chief mate's face took on a satisfied expression, this is just what was needed.

'I have good news for you, take these two and show them how clean we want the heads and don't leave anything out, they are to scrub the area and make it fit for the captain to piss on.' The sailor looked a little surprised, he was not going to clean the heads he was just going to see what state they were in but if the chief mate said they were to be cleaned then so be it. 'You two will go with Joseph and clean all that he shows you, and Joseph if they give you any trouble then send for me and I will place the whole matter in the captain's hands and that my friends could result in a flogging for the two of you.' The two men looked at each other, they were aware of the terrible floggings that took place on naval vessels and did not relish the thought of the cat being used on their backs. The chief mate watched as they followed the sailor towards the bow of the ship and the two boxes that were used by both crew and passengers when the weather permitted.

Satisfied that he had made the right call, Dimmock made his way to the captain's cabin.

Edward Carrick was hunched over a chart studying the coast of the new world he would have to get the Neptune into the right position to manoeuvre the ship between Cape Henry and Cape Charles then into the James River and up to Jamestown itself. There were still approximately ten days to go but he wanted to get a clear picture in his mind. He had brought the ship into Jamestown before but needed to refresh his memory and looking at the chart he could visualise the landscape. If all went well, they should make landfall without problem. There was a knock on his door and after a pause the chief mate entered the cabin.

'Mr Dimmock, not another death?'

'No Captain, just a slight unrest amongst some passengers, two men came to blows over a woman. I have dealt with it, however if you think I have been too lenient I will bow to your judgement.'

'How serious was the incident?'

'It was two men who were led by what is in their breeches not in their heads. They tried to lay with the woman who lost her son and they came to blows arguing over who should claim the her.'

'Was this a case of rape. If it was then the men should be punished accordingly.'

'It was not rape, the two men involved are too stupid to carry out a crime such as that and they both sustained injuries during their fight, one with a broken nose together with cuts and bruises the other with half his ear bitten off.'

'What punishment did you give them?'

'They are to clean the heads until they are fit for you to use, not only today but for the rest of the voyage and they are to be kept from the passenger deck they will sleep with the animals which is where they belong.' The captain thought for a moment, if this had been a Naval vessel the men would have suffered a severe penalty which may have resulted in keel hauling but that was unlikely as there should be no women on a naval ship of the line.

'What of the woman?'

'That is a more difficult problem, she suffered greatly when her son died, she communicates little with other passengers she only moves to eat and then it is only to keep herself alive, I think she may not survive the remainder of the journey and if she does what her husband will do with her is hard to imagine.'

'We are not nursemaids we are responsible for transporting the commodities onboard from England to Virginia, if the cargo becomes damaged through no fault of ours then whoever paid for it to be shipped to the new world will have to accept the condition that it arrives in. What I cannot do is punish the two men in such a way that it may cause their deaths so Mr Dimmock I think you did the right thing. Please make sure that those involved do not get off lightly, they are to be watched and if necessary, beaten by whoever you have detailed to oversee them, but any beating is not to be so severe that it kills them.'

'Aye, captain.' The chief mate was pleased with the outcome of his meeting with the captain, he would pass the message onto the crew who would probably take great delight in making the two men suffer.

Chapter 13

Following his attendance on the two fighters Richard Hinds returned to his cabin and slumped down on his bunk. There was enough room for him to stretch out, he closed his eyes and tried to think of how he was going to include the Saurin family in his future plans. He would speak to Martin Saurin as soon as possible and sound him out on how he envisaged life in Virginia. He had an idea in his mind that would involve the apothecary but how he would accommodate the whole family would be difficult. His knowledge of the family was only that which he had gained on the voyage. Questions kept leaping into his mind.

'How would the son be employed? What about Adele what did her father have in mind for her? He thought a lot about her and would be willing to take her into his life but would she be able to exist in his world? Life was not easy, he rolled over and faced the baulk head, the ship creaked and groaned, how many more miles had they to go? His eyes closed, maybe he would be able to answer his own questions after speaking to Saurin.'

Martin Saurin sat with his son going over the Latin they had been studying every day since their departure from England. He looked at his son and could see that the enthusiasm that was once there had gone Francois appeared to be in a trance like state when he recited the phrases and verse that had become embedded into his brain. As Richard Hinds approached Martin closed the book to the relief of Francois, Richards clear voice came through the gloomy air of their primitive accommodation.

'Good day to you, might I have a moment of your time Mr Saurin?' Martin Saurin looked at the surgeon with some apprehension, when they had cause to speak before it was normally regarding some dead or injured person.

'Please.' Martin gestured to the end of the bunk that Francois had stood up from. Richard sat and looking at the state of the area where Saurin and his children had been living for the last eight weeks, he felt a great deal of sympathy for them.

'This may seem a little strange but I have a question to ask.'

'If I can answer I will as long as it is within my knowledge.'

'It is not of a medical nature, I wish to ask you of your plans when we arrive in Virginia.' Martin was

188

surprised, why would the surgeon need to know about his plans they had only met at the beginning of the voyage and although the situations that they had both been involved with had been traumatic he felt that they had both acquitted themselves well. Martin did not immediately respond but tried to gather his thoughts then he looked from Francois to Richard,

'With God's grace I hope to find some accommodation for my family and try to establish myself as an apothecary in Jamestown.'

'Forgive me for asking but have you sufficient funds to carry out such a plan?' Martin felt a little affronted by Richard prying into his personal affairs, he would not discuss his finances with anyone particularly not within earshot of those on the passenger deck.

'Perhaps you would like to walk with me, a trip on deck may do us both good.' Richard was a little surprised but agreed then asked,

'Perhaps you would prefer to carry on this conversation in my cabin?' Martin was intrigued by the surgeon.

'That would be satisfactory, Francois you are to continue with your studies and I will test you on my return.' The look on Francois's face told a story of a young man who was close to the end of his tether as

189

far as Latin was concerned. His faced dropped as he answered his father,

'Yes, father whatever you say.' The surgeon stood and Francois resumed his place on the bunk.

Richard and Martin made their way through the ships decks until they arrived at Richards small cabin. There was just enough space for them to sit on a bunk without causing any great problem. Martin could smell some of the solutions that Richard kept, his eyes cast themselves around he could see various tools of Richards profession everything was in its place, everything had a use and every item gleamed as if it had just been meticulously cleaned.

'Well, what could you not tell me below?' His curiosity was apparent.

'You asked me about my ability to support my family.' The pause was for him to gather courage enough to tell the items he had with him. 'I have certain family heirlooms that I intend to sell thereby raising enough to rent or even buy a dwelling for my family and as for income, I am not afraid of any work, nor is my son. We will gain employment wherever we can. Adele will also work, she has a good brain and is not afraid to clean and wash for others and she will care for any property we may get.' Richard could see the determination in Martin's face, he was a man who would succeed no matter what the cost.

'Thank you for being so honest with me.' Richard said as he looked at Martins face, his expression was one of aggression, not against Richard but against the life that lay before him. It was then that Richard took a deep breath and launched into what he had been thinking about. 'Perhaps I should start by telling you a little of myself.' Martin watched the man in front of him get a little more comfortable before he started. 'I am from a fairly wealthy family, our wealth came with the gifts of land to my predecessors and their investment in their children. The law was an area that most of my immediate family entered into. My father and his father before him were established legal advisors and lawyers in the upper echelons of the state. They had both been called to the bar after studying at the Inns of Court. My eldest brother has followed in their footsteps, I have another brother who is, as we speak, serving at court and then there is me. I was destined for the church but through good luck and circumstance I had the good fortune to study medicine although my father thought that a surgeon was nothing more than a butcher, he changed his attitude when I studied both natural and human philosophy as well as surgery and pharmacy at the Royal College of Physicians. Although I learnt a great deal, I had no real knowledge of life so I pleaded with my father to

191

allow me to leave England for Virginia. Once he had become use to the idea of his son wasting his life in a land on the far side of the ocean, he made enquiries through his various sources and managed to secure me a property in Jamestown and letters of introduction that will hopefully start me off on a good foot. So, I have a place to live letters of introduction and an opportunity to offer my services to the people of Virginia.'

Martin had listened to Richard and he was interested in his life story but, he thought, how does that affect him?

'You seem to have your future well planned, Richard, I feel I have a great deal to achieve when we reach landfall.' He looked at the surgeon who had a look of excitement on his face, Richard took some papers from a folder and looked carefully at the wording.

'The property that has been acquired for me has enough rooms to accommodate at least four if not five people. There is ample room for the preparation of drugs and also space to live. It has two storeys and although it may be constructed in the same way as those in England it appears to have a more solid base than others.' He looked at Martin who still was unsure of what Richard was alluding to. 'My suggestion is that I need a trustworthy apothecary to assist me and you need a place to live and work while you establish yourself.' For some reason Martin blushed, his mind raced, this could be a solution to his initial problems,

'What would the cost be, as I have told you I have funds but I am not a rich man by any means.'

'The cost would be that you perform your duties as an apothecary, your son maintains the house and performs the duties of an apprentice to you, he will also be required to repair and service the house. As for Adele, I would like to engage her as my housekeeper. Her duties would be to run the house, keep it clean and control any servants I may employ.'

Martin looked a little confused, how and why did his luck change so rapidly, this was an offer he could not afford to refuse.

'If you would permit me to discuss this with my children, I would be grateful, however my immediate answer would be that I would be delighted to accept your offer and would assure you that you would not regret employing my family.' Richard held out his hand which was readily taken by Martin.

'So, please speak to Francois and Adele and let me know their feelings, I am sure that they will come to the same decision as you.' Martin rose from the bunk his mind in a whirl, this could be the making of a new start for him, he hurried back to his sleeping area.

*

Adele was keeping her promise to visit William daily and discuss whatever he wanted. She had told him of her family and how it came to The Netherlands but had yet to explain how they had arrived in England, she would carry on the story telling him of the troubles her father had when they reached England, how his religion had caused problems and how he had been shunned by the people where he had tried to settle. Adele knocked on the cabin door and waited, William's voice beckoned her in, he felt a certain amount of regret as she stepped into the cabin and he saw her face. He had a feeling that he would never be more than a friend to her. William had dreamt that one day they may become man and wife, however that feeling had been destroyed when he had seen her with the surgeon. It was the way she had spoken to Richard Hinds and her movements around him, William knew that he would have to settle for friendship.

'You seem a little disturbed.' She could see clearly that he was not in the best frame of mind. 'What troubles you?' William eased his leg into a more comfortable position,

'I have a great deal to learn before we reach Virginia, Alec and Robert have given me so much I don't think I shall be able to remember half of it.' His voice seemed a little sad and she could tell that it was not the amount of information alone that was causing him to take on such a mood.

'Are you sure there is nothing else?'

'No, but I fear that we may have to forego our meetings to allow me to try to absorb everything I need to know before we reach our destination.' This was unexpected Adele had thought that they would continue with their sessions until they landed,

'If that is what you wish then I will not intrude on your time.' He looked at her and could see that she had not fully understood his reasoning which was understandable.

'I am sorry but I really do need to prepare myself for a new life.' He looked down at his hands and then raised his head so that it was level with hers. 'I will not be confined to this rabbit hutch all of the time and hope that we will be able to see each other often during the final stage of our journey.' She could see that for some reason there was a tear forming in the corner of his eye.

'I shall insist on our meeting at least every day even if it is only to talk about the weather.' This brought a smile to his face he hoped that they would remain in contact both on the ship and when they landed. She stood and readied herself to go, 'We shall meet at the deck entrance each morning when the ships bell strikes twice in the forenoon, is that agreed?' He raised himself as best he could,

'Agreed, and when I get this thing off of my leg, I hope to be able to get around a lot more easily.' She paused and looked at the splint contraption that covered his lower leg,

'When do you think that will be done away with?' He tapped the splint,

'As soon as Mr Hinds thinks it wise, I shall see him in the morning and pray that all is well and this thing can be removed.' She did an odd thing she made a little curtsey, gave him a wonderful smile then disappeared from the cabin.

William had not been as attentive to Alec and Robert as he should have been. His mind had been else where he knew that if he was to succeed in the new world, he would be reliant on his two friends for all the help they could give. His friends had both gone to inspect what they had in the hold of the ship, it was the main reason for their return to England, although the sale of the tobacco that they had brought from Virginia paid for the most of it. Robert carried a ledger they identified each item, there were bales of cloth, good solid iron ware, oil lamps with decorated glass which were carefully wrapped, saddles and horse furniture gave off the smell of leather, the list was long and it took time for them to complete their task. On returning to their cabin William asked if they would continue with his education about the tobacco crops and anything else that he might experience in Virginia.

'There is so much for you to know, we can give you a glimpse into life on the plantation but you will have to wait and see for yourself the way that life is led there.'

'What about the people? Are they the same as in England, surely, they cannot be.' Alec laughed,

'You will see some strange sights, there are those that will be familiar to you but you must remember that we will be in a land that has been lived in and ruled by a different race of people who look and sound totally different to those in Bristol or Cambridge.' William seemed to regain his interest in what he was being told,

'What sort of people are they, are they savages as I have heard?' He had spoken to very few people who had experienced a meeting with other races and they had called them all savages and heathens. Robert reached out and touched William's arm,

197

'Your colour may not be the same as many, some are brown and some are black, some have a history that goes back into the time before Christ whilst others have been brought against their will. Do not view them as savages, it is vital that we, on the plantation, treat them as human beings because without them we would have no crops and therefore no money.' He looked at Alec who turned towards William,

'The savages you may have heard of have at times resented us,' he pointed to William and Robert, 'to the point where they have tried to rid their land of those who have claimed it for themselves. There have been many deaths not only from fighting that has erupted between us interlopers and those that rightly claim the land as their own. We have claimed land to be ours, we have cleared forests and built houses, we have planted unfamiliar crops and we have brought with us disease which has killed many.' He looked at William with eyes that were stern and fixed on his. 'Don't think of them as beasts of burden as most do, think of them as a part of life that is necessary to achieve our aim and wealth.' Robert shook his head at thoughts of some of the treatment he had witnessed.

'Alec and I have seen many horrors both in England and in Viginia, we have been lucky to survive and even luckier to have ended in the situation that we find ourselves today. We know that if you understand your workers and feed and house them accordingly you will get the best out of them and also you will not have to replace those that die which is an expensive practice. You will see many fall with disease, that we cannot stop, what we can do is get the most out of our workers without killing them.'

William tried to understand but found it difficult, he would be in a better position to understand when they arrived.

'These people that had the land, who are they?' Robert cleared his throat,

'There are many tribes or families that have ruled the land for hundreds of years, they have their own way of life, their chief's rule as elders and councils do in England. They have their own beliefs which are linked to nature which we find hard to understand and they can be fearsome warriors, never underestimate them for you will come into contact with many.'

'What are they called these people?' Alec smiled,

'This is the strangest thing, when the first men arrived in this land, they thought they had found the Indies, with spices, gold and other treasures, so they called those that lived in this land Indians. They have their own tribal names which you will get to know as time goes on, some are called Powhatan others have names that we find hard to pronounce such as the Algonquin or Iroquoian. You will get to know their names once you begin dealing with them.

'Do we actually trade with them?'

'Yes, trade is something that we have learnt from, they have many good ways of growing crops of maize and corn, which is another thing you will become use to. They hunt well but are fascinated by our weapons which we take good care not to allow them to get hold of.' William had now become very interested in what lay ahead of him, he would continue to ask about these 'Indians' and what they stood for.

*

Edward Carrick was not happy with the speed in which they were travelling, his particular worry was the state of the provisions particularly drink. The fish that had been caught had quickly been consumed and although the crew took great care in trying to supplement their rations with whatever they could catch even they had become anxious about the stale and sour beer they were given. Washing clothes and bodies in sea water helped in some ways but salt was on everything. The food had been salted, there was no fresh anything, all those on board were suffering from loose teeth, poor skin and bowels that did not function as they should. He had a decision to make, he could forge on and hope that what they had on board lasted or he could make for Bermuda, replenish his supplies then make the last six hundred miles with sufficient victuals. He sent word for his chief mate, bosun and coxswain to join him. They arrived each with a worried frown on their face.

'Gentlemen come in and sit.' They could see the charts on the captain's desk but they were not aware of why he had called for them. 'You are aware of the state of the food and drink we have,' there were nods from the three men, 'I have looked at the charts and I have a choice to make whether we continue on our course and hope to reach Jamestown before our supplies are exhausted or we make for Bermuda and seek replenishment there.' The men looked at each other. It was the chief mate who spoke,

'The passengers are reaching their limit, however I think we should maintain our course and make for Jamestown. The wind is in our favour and with god's grace we will be able to run before it and make good speed.' The captain looked at the chart on his desk,

'If we were to head for the Bermudas it will take two or three days and then a further ten to twelve days to reach Jamestown, if we maintain our course, as the chief mate suggests, we should reach our destination in no more than ten days.' The bosun then spoke,

'The victuals we have left would need to be strictly rationed, especially the drink. That may cause problems with not only the passengers but the crew will not take kindly to having their allotted rations reduced.' The captain then turned to the coxswain,

'What do you think Mr Leigh?' The coxswain took a breath,

'If the weather holds and the seas do not pick up, we could make Jamestown, it is a risk but isn't every move we make a risk?' Carrick knew that the experience his men had was based on many voyages, they knew the weather and the sea, he looked up,

'We shall head for Jamestown and Mr Dimmock start to ration what we have immediately. I shall need you to keep me informed of the state of both crew and passengers on a daily basis so gentlemen pray that God is with us.' With that the meeting came to an end, the chief mate and bosun made for the galley and the coxswain back to his post. The captain sent for the parson, if there was a time to ask for help from above it would be during the days ahead.

Chapter 14

Geoffry Peters had spent most of the voyage with the passengers, he felt that was where he could be of most help. The deaths that had occurred were truly devastating and the deterioration of those cooped up in the damp and dark of the passenger's quarters was rapidly becoming a major concern of his. He had spoken to the surgeon on many occasions but he could only do so much he felt that the moral welfare of those on board fell to him. He had held regular prayer meetings those that listened to him grew less and less until the tragic deaths occurred then prayers became not only popular but necessary. He reached the captain's cabin a little out of breath, he knocked and entered, the captains greeting was matter of fact,

'Come in Parson, I need your assistance.' Peters was a little taken aback, the captain seemed to have little time for religion, his faith was in the tides and weather.

'I am at your service, whatever I can do to assist I will.'

'Good, there is a need to ration our food and drink which will be hard on all. I have seen how you communicate with those on board and want you to ease the path we are about to take as best you can.' Peters was a little confused, the rations that the passengers were given were just enough to keep them alive as it was if they were to be reduced some would fall ill and those that were already suffering from ailment could possibly die.

'Captain, it is my belief that to cut the food that these people have will have a detrimental effect on many of them.' Edward Carrick was aware that there may be casualties and he would do all in his power to keep the numbers to a minimum. He knew that there were those amongst the passengers that may not survive under any circumstances, there were several older servants who he had seen embark and was surprised that they had lasted until then.

'I am aware of the situation, that is why I need your help. I need you to be with them, to help them through their suffering and to guide them along the path which lies before them.'

'I can do only what my conscience will allow me to do. I will try to keep their faith alive as well as their bodies. I may need the help of the surgeon and the apothecary if I am to succeed.'

'You will have their assistance I will make sure of that. Please carry out your duty and try to keep their faith alive.' At this point Carrick asked the Parson to contact both the surgeon and the apothecary and ask them to come to his cabin. The parson left his mind screaming, how was he to keep over one hundred hungry and thirsty men women and children from despair. He shook his head trying to think how he was going to help them.

Edward Carrick had been in similar situations and he had been able to get through the toughest of times. He took out the passenger list and carefully ran his finger down the list of names. He could see the mixture of individuals, their origins, professions and trades were many. The more wealthy had their own areas, some had the few cabins that were available others had to do the best they could in the space they were given. At the top of the list was a member of the aristocracy, the son of a Lord no less, together with a servant and an estate manager. Carrick had made it his business to see that they were well cared for, the man's father's investment in the ship and the cargo it carried was substantial. Although the son was not in the highest of echelons, he still had the ability to influence the profitability of the voyage. The livestock in the hold belonged to his family although their property in Virginia had sufficient numbers of cattle, sheep and pigs, his father's plan was to improve the bloodline with good quality beasts from English breeders. Carrick would ensure that the passenger in question would be cared for throughout the voyage.

The surgeon and apothecary met outside the captain's cabin, they greeted one another asking what the problem was.

'I fear we are in for troubled times I passed the chief mate on the deck, his face told a story of worry, so prepare yourself for something that may take a great deal of thought and action.' The captain's voice sang out,

'Come in.' He was not in his customary position standing looking at charts, on this occasion he sat behind his desk with the passenger list in front of him. 'Mr Hinds and Mr Saurin, we shall be entering a stage of our journey which will take all the skill and care to see us through. You may be aware that the provisions onboard are running perilously low and we still lie some considerable distance from Jamestown, I have decided to carry on our course and rely on wind and weather to get us to port in the earliest possible time.' The two men stood in front of the desk and glanced at each other, they were aware of how the food and water was deteriorating in standard and quantity. 'It will be necessary to ration what we have and that may increase the problems that the passengers are experiencing. Hunger and thirst are the two biggest dilemma's that we will have, every chance we get we will try to fish and if it should rain then we will capture as much water that the buckets onboard can hold'. Richard leaned forward,

'Is there not livestock on board, can we not slaughter a beast to feed those whose hunger may drive them to the limit?'

'You are right we do have cattle, sheep and some pigs in the hold, they are cargo as are the passengers and the livestock pay more for their passage than the indentured servants.' He paused and looked up, he could see the look of amazement on Richard Hinds' face. The surgeon blurted out,

'Are you saying that the cattle and sheep have a higher value that of the people on the passenger list?' Edward expected an outburst especially when the value of human life was discussed.

'If you were to ask the owners of the stock, what do you think their answer would be, is it the cattle or the servants that hold the most value?' Martin Saurin could not believe what he was hearing,

'Surely in the name of all that is holy one cow or sheep could be sacrificed to feed those who may otherwise starve.' The captain moved uncomfortably,

'It is not your decision or mine, what I can do is ask the question to the owner's representative who travels with us but please remember that in the eyes of those that rule, the peasants and servants are of lesser value than that of their prized beasts.' Martin had seen the results of the ruling class viewing labourers in the same way as they viewed any other piece of property. He had witnessed dreadful punishments for those who had not obeyed the laws laid down by the elite, the persecution of those in France had left him with scars that would remain with him for the rest of his life.

'How can we influence those who own the livestock?' It was almost a plea from Martin.

'There is very little, only to put the case that if the ship were to be caught in bad weather that the livestock would not be of any use when it came to saving the ship.' The captain smiled ironically. 'Nor for that matter would the passengers.' The three men were silent their predicament seemed to have no answer. 'I will speak this day with the owner's representatives and will do my utmost to get agreement for at least one beast, whether it be cow, sheep or pig to be slaughtered.' Richard and Martin felt a little relieved at least there may be some hope in avoiding starvation amongst the passengers. Richard then spoke,

'We will use our skill and knowledge to keep those on the passenger deck alive, as for their overall health that will be in the lap of the gods and the owners of the livestock.' All three men's faces did not display confidence least of all Edward Carrick, he had dealt with those who placed themselves on a pedestal before and his success had not been as good as he would have liked. The surgeon and apothecary left the captain's cabin with a great deal of trouble on their minds.

Lord Spilsby's son lay on his bed, his cabin was roomy enough for one but he felt enclosed. The wine had become unpalatable although he drank it mainly to help him endure the conditions, he found himself in.

'Whitmore. He called for his manservant. 'Where the devil are you, get yourself in here as quick as you like.' There was a sound of scurrying as John Whitmore rushed to answer his master's call. He had been in service all his life, born on the estate, his family had been linked to the Lord and the estate for as long as he or anyone else could remember. His current master was the youngest son, David, a man of some twenty-five years who had been raised on the family estate and had been doted on by his mother, in her eyes he could do no wrong. His father on the other hand knew exactly what he was like, a wastrel, a drunkard and a womaniser. Things had come to a head when he had become involved with a married woman and then sited in a divorce case which swept through society like a raging fire. His father had been disgusted by his actions and embarrassed at court.

'You, Sir, are a reprobate, nothing more nothing less and I will not have you in my house a moment longer. You will be out of here as soon as a horse can be saddled.' There was nothing his mother could do to persuade her husband to change his mind.

'You will leave this place and take ship to the Americas, I have stock to be taken and you will go with it.' He had pleaded with his father but this time things had gone one step too far, even his mother could not help.

'What am I to do on the other side of the world?'

'You will start a new life, you will be away from the gambling and womanising that you currently frequent, you will be exiled from this land for as long as it takes you to come to your senses.'

'But father there are nothing but savages and religious zealots in the colonies.'

'And that my boy is exactly what you need to focus your mind on your duty not only to me but to your family.'

David Spilsby had departed shortly before he was involved even further in the scandal over his affair with the married woman in question. He had been told, by his father, that he would be accompanied by an Estate Steward by the name of Norris and that he could take his manservant but that was all. He would be responsible for getting the stock to his father's property in Virginia and after that he was to continue to govern his family's property. His father had written to the governor of the area and requested guidance for his son. The family land was in good hands and made a substantial amount from various crops, his father had warned him that if David interfered with the running of the property, he should not think of ever returning to England.

Whitmore opened the cabin door,

'Yes, My Lord,' David Spilsby looked at the retch of a man standing before him, he had little flesh on his face or any other part of his frame, his eyes stood out from his head and his lips were almost blue.

'What is wrong with you man are you deaf?' Whitmore looked at the figure lounging on his bed, it was not a bunk but a bed such as Whitmore would have been thankful to just spend an hour in instead of sleeping on a rolled blanket filled with straw.

'I require wine, Whitmore and try to get something a little more palatable than this vomit.' He tipped what was left of his glass onto the floor.

'Straight away m'lord.' He turned and almost ran from the cabin. There was some wine but it was all from the same barrel so there would be no difference but Whitmore knew that his master would not be able to tell once the first glass had been emptied.

*

Edward Carrick did not like the pompous creature that paid the majority of the costs of the voyage. He knew he would have to approach him for permission to slaughter one of his cattle to feed those onboard. His approach would not be to plead his case but to be matter of fact and hope that the pathetic specimen would understand the importance of keeping people alive. As he approached David Spilsby's cabin he passed the servant who he had seen fetching and carrying for his master, he looked in no fit state to carry out any duties let alone dash and tear about for some lazy good for nothing. Knocking on the door he drew in a breath and waited for the answer.

'Come.' The call was one filled with boredom, Carrick entered what he saw did not surprise him. The manservant had done his best in keeping the cabin clean and respectable but the idiot he saw before him had no sense of cleanliness.

'Ah, the captain, now for what do I owe this pleasure, have you come with news of our arrival, will I be able to see land soon and get off this hulk?' Carrick looked around and then back at the face that without a wig looked blotchy and lined.

'I am here to discuss the state of the ship.' David Spilsby looked up with a lack of interest,

'What, pray tell, has that to do with me, the running of this ship is in your hands is it not?'

'It is and that is what I am doing in speaking to you.'

'Well man, what is it?' Edward Carrick did not like this individual at all, it was his lack of purpose that appalled him most.'

'Our voyage has a further ten days or so to go, our supplies are running precariously low, those on the passenger deck have been without a decent meal for some time now. The health of those who want for food is deteriorating and sickness is beginning to run rife.' Edward could see no sign of concern or interest on the face of the man before him.

'And, I ask again what has that to do with me.'
Edward knew that the only way to get through would
be to speak as plainly as he could.

'You have livestock in the hold, the passengers
are close to starvation, we need to slaughter one of
those animals to prevent death and sickness.' Nothing
came from David Spilsby, he was not interested in the
problems of those who he considered far below his
station in life. Edward tried again to get through to
this excuse for a human being. 'Can I have your
permission to slaughter a cow and use it to feed those
on board?' The face of the man in front of him looked
up, he was annoyed,

'Whitmore,' he called again, 'Whitmore,
where is that man?' The door opened and Whitmore
stood on the threshold.

'Yes, my lord?'

'Fetch Norris, get him hear immediately.' The
servant nodded in a servile way that held a certain
amount of contempt. 'We will wait for the man who
has been sent to care for the beasts and see what he has
to say about losing one of his precious animals.'
Spilsby poured more wine into his glass, his attitude
remained one of idle annoyance. Whitmore ran to the
hold where he knew he would find Norris,

'Come quickly, you are needed, our master wants you to give him guidance on the use of the livestock.' Norris stood away from the young bull calf, it was around ten months old, he had seen it lose weight and was concerned over its condition. There were three other calves that had managed better however none of his charges were in the peak of fitness.

'Does he need me now?'

'Yes, straight away.' Please do not antagonise him, I have enough to deal with without his anger growing.' The husbandman let his hand run over the calf's flank,

'Lead the way.' Whitmore climbed the stairway to the upper deck with Norris in his wake. On reaching the cabin Whitmore knocked and waited,

'Come.' They entered Whitmore in front. Spilsby pointed at Whitmore, 'You can go but stay close I may have need of you.' The servant left glancing at Norris as he passed neither man knowing of what was to follow. 'Ah, Norris, what is the state of your charges?' He answered with a look of puzzlement on his face,

'My lord?'

'How many times do I have to repeat myself, in what condition are the animals?' Norris rubbed his tired eyes, his role meant that he spent many hours in the hold with the livestock and he had little sleep.

'They are suffering from the lack of water, we have enough at the moment but there may be difficulties ahead if we do not have rain.' David Spilsby had no interest in farming, livestock or otherwise,

'Are they alive?' His voice became even more irritated.

'Yes, they are alive my lord but for how long I cannot say.'

'Well, the captain here,' he waved his hand in the direction of Carrick, 'Wants me to let him slaughter one of the stock, what do you say to that?' This came as a surprise to Norris.

'Why?'

'To feed the hungry mob that inhabit the lower deck, that's why.' Norris looked from his lord to the captain,

'Are there no victuals on board, I have seen food in the galley, is there not salted fish and meat?'

'That is a very good question, captain what do you have to say about that?' Carrick could sense that this was not going to be easy.

'The salted and dried food that we have is almost at an end, we do not have sufficient to see us to port unless drastic action is taken.'

'And what action would that be, pray tell?'

'Rations would need to be cut and those without any means of support would starve.' He was blunt with his reply, he needed to be this idiot before him could not tell day from night when it involved those of the lower order.

'How many would starve?' His question was ludicrous.

'I cannot say but if the passengers were to get sick with the bloody flux and that illness got to the crew then we all may die.' For the first time it may have registered with Spilsby that he was in danger. Norris spoke,

'If we were to slaughter an animal enough to feed the crew then their rations could be given to the passengers, would that not suffice?' Spilsby looked directly at the captain,

'That's a good point, what do you say to that heh captain?'

'I have upwards of one hundred passengers, including yourselves, the crew numbers no more than fifty the supplies that we currently have would not feed all.' Spilsby turned, he was bored and had no thought about those passengers who might suffer or even die.

'Well, as long as my plate is served warm and is full, I do not really care.' Spilsby turned back to Norris. 'What would be the repercussions if one animal was slaughtered?' Norris was a little sickened by what his master had said,

'The livestock are of good blood lines and would enhance your father's herd in the Americas. Your father, my lord, has given me the responsibility of getting the stock to his estate but in this situation, I feel that the loss of one bull calf would be acceptable.' Spilsby almost jumped up,

'You are in agreement with the captain!' His voice was almost that of a woman high pitched near hysterical. Do you know what you are agreeing to, a bull calf is worth more than several of the indentured servants.' The captain then asked a flippant question,

'So, what are you advocating, that we save the calf and eat the passengers?' Spilsby clenched his fist and brought it down onto the desk top,

'Do not speak to me as if I were a member of your god forsaken crew, as far as I am concerned the people on the lower deck are things, they are not people and whatever happens to them is of no interest to me.' Carrick reached out, grabbed Spilsby by the collar and pulled him across the desk.

'On this vessel I am judge and jury, I am the law. Any crime against man or woman will be for me to adjudicate. No passenger will suffer as long as I can help it.' Spilsby's face was turning red as he gasped for air, Carrick released his grip and Spilsby straightened himself, he croaked,

'Your action will be reported and you, captain, will no longer command any ship that my family has an interest in.' Carrick smiled,

'That matters little to me as this is to be my final voyage across the ocean.' This took the wind out of Spilsby's sails,

'I shall report you to the authorities when we reach Virginia, you will not go unpunished for your actions.' Carrick knew that the vindictive specimen before him was capable of causing him a great deal of trouble, he controlled himself,

'That is for you to action if and when we reach the shore.'

It was then that something strange happened. Spilsby dropped into his chair, he clasped his hands to his head and in a muffled voice said,

'Do as you please, just leave me alone.' His shoulders shook and it appeared to the three men standing in front of him that this creature was crying. Carrick could not leave without a decision being made over the bull calf,

'What of the calf, what is your decision?' From behind his hands Spilsby said,

'Whatever you want, just leave.' Carrick looked at Norris and nodded they both turned and left the cabin leaving Whitmore to deal with his lord and master.

As the captain and Norris walked away from the troubled young aristocrat Norris spoke,

'If I am to sacrifice a bull calf, I need your word that it will not be in vain and that every part of the beast will be put to good use.'

'Have no fear, all that will remain is its hooves, and if the cook can use those for anything they will go to.'

In Spilsby's cabin Whitmore circled the desk and carefully removed the glass that his master had been using. He gently helped his master get to his feet and then led him to the bed and easing him slowly down he stepped back, his master turned over and buried his face into a pillow trying to hide his sense of failure. Whitmore knew when to leave his master and this was the time to let him sleep off the wine, he had been drinking that day. As he stepped away from the bed, he heard a strange sound and turning towards the cabins small row of windows he could see through the opening that rain had started to fall,

'At least God has answered one prayer.' He thought.

The captain took Norris to the galley where he called for the cook, as he approached Carrick spoke,

'Good news, we have a bull calf to add to the store.' The cook's eyes opened wide,

'God be praised and together with the water that is currently falling in a steady shower we may be able to survive this journey.' The captain had not been aware that the rain had started to fall, he stopped and listened, he could just make out the sound of rain hitting the ship.

'Mr Norris I will leave you with our cook, if you could show him the animal that you have chosen, I will let you make any arrangements needed to make use of every inch of the beast.' He left the two men discussing the size and age of the animal. On the deck the activity was all about capturing as much water as they possibly could. Carrick could hear the chief mate giving orders, the crew were bringing out sail cloth and positioning it so that any rain could be channelled into the barrels that had been made ready. He was satisfied that all that could be done was being done, he looked towards the sky and felt the rain hit his face, opening his mouth he managed to take in the life saving liquid,

'Mr Dimmock, how goes the water?'

'It goes well captain, if this continues for the next day or so we will be able to replenish our stock.' Carrick smiled, 'Carry on Mr Dimmock and see me when you have all under control, I may have some further good news for you.'

'Aye, Aye captain.'

Edward Carrick felt a sense of relief as he walked back to his cabin but peace was not to be his. The two men who had been most concerned about the state of the people on board were waiting for him,

The captain greeted them with, 'I have news to tell.' The captain gestured towards his cabin,

'Follow me and I will tell all.' Richard Hinds and Martin Saurin followed the captain hoping that what he had to say would be of help to all. In the cabin Edward Carrick took his seat behind his desk,

'The information I have could be the saving of us, however I do not want anyone to think that we are secure in our venture.' He explained what had happened in Spilsby's cabin, 'I will expect that you, together with the parson and others, to ensure that whatever food and water is now available will be treated as if it were our last. The last of the salted fish and meat is to be saved until all fresh meat has been consumed. The cook will make the best of the carcass, he will need assistance to butcher and cook the animal so I need you to seek out any man or woman who has the skill to make good of everything the bull calf can offer up.' The two men looked at each other then turned towards the captain,

'Thank you.' They said almost in unison. There was little more to say, Richard and Martin left with smiles on their faces, perhaps God was with them.

The chief mate and bosun had made sure that every drop of rain that could be saved had been carefully collected in barrels and it was still raining. The bosun turned to the chief mate,

'This should do us for the remainder of the voyage.' The bosun rubbed his chin,

223

'Yes, but water will satisfy thirst but not hunger, how will we feed these people?'

It was then that they saw the cook hurrying towards the lower deck, the bosun called to him,

'And where are you off to in such a hurry Jacob Standish?'

'You have not heard we are to have one of the bull calves and I am to butcher it as quickly and as fast as I can.' A look of surprise spread across the chief mates and bosun's faces,

'A bull calf you say.'

'Yes, and I am in need of a person to help me deliver every sinew of the beast, do you know of any person who could help?' The bosun thought for a moment and turned to the chief mate,

'There is a couple, man and wife, who were in the service of a wealthy land owner, he was a gardener and she a cook may be they could assist.' The cook's eyes lit up,

'Most women know the kitchen but if she knows how to make the best out of the offal that would help what we have go further. Could you send her to the galley please.'

'I will and I will find out if there are any others who might help.'

The cook went on his way with Norris and the bosun left the chief mate and headed towards the passenger deck. The chief mate looked through the rain at the crew still directing the rain into barrels. He thought, 'this was good, this was very good, but would it last.'

Chapter 15

Martin Saurin had a great deal to consider, the offer made by Richard Hinds rang around his head, he needed to sit with his son and daughter to find out how they felt about working for the surgeon. He found them together, news had reached them about the meat that would, hopefully, reach them soon. Martin sat in front of them,

'I have a proposal to put to you, it concerns our lives when we reach Virginia.' He looked at the two young people before him, they were no longer children, they were man and woman and they had their lives ahead of them. Martin told them of his conversation with the surgeon and as he did surprise and curiosity spread across Adele and Francois faces,

'Would this mean that we would be indentured to the surgeon?' It was Adele asking the question.

'No, I would be in charge of my own business and run it alongside the surgeons practice.'

'But father, we would be beholding to the surgeon for many years.'

'Yes, but as soon as I can become established, I will become independent of him. This is a way that would allow me to start working for us as soon as we reach Virginia, you know that if we try to find somewhere to live and work it might mean that we would have to take on any employment that we could find for many months or even years before I could become established.' Adele could see that her father was desperate to accept the surgeons offer.

'I would be nothing more than a maid and for how long would I have to carry out the wishes of the surgeon.' Martin heard the tone of voice his daughter had used which saddened him. He did not want them to think he was selling them into servitude.

'You would be the mistress of the house, your duties would be to direct those who cleaned and fetched for the surgeon, you would be responsible for any money spent in the house, the ordering of food and materials, you would not be a skivvy.' He then turned to his son,

'Francois, what do you think of this?'

'My concern, father, is that we will become tied too closely to the surgeon, if I were to seek another path to follow would I be able to. You must believe, father, that in this new world there may be opportunities for me to learn and grow with the land.'

This was not what Martin expected from his son, he had thought that his son would naturally follow him and become an apothecary.

'Do you have any thoughts of what you may do or become?'

'I feel that this new land we are about to reach will offer me opportunities that I may never have thought of and I want to be able to follow any path that I think will create a new life for me.' Francios looked directly into his father's eyes almost pleading with him not to hold him back from his dreams.

'I have always thought that....' his voice trailed off as he let what had been said by his children sink in.

'If I were to promise you that I will not stop either of you from taking any action you wish after we have been with the surgeon for one year would that allay your fears?'

Adele looked at her brother and they nodded. They both knew that if their farther wanted to he could stop them doing anything if he put his mind to it. They were of an age that they could leave him if they so desired but their love and respect for him over ruled any such thoughts.

'So, I will tell the surgeon of our decision and we can look forward to starting a new life in Virginia.' He stood and made his way towards the stairs leading to the upper deck.

Richard Hinds was delighted to hear that the Saurin family had decided to start their life in the new world with him. He had discussed again the roles that they could adopt on arrival and he had agreed that if, after a year, either Adele or Francois decided to go along another path he would not stand in their way.

William sat on the edge of his bunk and awaited a visit from the surgeon, he hoped that today would be the day when he regained the full use of his leg. He was aware that he would have to be cautious with his movements, he did not want to jeopardise his acceptance by the plantation owner when he finally reached his destination. Alec stood in front of him,

'Today we will see how well you can get about without the splint.' He looked at the slightly worried look on William's face. 'I am sure you will be fine, you have done all that you can to ensure your leg would heal without problem and I for one can't wait to see that thing cast into the sea.' He pointed to the rows of wooden slats that made up the splint. Alec then stood back a little, his mind was on how close they were getting to Jamestown. 'There are other things you need to be aware of when we land that affect both those that live in Jamestown and those that run the plantations. There is a certain amount of unrest and debate that goes on between those that grow and those that make. It is something that has been fermenting for some time within those that govern. The argument is that the Indians prevent the development of land that could be used to cultivate more produce, it was also said that the Indians are increasingly encroaching on land cultivated by settlers.' Alec then went on to describe some of the disputes that had taken place between settlers and the Indians. 'So, be aware that things are not as rosy as some may say. There is a General Assembly that, when we left, was led by Sir William Berkeley he was not in favour of moving the Indians on which has created an amount of unease in the colony. My advice to you is to keep well away from politics and concentrate on the job in hand, which is tobacco.' William shook his head there was so much to take in and although they had spent weeks at sea, he did not think he had retained more than half of what he needed.

There was a knock on the door, it opened to reveal the surgeon who had a look of one that had lost a penny and found a guinea.

'How are you William, I hope the leg has not given you any problem?' He started to lift William's splinted leg.

'It is holding together well, I have very little discomfort and I am eager to get this thing off of my leg.' The surgeon started to dismantle the splint, as he removed it he could see that William's leg was in good shape, he felt the leg and could tell that the bone had knitted well.

'I think that this can be discarded.' He tossed the splint onto the floor. 'What I require of you is that you do not place any more weight than you need to on the leg and treat it with some delicacy until the muscles have strengthened.' William eased his way from the bunk and stood for the first time without the splint. His leg felt as sturdy as it could after weeks of being supported by the splint. He would do as he had been told and would treat the leg with care. The surgeon told William to sit and then ran his hand once more over the leg.

'It seems that you have made a successful recovery which in the circumstances is rare. Some who have suffered broken bones on board ship have lost a limb or in some cases have died so, consider yourself very fortunate.'

William looked at the surgeon and was pleased with his comments but inside he felt the pangs of jealousy start to well up. He could not get the vision of Adele after she had spoken to the surgeon, she had not looked at him in such a way. As the surgeon stood to leave William shook his head and cast the memory from his mind, if a relationship between him and Adele was not to be then he would accept his fate, he would not like it but he would accept it.

Chapter 16

On the main deck the rain still fell, the barrels were filling and it appeared that the ship would be able to fully replenish its stocks. The bosun had looked through the passenger list and had selected a man and wife to seek out regarding help for the cook in dealing with the bull calf. He stooped as he walked through the passenger deck and asked if there were a couple by the name of Taunton, he eventually came across the couple, it was man and wife, he had been employed in the stables and she in the kitchen of a grand house whose owner had fallen on very hard times during and after the war between Parliament and the King. They were Catholics and had suffered for their faith. The man and woman who stood before him had retained their catholic faith but could not practice it openly any more in England so they had made the decision to seek a place in the new world where they could worship how and when they wanted to.

The bosun studied the two before him, they were of a similar age of about twenty-four or five, they had the look of most passengers, tired dark eyed and with skin that showed signs of poor food and drink.

'You, I understand, have knowledge of how to prepare meat after it has been butchered, is that right?' The woman looked with some dismay at the bosun,

'Yes, I know how to prepare meat.'

'Do you know how to make a good sausage, and use the offal to create stews and soups?'

'Yes, I do but we have nothing on this ship that needs such talents.'

'That is where you are wrong, we have a bull calf that is to be slaughtered and the cook needs someone with your knowledge to help him, so get yourself clean and go to the galley, ask for the cook and tell him I have sent you to help,'

'What about my husband, cannot he help too?' The bosun thought for a moment,

'Yes, take him with you, I am sure that the cook can find work for him as well.' The couple looked at each other in amazement, it seemed that they had a turn of good fortune. The process of butchering the bull began, it was killed as swiftly as possible then without further ado it was hung to let it bleed. The blood, a precious commodity, dripped into the ready prepared buckets. The cook used his skill in skinning the animal and then dissecting it into joints of good size. The offal that had been removed was handed over to the woman, she took the lights and placed them to one side she then looked at the mound of bloody organs that were left, rolling up her sleeves she went to work.

Away from the galley the passengers were interested in the rain that was falling and how to get enough to satisfy their thirst. Those that could manage to get to the open deck and with any container that they could lay their hands on collected the rain water and drank it eagerly. It was only when they had enough that they took what they could to the other passengers.

Edward Carrick studied the charts laid out before him, he could see the passage he needed to take and measuring the distance computed that they should be in sight of land within the next seven days. He was a skilful navigator, he had brought many ships into harbour and this should not be any different from the last. It was now that the he turned his mind to what would take place on landing. There were many on board who would have places to go and contacts to make, there were others who had been put on board without knowing exactly who they were to meet and some would not have any knowledge of who or what they were supposed to do on arrival. It was always a time of jubilation for some and desolation for others. He knew those such as the surgeon and apothecary would do well, as would the creature who was probably laying drunk in his cabin. Those without any sponsor would have to remain on the ship until a place for them could be found. These were the servants who for some reason had lost or never had knowledge of the person who had paid for their crossing. What would happen to them would not be pleasant, they would be put up for auction. If there were women they would be taken quickly if they were of childbearing age, otherwise they may end up in the most menial of circumstances. That was in the future his mind came back to the present. He called out for his boy,

'Fetch me the chief mate and be quick.' The boy nodded and turning made a fast exit from the captain's cabin. Mr Dimmock was trying to get dry after watching the crew directing the rain into barrels, both he and the bosun had watched as the levels grew steadily higher and the full barrels taken into the hold. He saw the cabin boy coming towards him, he was soaked, his hair was plastered against his face and head,

'Boy, what are you after?' The lad came to an unsteady halt and brushing the water from his eyes said,

'The captain has asked for you, can you go to his cabin?' Dimmock rubbed his face one more time, dropped his towel then followed the boy back to the captain's quarters.

'Ah, Mr Dimmock.' The captain looked up at his chief mate, 'We are getting close enough to Jamestown to start to think about the approach we are going to take.' He pointed to the chart, 'You and I have been here several times before so there should be no problem in us reaching the harbour safely but as you know things don't often turn out the way they are expected. I will need you, the bosun and the coxswain to work in unison, you know how I work as do the other two. We should have enough victuals between now and when we land to see us through, however there are in excess of one hundred and fifty mouths on this ship and the bull calf will have to be rationed if it is to last.' The chief mate looked at his captain he knew what he said was right and that if they were not careful things could turn out very difficult.

'My concern,' he said, 'was the water, no matter how much we have been able to capture, the weather will become warmer and the need of the people on board will grow.' Edward Carrick was aware that no matter how much they gathered it would never be enough especially as his chief mate said with the temperature rising.

'I appreciate what you are saying, as you know that feelings will turn in the coming days especially when land is sighted. The highest number of those on the passenger deck are young men, who are on this ship for various reasons, they may be difficult to handle when we reach port, please inform the crew that if any of these young men were to jump ship, we will be held responsible which may result in money being taken from our profits.' The chief mate smiled,

'I will make sure that the crew are aware that their pockets may be lighter if any man were to leave without being first checked off the passenger list.'

The chief mate returned to the main deck of the ship, the rain continued, he looked up into the sails, although the rain was heavy the winds kept them moving, the last thing he wanted was another period of either storms or doldrums. As he surveyed the scene on the main deck, he realised that the sea had been a major part of his life and that his dedication to the waves had brought him fear and pleasure. He watched as the crew went about their duties, he had seen many men and boys on many ships, his future would be at sea and if he could choose, he would pick the ocean to be his resting place when his time came. A figure approached him, it was the body of the parson, hunched against the rain he seemed to have something troubling his mind of sermons and prayers.

'Mr Dimmock, a moment please.' The chief mate grabbed him by the arm and led him to a sheltered area of the deck,

'What is it that brings you to me.' He could see the face of the parson was in some quandary,

'It is the man who lost his wife and child, he may be thinking of self-murder.'

'What makes you believe such a thing?' The chief mate looked at the parsons features through the dripping brow he could see the concern etched into his face.

'He has not spoken to any of the other passengers, he sits by himself with what he has left of his wife's clothing, he has not eaten for some time and he has become infested with lice.'

'Is he a danger to others or just himself?'

'To himself only, but I fear his condition may worsen as we approach the end of our journey.' The chief mate had seen many a man fall to pieces following the death of a child but this man had lost his wife as well.

'Show me this man.' The parson led the way.

They found the man, a carpenter by trade, in a bundle of rags clutching a woman's shawl. The chief mate could see he was in a bad way, his hair was matted and there were signs of life on his scalp. The chief mate asked the parson for the man's name,

'I don't know it, I have tried to speak to the fellow but have had no success.' Dimmock took the shoulder of the man and turned his face so that he could see what he was dealing with. The sunken eyes above an unwashed bearded face told the chief mate that the man was nearing the end of his tether and possibly the end of his life.

'What's your name?' He shook the man gently to begin with then with some force. There was no reaction, he asked again,

'What's your name?' He looked directly into the man's bloodshot eyes, there seemed to be no life behind them, his gaze was fixed on nothing, still no response. The chief mate told the parson to make ready to assist him, the parson didn't understand but braced himself for whatever the chief mate was about to do. Dimmock stood and took a deep breath then he bent low and reached out taking hold of the shawl that the man was clutching and pulled. As he did a scream filled the air, it was not that of a man or woman but that of someone in dire straits, the man's arms shot out reaching for the shawl but the chief mate was quick in his action, he pulled the shawl out of the man's reach and pushed him to the ground with his free hand. He felt no resistance and the creature before him was just a bag of bones. The face looked up at the chief mate who could see it was filled with fire and anger, again he lunged at the chief mate, this time he managed to grab a handful of the shawl but he did not have the strength to take it from Dimmock's grip. The man fell back and as he did, he wailed for a second time causing all those nearby to stop what they were doing and watch the scene that was unfolding. The skeleton like figure curled up into a ball trying to hide his face from the world it was at this point that the chief mate pulled him by the arm and showing him the shawl said,

'I will destroy this if you do not speak to me.' He held the shawl at arm's length and the sunken eyes followed its path.

'Give it to me.' The voice could hardly be heard, a frail arm reached out towards the ragged shawl. 'Give it to me.' This time the voice was louder still with a hoarseness that came without use. The chief mate thought that progress had been made,

'Now what is your name?' No reply. 'I promise you by all that is holy that I shall destroy this,' he held the shawl aloft, 'If you do not speak to me.' There was a reply of sorts, the chief mate could hardly make out what was being said. 'Tell me again, I can't hear you,' he still held the rag at arm's length.

'David, my name is David.' The parson watched as the chief mate coaxed the man into speaking.

'And your second name.' Dimmock did not want the man to stop now that he had got him to utter his first words for some time. The man coughed and phlegm filled his mouth, he spat out the green slime onto the floor of the deck,

'Stephenson, my family name is Stephenson.' The parson then recalled that the man was a carpenter by trade, he bent forward,

'You are a carpenter, a skilled man, you are needed here to help make sure that this vessel reaches harbour.' The chief mate thought this was a good move by the parson. The carpenter raised his head with some difficulty,

'My wife, my child, lost, all is lost.' His blank eyes did not see the faces of the two men before him. The parson tried to comfort him,

'Take heart, you have your life ahead of you, come now try to look to the future.'

'I have no future, my life is gone.' His voice grew weaker and again he coughed and spat out the product of his sick lungs. His body slumped back but as he did so he reached up to the chief mate who, realising that the man was reaching for the shawl placed it into the bony fingers that were outstretched towards him. The carpenter brought the ragged cloth to his mouth and kissed it, his body then heaved and coughed which almost tore his body apart, his head fell forward the rag against his lips. The parson turned and looking up at the chief mate said,

'He has now joined his wife and unborn child, we can do no more for the man accept pray that his soul finds peace.' Dimmock could see that the body was curled almost into a ball, it would take some doing to get it straight he could see the lice moving the skin on the man's head, it would take men with strong stomachs to deal with this.

'I will leave you here, parson, and inform the captain of yet another death.' He stood up from the body and made his way to the captain's cabin.

The parson, Peters, stared at the body of the carpenter, the end of his life had been one of sadness and pain, he was at rest now and the state of the body mattered not. He quietly recited the lord's prayer as he waited for members of the crew to come and deal with the corpse.

As the chief mate stepped towards the door of the captain's cabin, he still had a vision of the poor man's body, it may have been a blessing in disguise as the problem of dealing with the carpenter on arrival in Jamestown no longer existed. He knocked and entered,

'Another death, captain.' Edward Carrick looked at the face of his chief mate, he could see that what he was about to tell him was not pleasant.

'Who and how?' The captains voice displayed an amount of annoyance.

'It is the carpenter, Stephenson, the man whose wife died in child birth soon after we had left Bristol.' Carrick remembered entering the details of the woman's death into the log and noting it on the passenger list.

'What caused his death?' The question was posed in a matter-of-fact way.

'It could be said that it was brought on by the man himself however the state of what he was spewing up looked very much like a case of the old man's disease, his lungs were filled with fluid and he could hardly draw a breath. It was not only sickness of the body that did for him, it was sickness of the mind that stopped him fighting whatever ailment he had.

'How have you left the body?'

'The parson is with it and I have sent two men to deal with what is left of the man.'

'Can I leave it to you to see that the body is taken care of, a short prayer on deck and then.., well you know what to do.'

'Very well, captain,'

'And Mr Dimmock, if the man was in the state you say he was, his possessions will no doubt, not be worth saving, so if you would dispose of them, I would be grateful.'

'As you wish.' The chief mate turned and made his way back to the body.

Edward Carrick opened the log and made the entry recording the death of the carpenter it was another story of a family that had dreams of a new life in a new world but had been cruelly prevented from reaching the shores of the new world. He went back to studying his charts, they should be in a position that required a good pair of eyes aloft to search for the first signs of land. He reached into the bottom draw of his desk and withdrew his most prized possession, his spy glass. The glass had cost him a pretty penny and he was determined to put it to good use. This was the second voyage on which he had taken the instrument, as he reached the deck, he put the glass to his eye. Although the horizon was brought into focus and he could clearly see for a good distance that land was not evident

The bosun and coxswain were together scanning the horizon,

'Ah just the two I hoped to see, Mr Truscott, could you make sure there is a man with good vision in the nest, we need the sight of all from now on to make sure we do not encounter any obstacles that may prevent us from completing our journey.' The bosun touched the tip of his cap,

'Aye, captain.' He called out to one of the crew,

'Up you go, Harry, to the nest and keep a good look out.' The sailor went to the side of the ship and started the long climb to the crow's nest.

'Keep me informed of any sightings you may get, If I am right, we should be in sight of land within the next twenty-four to thirty-six hours.' The confidence in the captain's voice filled all that heard it with hope.

The bosun watched as the sailor climbed the ropes, it was not the best loved task of many of the crew but some liked the isolation of the crow's nest away from the problems that surrounded those trying to keep the ship on course. As he reached the small platform that held a barrel shaped container in which the sailor would stand and keep watch he rubbed his eyes making sure that all was well with his vision. The ocean seemed never ending, just wave after wave rolled over the surface of the water. He could see the white of the horses' tails break and some of the larger creatures that swam alongside the ship, he settled down and watched for land.

Chapter 17

William looked at his two companions, they were discussing what was needed when they eventually reached Jamestown. Alec frowned as he spoke,

'I don't know if the news from England has reached the colony regarding the price of tobacco, if it has then we may be in for a rough time.' Robert looked at the ledger in front of him,

'The downward price has bound to have had an effect on the trading of the leaf. Those that have small plantations will be in need of support or they will surely suffer.' He looked up from the ledger. 'Thank god that we had an agreed price for the shipment we brought to England.' William looked from one man to the other,

'What bad news is there?' His voice was full of curiosity.

'Things happen in London that take an age to reach Virginia, the law seems to be ever changing and the Navigation Act that is in force restricts us, we have to find ways to get over or around the obstacles that are placed before us.' There was so much that William needed to know, he had never heard of the Navigation Act and was totally unaware of the changing price of tobacco. He asked,

'What is this Act and why does anything laid down on one side of the ocean have an effect on those thousands of miles away?' Alec could see that William was eager to understand the business of tobacco trading but there was more than just sailing with a cargo from one side of the Atlantic to the other.

'When we arrive at our destination Robert and I will be in a better position to take you through the why's and wherefores of our trading and all that influences it, for now just try to get the planting, growing and harvesting in your head, what follows after that we will explain to you in the days and weeks to come.'

William sighed, he was eager to learn but became bored with the methods used in cultivating the crops. His mind turned to Adele, he wondered what she was doing and if her father had made any plans for her when they reached Jamestown.

'Are you in need of me? I would like to get some fresh air, I know that the rain is still falling but just the sight of the sky might help to clear my head of all the information you have given me.' Alec looked at his young companion,

'No, you go ahead, you can tell us of what you see on deck especially if there is any sign of land.' William stood and carefully placed his damaged leg on the floor of the cabin, it felt firm enough but he knew he had to take care. On reaching the deck he could see the parson together with the chief mate watching while three or four of the crew were moving what appeared to be another body wrapped in sailcloth close to the ships rail. The rain had eased slightly making it easy for William to ask one of the sailors what was happening.

'There has been another death.' He said in a matter-of-fact way that those who have seen many corpses used.

'Do you know who it is?' William asked as the body was lifted and taken closer to the edge of the ship.

'I believe it was the poor soul who lost his wife and unborn son not long after we set sail, he was in a bad state of mind and some say that he killed himself through lack of food and water.'

William watched with a morbid sense of fascination as the corpse was lifted and dropped over the side of the ship. The rain continued to fall as the parson read a prayer for the departed. There was a delay and then as the wrapped corpse hit the waves

William thought he heard a splash as it entered its watery grave. He turned to the sailor,

'How many is that who have perished on this journey?'

'It must be four or five.' William looked at the rail over which the corpse had been dropped.

'Is that normal for that many to lose their lives on a voyage such as ours?' The sailor looked through the rain at the sea,

'It has been known that all on board a ship sailing this passage have been lost through the captain's failure to keep a steady course and it has been known that ships have had an outbreak of disease, possibly pox, and have lost almost all passengers and crew, so we can thank the heavens that we have lost only few.' William thought on what the sailor said, he had experienced death during his life but not as close as this. The rain had lifted and William could see some blue patches between the clouds,

'And what of the land that we are heading for, do you know much about it?' The sailor lifted the rope he was gathering,

'I know of some things and a little of the land. There is good land and bad land, there are many rivers and forest. I am told that the hunting of deer, wildfowl and other things is good.' William tried to picture the land but found it difficult.

'How big are the rivers and is the land good for crops?'

'The rivers are wider than the Severn but may be not as fast flowing, there is fish a plenty and reeds grow well along the banks.'

'What of the people, I am told they are called Indians?'

'I know little of them, they can be seen near the harbour but they are few, there are others such as the people from Africa whose number seems to grow each time I reach these shores.' He stopped and looking around saw that he was needed towards the bow of the ship.

'I must be about my duties, you will have to ask those you travel with for more information of the land we are nearing.' William asked one last question,

'How long before we reach our destination?'

'I think I told you before, you will know when you can see where the seagulls land.' With that he stood and headed towards the bow of the ship.

William stood and shook some of the rain water from his hair and clothes, he would ask Alec and

Robert about the land and the people that inhabit it. He took care as he made his way back to the cabin the rain had made the deck slippery and he could not afford to damage his leg. In the cabin he found Alec and Robert with their heads together discussing prices and weight of tobacco, the news they brought from England would not please those on the plantation, William's entry made them both stop and look up,

'I have been speaking to one of the crew and he has made me realise how little I know of where we are headed, could you please give me some idea of the land I am about to enter?' Alec spoke,

'If you are willing to wait until the next bell ring's I will then answer your questions as best I can but for the moment Robert and I need to assess our visit to England and to judge whether it has been profitable, so if you could leave us until then it would be good.' William felt a little spurned but realised that his companions had much to do before they landed. He left the cabin and made his way to the passenger deck, he was almost in a dream like state his mind tried to imagine the land he was headed for in his thoughts he could see forests and rivers, strange men in clothes he had not seen before, different coloured skin, people talking in languages he had never heard before, but this was his imagination he needed to see for himself and excitement started to build inside him.

There was a smell coming from the galley, one that made his mouth start to water, he would try to see what was going on but knew that the cook was a fearful being and would probably chase him off. The sight that met him when he reached the galley was one of almost horror, there was blood to be seen and animal parts being severed by the cook, there was a woman cutting and chopping the entrails of an animal.

'Are we to have this to eat?' The cook stopped for a moment,

'If you do not move yourself you may end up in the pot with it, so get out of my galley and let us do our jobs.' He realised as he left the madness of the galley that he had not really been able to get around the ship so well when he had the splint on his leg. As he left the blood-soaked hell that was the galley, he met Francios who, like him seemed to be at a loss.

'Good day, Francios, are you well?'

'I am as well as can be expected, I will be a lot better if I can get something to eat other than dried or salted fish.' William smiled,

'I think everyone will be in a far better mind when the cook has finished. Do you know where this bounty has come from?' Francois glanced toward the galley door,

'It is one of the cattle that the wealthy owner gave to the ship to prevent starvation amongst us.'

'Very generous of him, a kindly gesture.'

'My father has told me that it was not done easily and that the captain had to struggle with the man to give up a bull calf.'

'Who is this man to have enough livestock to be able to sacrifice an animal?' Francois walked towards the place that he had called home for the last six weeks and William followed him.

'He is a lord who, so the story goes has been exiled by his family for some wrong doing.' They walked to the passenger deck and stopped as Francois' father and sister came into view. William didn't know how to address Adele, he wanted to continue his friendship with her but felt as if something was restraining him. Francois stopped,

'I have brought a stranger to see you.' Adele and her father put down the book they were reading.

'William, how are you, how is your leg.' Her voice brought pangs of want into the pit of his stomach.

'My leg is good, I no longer need the support of a splint and should be as good as new in a few days.' He was about to ask her if she would like to continue with the story of her family when the ships bell rang out. 'I have to go, Alec and Robert are going to give me more information about the plantation that I shall be working on so please forgive me but I must go.' Adele looked a little upset, she had wanted to speak to William about his plans for the future and she wanted to tell him of the offer made by Richard Hinds but that could wait for another day. William said his farewells and returned to his cabin. He passed the galley and could hear the chief mate's voice, he was trying to find out how long the meat from the bull calf would last. William stopped and listened,

'Mr Dimmock.' The voice was that of an irate cook. 'I have been given a bull calf that is more the size of a sheep, I know that it was the poorest of those we have but this creature was underweight and undernourished, I can only use what I have. This good woman,' he pointed to Joan who was busy stretching the bull's intestines, 'is working miracles but we will only have enough for several days even if it is strictly rationed.' The chief mate watched as the woman drew out the intestines, presumably, he thought for some sort of sausage,

'What weight of meat do you have?' The cook wiped his hands on a blood-stained apron,

'Overall, we may have some hundred and fifty pounds of meat, which does not seem much but that is all we could use. We will have some form of blood sausage and the offal can go into some form of pottage, there is a small amount of grain left with some oats and I will use that to stretch the meat out as best I can.' It was far less than the chief mate or the captain had anticipated. He looked at the butchered meat,

'So, we have about a pound of meat per person, will that last them seven days?' The cook shook his head,

'I doubt it but we have no choice, will the captain bring us to port in seven days?' The look on the chief mate's face did not inspire confidence.

'You will allow no more than several ounces per day for the passengers more for the crew and as for his lordship, he will probably demand a steak for every meal.' The cook knew that a certain amount would be available from boiling the bones and making whatever he could from every part of the animal. 'I will let the captain know of the state of the rations, if you have any discontent from either crew or passengers let me know immediately.'

William did not like what he heard, it would be good to taste beef, but so little would not feed those on board for very long. He continued his journey back to the cabin. As soon as he could he passed what he had heard to Alec and Robert, they did not seem surprised,

'We have had a similar experience, prepare yourself William to suck on the hide of the calf if there is nothing left.'

'What about the other livestock on board, surely, we could use that to feed all?'

'You forget William that the owner of what remains has no thought of anything other than getting the livestock to Jamestown safely and if that means certain passengers have to pay the ultimate price then so be it.' Alec looked seriously concerned, then Robert said,

'If it is controlled, I am sure that we will survive, there is still some salted fish and a small amount of salted pork that can be used, remember we have an ocean surrounding us and I am sure that the crew will be trying to catch as much as possible.' Alec cleared the ledger away and brought out a sheet of parchment, as he unrolled it William could see the drawing of a coastline appear, there were rivers leading from it, he tried to read the names written against them.

'This is a map that shows where the plantation lies, we use this to explain what we are growing to the buyers in London, now look closely you can see rivers marked James, York and Rappahannock, the Rappahannock runs through Lancaster County, we have to travel from Jamestown which is here.' He pointed to a clearly marked area. 'Across York River then through Gloucester County then across the Rappahannock the plantation is no more than forty miles and if the weather is good, we should make it in two days. We have good friends who will give us a place to rest overnight.' William stared at the map, so this was to be his new home he thought.

'Are the rivers wide and what of the land is it flat and are there savages?' Robert leant towards the map,

'This land is relatively flat, the land rises to the north but we shall not be going that far and as for the rivers, yes they are wide and we will need assistance in crossing them, as for the Indians, you may see some however, when we left for England, there was no trouble with them but that is not to say that while we have been away things have changed.' William's curiosity got the better of him,

'What are they like, these Indians? Do they grow crops and herd livestock?

'Yes, they have their own crops, which we have learnt to grow such as maize and corn which can be made into flour, the bread it makes takes a little time to become accustomed to. As for livestock, they are hunters rather than farmers, there is far more game in the woodlands than we have in England and they make use of every part of whatever they kill. You, no doubt have a hundred more questions to ask but they will have to wait until we reach land.'

*

David Spilsby opened his eyes only to be met with the same disorganised room that he had seen before he had fallen asleep, his mouth was dry and his stomach ached.

'Whitmore,' he called in a croaky hungover voice. 'Whitmore', this time he raised his voice, the effort made him gag on something unpleasant that rose into his mouth. His servant heard the call and hurried to find out what his master wanted. John Whitmore knew by the sound of his voice that his lord and master was not in a good mood which was not unusual.

'Whitmore, get yourself in here.' His servant brushed himself down then knocked on the cabin door,

'Come in, damn you.' There was no doubt in Whitmore's' mind, this was not going to be easy. As he opened the door, he could see the young lord half spread on the bunk, in one hand he held a glass which he tried to fill from a bottle that he picked up from the floor.

'Yes, my lord.' Whitmore stood waiting for the abuse to start.

'Get me something to eat and be quick about it, I have given this ship a bull calf and now I want them to give me a decent meal, now go and make sure that what you get is something I am fond of.' Whitmore turned and quickly headed for the galley. He knew his master was partial to steak and that he liked it done in a particular way. He found the cook rushing around trying to do several things at once, Whitmore put a hand out to stop him,

'Can't you see I am busy, what do you want?'

'My lord wants something to eat.'

'He and everyone else aboard this ship, he will have to take his turn.' Whitmore was a worried man, if he did not deliver the requested meal, he would surely get a beating. The cook realised who Whitmore was and that if he didn't supply a meal for the young lord the captain would be on his back. The expression on Whitmore's face changed when the cook asked exactly what his master wanted.

'A steak cut from the rump of the animal and done not too well.' The cook looked at the mass of meat that he had butchered and lifted a joint. He took a thick slice and laid it onto a griddle which had the flames of the fire passing through it.

'If he does not like it done to well it will not take long, I have nothing to go with it but perhaps some mustard seed may please his palate?'

'Yes, that would please him.' Whitmore watched as the cook waited for the meat to brown and with skill, he turned it making sure that it was cooked but not overdone. Once the cook was satisfied, he lifted the steak onto a pewter plate reserved for the young master.

'There you are.' He held out the plate towards Whitmore who with care held it in a tight grip. The cook laid a spoonful of mustard alongside the steak and wished Whitmore luck.

Opening the cabin door, Whitmore eased his way in holding the plate firmly, his master was sat at his desk.

'Come on man, I am starving.' Whitmore put the plate down in front of his master who took up a knife and started to cut into the steak. To Whitmore's surprise there was no immediate comment but as Spilsby put a portion of steak into his mouth he let out a scream, he like all others onboard had suffered from a weaking of the teeth and gums, his effort to chew the steak caused a tooth to come lose and then drop from Spilsby's mouth, he spat out both the steak and the tooth then he picked up the plate and threw it at Whitmore.

'You fool, you idiot, look what you have done!' John Whitmore looked down at the steak on the floor, so many would have given anything for such a meal. 'Take this away.' He pushed the meat that was now on the floor of the cabin with his foot. 'And get me something that I can swallow.' Picking up what was left of the steak he wrapped it into a cloth, he would eat it later once he had seen to his master's meal. He made his way back to the galley. Taking a deep breath, Whitmore entered the galley, the cook looked at him with surprise,

'Now what do you want, was the beef not enough?' With embarrassment Whitmore shook his head.

'He tried to bite into it and it took a tooth from his mouth.' The cooked didn't know whether to laugh or swear.

'So, what does he want now?'

'He wants something that will fill his belly but not take his teeth out.' The cook looked around the galley, through the steam he could see that a broth was almost ready and that if he served that with perhaps some blood sausage it could be eaten without mishap to teeth. He took a bowl and ladled out some broth making sure that any meat was falling apart. Whitmore returned to the cabin carrying the second meal, he placed it before his master who, looking at the broth clutched the bowl and nearly threw it at Whitmore but the smell of the broth hit his nose and he suddenly realised just how hungry he was.

'Leave it here and what is this.' He held up the blood sausage. Whitmore didn't know what reaction he would get.

'It is a sausage that is soft to eat and it will fill the stomach without harming the teeth.' The young aristocrat sliced the sausage and placed it into his mouth, he found that taste to be not unpleasant and as Whitmore had said, easy on the teeth. After he had dealt with the meal, he took himself off to a quiet corner between his master's cabin and the bulkhead, he took out a knife that he had kept as sharp as a razor and with an unsteady hand began to slice the steak into very thin pieces. He consumed each slice by letting it slither down his throat, it didn't matter about the taste, it was food and good food at that. Whitmore felt as if he had achieved something as he felt that his stomach had reasonable food in it after such a long time of salt this and salt that, he smiled at himself he had done good.

William had made daily trips to the passenger deck hoping to catch Adele on her own but each time he had visited it was only Francois who he got to see.

'Where is Adele and your father, every day they seem to be engaged elsewhere?' Francois could see the frustration building in William's face.

'They are discussing matters with the surgeon.'

'They must be serious matters if they are with him every day.'

'You do not know of our arrangement for our new life do you.' William was a little bemused, he had no idea of what Francois was talking about.

'Pray, please tell, what are these arrangements.'

Francois pointed to a space on the bunk beds,

'Sit and I will tell you of what is to become of us.' When William had made himself comfortable Francois began to tell him of how his father had agreed with the surgeon that he would set up his apothecary alongside the surgeon and that both Adele and he would be employed by the Richard Hinds.

'How was that to be?' There was anxiety in William's voice.

Francios explained how he was to be employed with his father and that Adele was to be in control of the surgeon's household. It took William several minutes to take in exactly what this meant. Adele would be beyond his reach and the way she had responded to the surgeon's company made him feel as if his world had just collapsed.

'Do you agree with your father that this is the right thing to do?' Francois looked William in the eye,

'Both Adele and I have agreed to spend one year in the surgeons employ and then if we decide that there is another path we wish to follow we will leave.' William thought for a moment, a year was a long time and he did not know how many times he would be able to see Adele during the year.

'What is it that you truly wish to do once we arrive in Virginia?'

'What I want and what my father wants me to do are very different. I would like to seek my fortune, whether that be by clearing the land and creating a plantation of my own or venturing out into the unknown to explore what treasures lie in wait for those with enough courage to look for it.' William heard the words and thought how close they were to his own wishes and desires.

'We must stay in contact when we reach Virginia as your thoughts are very similar to my own and perhaps, we might join forces in an effort to achieve our goals.'

'Can you wait for a year? We may find ourselves in positions that that we cannot leave.' Francois wanted to believe that he could and would venture out on his own and if William was to join him all the better but a year, he thought, was a long time.

Willliam stood to leave and as he did there was a commotion in the entrance to the passenger deck. He stopped one of the men trying to get to the stairway leading up to the main deck.

'What is it, why the excitement?'

'It is land, land has been sighted.' Francois stood and joined William and others as they tried to get to the main deck. There were two sailors holding them back one had his arms outstretched,

'Wait your turn, you will not be able to see land yet and the crew have work to do so wait your turn.' There was a sagging of shoulders as the passengers turned and went back to their living area. William took Francois' arm,

'Land, we are there it has been so long but we have made it.'

'And I think we have enough food and water to see us safely to our destination.'

The two young men grabbed each other the thoughts of problems yet to come left them as they eagerly waited for their turn to get on deck.

Chapter 18

In David Spilsby's cabin there was no joy only boredom and drink. He grasped the brandy bottle and poured some of the golden liquid into a glass, he was about to take a sip when he heard the footsteps of crewmen running past his door.

'Whitmore, Whitmore, what the hell is going on, what is all this noise and commotion?' Two days had passed since the saga of the meal, John Whitmore was trying to stop a member of the crew to ask the question, he managed to grab a man by the sleeve,

'What is happening, why all the activity?'

'Land has been sighted.' He said before he broke loose from Whitmore's grip. Turning towards his master he repeated what he had just heard.

'Land you say.'

'Yes, my lord. It appears that it has been sighted.' David Spilsby got up a little unsteadily from his bunk.

'This is something I must see.' He placed his glass onto a table and made his way to the opening that led to the main deck. Whitmore started to follow but was stopped when his master told him to go back and clear up the mess in his cabin, Whitmore turned feeling only hatred for the man he called master.

As he got out into the fresh air David Spilsby looked around for a suitable place to see the land that everyone was yelling about. He walked to the side of the ship but could see nothing, he called out.

'Where is this land, I cannot see anything.' The person standing next to him said that it had been spotted from the crow's nest and to see anything you needed to be higher. With that Spilsby moved closer to the ships rigging, he was unsteady and the roll of the ship made his balance even worse. He took hold of the lower rope of the rigging and pulled himself up. From the far side of the deck the bosun watched as Spilsby tried to raise himself,

'Stop him!' he called out, 'Stop that man.' Two of the crew started to make their way towards Spilsby who had managed to get onto the ships rail and grasped ropes in one hand whilst trying to shield his eyes with the other. The ship dropped unexpectedly, the rope that Spilsby was holding on to started to slip from his grasp and as the ship lurched for a second time, he lost his grip. The two crew men tried to catch hold of his clothes but failed, they watched as he fell, there was a look of both surprise and horror on

Spilsby's face, his arms flailed aimlessly as his body hit the ocean the air was knocked out of him. The speed of the ship drew him down and under the seamen looked on and watched his body disappear beneath the waves. As he fell David Spilsby thought of nothing but survival no thoughts of family of loved ones passed through his mind, he hit the water and struggled to fight the pull of the ship but no matter how hard he fought he could not hold off the ocean from rushing into his mouth and nose, his eyes almost left their sockets as his arms and legs thrashed about, he could not reach the surface. His movements slowed then stopped as the life he had abused left his body.

The bosun stood looking at the space where the young lord had been standing before he fell, he called out at the top of his voice,

'Can you see him?' He was running towards the two sailors who had tried to reach Spilsby before he fell.

'No, he has gone.' The bosun slid to a halt and bent over the ships rail. He could see no sign of the man, there was nothing except waves and the vast expanse of ocean.

'Stay here and watch.'

'But bosun no man could survive being dragged under by the ship.'

271

'Just watch, I will fetch the captain.'

The sailor shrugged his shoulders, he had seen a few men fall overboard some in calm seas others in storm, very few had been retrieved from the brine and it may be a blessing that they were not, a quick death rather than one that lingered. As the bosun pushed through the passengers he shouted for all to keep clear. His voice attracted the chief mate's attention, he was in conversation with the coxswain and had seen the commotion but did not know what the cause was. He saw the bosun disappear into the stern of the ship and then made his way to where two of the crew were looking over the side.

'What is happening here?' One of the men turned away from the sea,

'It is the young lord, he has fallen over the side.' The chief mate's reaction was,

'My god, this is not good, how did this happen?' The sailor explained how the young lord had climbed onto the ships rail and then lost his grip and fell.

'Did nobody see what he was doing?'

'All on deck were looking into the distance trying to see land.' The chief mate shook his head, this was not going to be easy to explain to those in authority.

'What!' Edward Carrick jumped from his chair, he could not believe his ears, they were no more than seven days away from Jamestown and now this disaster. 'Show me.' The bosun led the way to where the incident had occurred. The chief mate and the two crewmen were still searching the sea for any sign but in their hearts, they knew it was the end of the man that had fallen. Carrick pushed the two men aside and looked over the side of the ship, there was nothing to indicate that a man had fallen, the bosun pointed to the spot where Spilsby had stood trying to get a view of the land, the captain could see that anyone falling into the waves that the ship was creating would have little chance especially as they had gained a good speed with full sails. 'Mr Truscott, you with those two men will go directly to my cabin and Mr Dimmock get the lords man servant to my cabin as quick as you like.' While the bosun and the two crewmen made their way to the captain's cabin the chief mate sought out Whitmore. He found him gathering his master's clothes, trying to make the cabin a little more habitable.

'You are to come with me, leave what you are doing.' Whitmore looked up in surprise he had little to do with the crew of the ship and was at a loss as to why he was being summand. Stuttering he asked,

'I have done something wrong?'

'Just come with me and keep quiet.' Dimmock did not want a flood of questions coming from the servant.

The party of men stood before the captain's desk, Carrick looked at them he could see worried faces on all but the man who he recognised as the manservant. He took out a sheet of paper, moved his inkwell and made ready to write what was said.

'I need to know exactly what happened, every moment and movement made, I shall begin with you.' He pointed at Whitmore who jumped,

'Why me, what is this about, my master will have something to say about this, he will not take kindly to having me taken from my duties.' Carrick realised that things had happened so quickly that the servant was not aware of what had occurred. Carrick looked at the man, his sallow features gave him an almost pathetic appearance.

'There has been a tragic accident.' Whitmore raised his eyebrows, Carrick continued 'Your master has been killed, if you listen to what those gathered here have to say all will become clear.' Whitmore took a step back, his master dead, his head spun, he couldn't think straight. The captain then began his questions,

'When did you last see your master?' Whitmore was still recovering from the news that his lord was no longer, he looked around the room trying to take in the situation.

'This morning, I was with him when he first arose from his sleep.'

'And what happened then, did he eat and drink?'

'He did not eat but he did drink, he called for wine.'

'Was that normal for him to drink wine so early?'

'Oh yes, he would drink either wine or brandy whenever he could.'

'And today how much wine or brandy did he have?'

'Several small glasses of wine followed by a glass or two of brandy. I do remember his hands were trembling before the drink and as he drank, they became steadier.'

'Was it then that he left the cabin?' Carrick was trying to ascertain if Spilsby was incapable before he went on deck.

'He complained about the ruckus going on outside and sent me to find out what was happening.'

'And did you.'

'Yes, I returned and told him that land had been sighted and he then stood and pushed me aside making his way to the open deck. I was told to remain and clean the cabin. That was the last time I saw him.' Carrick looked at Whitmore and could see that the man was a bag of nerves.

'As your master left the cabin was he in control of himself?'

'He was very unsteady on his feet and swayed more than the ship would normally cause.' Carrick noted down all that had been said by Whitmore from whose statement it would appear that the young lord was drunk before he left his cabin, probably still suffering from what he had consumed the night before.

'Mr Whitmore you can go, I want you to note how much alcohol you master drank and his condition during the voyage so far, is that understood?'

'Yes captain, I still have the empty bottles if you should wish to see them?'

'No, I don't think that will be necessary just let me have the details by sunset.' Whitmore left the cabin not really knowing what to think, he would need to tell Norris and clean the cabin other than that he would have to await his future.

In the captain's cabin the bosun and the two sailors told of how they had rushed to try to prevent Spilsby from climbing the lower rigging and how they were too late. The three men left leaving the chief mate and Carrick.

'What a mess, I knew he was a drunken idiot but I didn't expect this.' He sighed and put down his quill. 'I will have to report this to the Governor of the Council when we arrive, as I understand it there was a family connection between him and Spilsby so it will not be an easy thing to do.' The chief mate did not envy the task that lay ahead of his captain, there may be repercussions which would affect his standing in the hierarchy of Jamestown.

As the bosun left the captain's cabin he could hear singing which he thought strange but then it came to him that the passengers knew little of what had happened and that they would be consumed by the fact that land was in sight. Those on deck were indeed singing hymns in thanks, he passed two young men who he recognised, they were staring at the horizon trying to see land, he smiled at them.

'Bosun, when will the land become clear?'
Their eagerness flooded from them.

'It may be a day or two before you get a clear
view of the Americas.'

Francois and William thanked him but
although they could see nothing, they still remained
staring at the horizon. William spoke,

'Just think that in six or seven days we shall be
treading on a strange and different land.' He glanced
at Francois who had a dream like look in his eyes,

'Yes, will it be fortune or famine, we can only
wait and see.'

Chapter 19

Richard Hinds heard of the loss of David Spilsby, he was not surprised that the man had been the cause of his own death. He had arranged a further meeting with Martin Saurin which had become even more important now that land was in sight. They met in Richard's cabin,

'We need to make sure that we are in agreement on what we are going to do when we arrive in Jamestown.' He took out a sheaf of paper. 'Perhaps if I were to make some notes it would serve us well.' Martin Saurin agreed. 'The house, I am led to believe is big enough for the four of us and if we need more space then there is a barn to the rear of the property.' They went through various scenarios, Richard making the necessary notes and Martin trying to fit his family into Richard's future.

'Do you know if there is any land with the house?'

'I believe so, why do you ask?'

'I shall need an area to grow plants both for creating lotions, pills and such like together with those that can be used to flavour our food.'

'There is an acre of cleared land which should be enough for your requirements.'

Martin conjured up a picture in his mind, he then shook his head he needed to stop fantasising about the role he was about to undertake. He had been through many hardships to reach this stage in his life and he needed it to be one of peace but he knew it was a dream. The death of the young lord brought home to him that death was on every one's shoulder and could visit at any time. He was not the only one who dreamt that the land they were approaching was one filled with a better life.

Geoffrey Peters had watched the passengers throughout their journey, he had seen them deteriorate and, in some cases, die. His faith had been tested to the limit but his belief in the almighty had stayed with him. The passengers had gathered to hear him preach and he hoped he had given them comfort during the times of poor victuals. He had seen the way that the surgeon and the apothecary had administered to those that they could help and he felt that all that could be done had been done. His role as parson did make him a point of contact for those with troubled minds. Many of the passengers had sought some sort of confirmation from him that their decision to commit themselves to working as an indentured servant for many years would give them a better life than that which they had in England. He could only tell them what he understood from others. His knowledge of Virginia was only what he had been told or read about which was nothing in the realm of things. All he could advise was that they work hard and keep their faith. They still asked the question of whether or not they would be able to gain their freedom in this new world that they were headed towards. He had asked the question to Alec Sinclair, who was the only person he could comfortably speak to, his reply was that those who were indentured would be worked hard and that their mortality rate would be high. The parson also asked,

'Would life for the passengers be the same as England in that would there be the same laws and justice?' Alec had told him that most things were the same as in England but all must realise that everything would be on a much smaller scale. The parson had been careful not to paint a picture of the promised land. He tried to be matter of fact but could see on the faces of those he spoke to that they still expected something better than the life they had left behind. For his own peace of mind, he had tried to discover what the state of the church was in Virginia and was astonished to find out that there were not that many men of the cloth and that churches had been erected but were still few and far between. Alec had explained that as a parson he would be required to officiated at the usual ceremonies, christenings, marriages and deaths he would also be asked to travel to plantations to hold services. This did not pose a problem for the parson as long as he had access to a good horse.

The information he gained from speaking to the chief mate, bosun and coxswain was a little different, more down to earth. They told of many challenges to those who said they had married but only in a common law way. Many were too far away from church or did not have the money to get married in a church and many a bride would be pregnant before they walked down the aisle. The high rate of illegitimate births was many but this was not questioned if the man and woman had given each other their pledge. This made life problematic for the church in recognising the offspring of such a union. As for sins that happened in the form of married men getting servants with child, they often occurred. This did make the parson think hard about how he would conduct himself in the role he was about to undertake.

Martin Saurin had also been in regular contact with the other passengers mainly when they had problems brought on by the conditions in which they were living. He had seen their aspirations go from a high when they first boarded the ship to an extreme low when the food became scarce and sickness started to spread. At the time of the deaths, he had seen even the young men, of which there were many, change, they had lost their initial hope and enthusiasm and as the days went by, both he and the parson saw their spirits plummet, however with the news of land being sighted it lifted them out of the trough that they had fallen into so much so that they could speak and think of nothing other than what they would do in this place called Virginia. The parson attempted to quell their enthusiasm but he soon realised it was a hopeless task, they would have to find out the truth of life in their chosen land for themselves.

It was on the second day after the first sighting of land that those on deck could make out the shore line in the distance. William, Alec and Robert stood at the ships rail and stared at the thin green line that could be seen in the distance.

'We will follow the coast then sail into the James River and that is when you will be able to see the land a little clearer.' Williams eyes lit up, they had made it, this was his future home. Alex and Robert had difficulty in getting William back to the cabin, as he seemed to be mesmerized by the land slowly appearing.

'I must speak to Adele and her brother.' His voice was that of an excited child.

'Give them time, they will want to take in this moment themselves, perhaps it may be better tomorrow.' Alec had seen the surgeon heading towards the passenger deck and he knew that it would not be a good time for William to see how Adele greeted the news with Richard Hinds.

Edward Carrick leant over his log carefully entering the events surrounding the death of David Spilsby. He had to be very precise as to what had taken place it would be in his interest to keep things as brief as possible. The date of death had been the 14th of October 1670, the time he had to estimate as five bells in the forenoon. He noted those in attendance as the bosun and two of the crew as for the cause of death he entered that it was an accident which happened when Spilsby had attempted to obtain a better view of the approaching shoreline, the matter of drink was something that he would explain to the Governor in person. The remaining details were simple enough, unable to retrieve the body due to high seas and that a prayer had been said by the parson. He then turned to the passenger list and drew a line through the name of Lord David Spilsby. Placing his quill back on his desk he blotted the entries and closed the log and list, he knew that he was in for a delicate meeting when he broke the news to the Governor. The captain then made his way to the deck carrying his spyglass, he passed several of the passengers eager to get a glimpse of what they thought was the promised land, reaching the coxswain he surveyed the ocean and the land that slowly appeared to the starboard side.

Mr Leigh you know the course as well as I do, can you foresee any difficulties?'

'No, captain, may be other vessels leaving port, other than that we should have an easy trip into the harbour.'

'Good, and what is your estimate of when we will arrive?'

'If all goes well, we should enter the harbour at Jamestown within three days.'

'If you need me, I shall be with the chief mate.'

'Aye, captain.'

He found the chief mate checking the rigging with the bosun,

'All is well Mr Dimmock?'

'Aye captain, now it is, we do not want any further accidents as we are so close to Jamestown.'

'We should be docking in the next twenty-four to thirty-six hours so I need both of you to ensure that all is in order with all parts of the cargo. Make sure that nobody jumps ship and that the crew are ready to unload as soon as we get alongside the wharf, there should be men ready to assist, as for the passengers make sure they have any papers ready and those that don't get them ready to answer any questions that may be asked of them. From now until we reach Jamestown, I will spend the majority of my time with the coxswain.' The two men touched the brim of their caps and then watched as their captain made his way back to the upper deck.

*

Alex Sinclair remembered when he had last been on a ship heading for the coast of Virginia. He had been a prisoner without hope or any future, he had seen many die not only on the ship but when they reached land. He shuddered and looked at his good friend, he was possibly the only one who could understand how he felt as he had a similar experience, he shook his shoulders and returned to the present, he needed to organise how and when his cargo would be unloaded and where it was to be taken and decide what to do about William, it would be good for him to watch what was happening but he had to be aware of the dangers that lurked during the unloading of the cargo.

'Robert, when we arrive can I leave William in your charge, I will need to get to the warehouse to check the space and make sure we have enough men to handle our cargo.' Robert looked around and could see William still with a glassy look in his eye, he seemed to be dreaming and that would not do so he took hold of a lump of tar and threw it at him. William was dreaming until something hit him on the side of the head, he looked around and saw Robert smiling at him,

'What was that for?' he asked.

'To bring you back to this world.' Robert said laughingly. 'When the ship finally docks you are to stay with me, do not get involved with things you know nothing about, I will find plenty to keep you busy and satisfy your curiosity, however before you do anything else you are to sit and write a letter to your mother you must remember the pledge we made to her that we would ensure you wrote on a regular basis. You have a great deal to tell her but I suggest that you leave out the injuries and deaths that we have seen.' Robert handed paper, quill and ink to him and he sat not knowing where to begin, his mind was racing, one moment he thought of the world that he was about to enter and then a picture of Adele flooded into his vision. Adele was sitting with her father and brother, they, like all others onboard were talking eagerly of what they would do on arrival in Virginia.

'Father, do you know what sort of house Mr Hinds has in Jamestown?'

'No, he has little knowledge of it himself, he knows that it has at least seven rooms and that it has a small parcel of land, you will have to curb your questions until we arrive.' Her brother also had many questions but knew that to ask them at that time would be worthless.

Chapter 20

As the shoreline grew evermore clearer, mixed feelings of anxiety and hope filled most of the passengers. The food, although reduced to salt fish and meat, had lasted and the water was still drinkable. Those that could get on deck stood with the parson as he preached, thanking God for their safe deliverance.

Martin Saurin stood at the side of the ship with Richard Hinds, they could both see the shoreline slowly come into sight.

'Is this Virginia?' Martin asked,

'So, I am led to believe.' A member of the crew passed them as he did Richard asked, 'Are we looking at Virginia?' The sailor stopped and answered in a lightly annoyed voice,

'What you see is the entrance to the Chesapeake.'

'Chesapeake, what is that?' The sailor's annoyance increased, he had work to do.

'It is the name of the bay which has given its name to this part of the coast, now no more questions there is a great deal to do before we enter the James

River.' Martin was about to ask about the river but thought better of it and asked Richard if he had any idea of the area they were about to enter.

'Like you this is my first visit to the new world and names are strange to me as they are to you.' They both continued to look at the land unfolding before them.

The Neptune passed between Cape Henry and Cape Charles, Edward Carrick had taken several ships into Jamestown, he had seen the town grow and the frontage to the sea develop to a point where ships could berth in the deep water alongside a sturdy wharf which had the facility to unload most of the cargo carried by the merchant ships that arrived in the colony. Carrick looked at the coast, he knew it well, the green he could see filled him with a sense of achievement, he had successfully brought another ship across the Atlantic Ocean and this would be his last voyage as captain. Carrick could not think that he would never venture back to England, perhaps he would take ship to other parts of the Americas he put that thought firmly to the back of his mind. Another ship came into sight, he could see by its draught that it was fully laden and probably bound for the mother country, through his eyeglass he could just make out some of the crew waving, their journey was about to begin and he was grateful to be at the end of his. He returned to his cabin and feeling his chin decided that he would need the services of the surgeon before they reached port. He sent the cabin boy to fetch Mr Hinds, then washed his face in readiness for a shave.

Richard Hinds saw the young boy approaching, what was it this time, another death or some senseless injury? The boy touched his forelock,

'Sir, the captain wishes to see you and could you please bring your razors.' Relief passed across Richard's face,

'Only a shave.' He turned to Martin, 'I have been summoned by the captain who wants rid of the growth on his face.'

'I'll keep watch on the land and we can meet later. there are more things we need to talk about.' Martin watched as Richard and the cabin boy made their way to the captain's quarters.

Alec and Robert had made sure that their cargo was in good order and then made their way to the main deck.

'It will soon be time to make our way back to the plantation and see those we left some nine months ago.' He looked at the green strip of land which grew wider by the minute. Robert followed his friends gaze and felt as if he was nearly home for that was what Virginia was to him.

'We have a lot to catch up on, you will be able to see your wife and children, they will have grown since we left.' Alec looked at his friend knowing that he had no such homecoming to look forward too, his wife had died and he was on his own but that did not seem to prevent him from living a good life.

'It is my hope that all is well and nothing troublesome awaits us.'

'Our only problem at the moment is keeping William's mind on what is needed of him and not dreaming of strange lands and of course the young woman who he has become fond of.' They both smiled they knew that William would be faced with many decisions when they arrived some of which would not be easy to make.

The ship entered the James River and made its way towards the port, the crew were in a heightened state of alert making sure that sails were trimmed and all things secure. Edward Carrick, now with a clean-shaven chin, watched the ships progress. It was now under sixty miles until they reached Jamestown and he had to get his thoughts in order particularly those relating to the death of David Spilsby and that was going to be difficult. He ran over the sequence of events in his mind, would he stress the young lord's fondness for wine and brandy, maybe his reputation for drink was already known by the Governor, who was distantly related to the man. He would see to the registering of the cargo then make his way to the Governor's house, taking with him his log. Once that had been completed, he could then concentrate not only on handing over the ship but also his own property and the state of his crops and profits. The sails were full and their speed steady, he would rest for an hour then see to the instructions for his chief mate, bosun and coxswain.

As the Neptune made its way towards its final goal those on board were fascinated by what they could see on the banks of the river. The flora and fauna delighted those who had seen nothing but ocean for the past eight weeks. William was surprised when he saw Adele standing, looking at the passing shoreline,

'Hello, I have not seen you for some time, are you well?' Adele's innocent face looked at William, he still felt his being tremble when he looked into her eyes.

'I am far better now than I have been since we set sail, but I must admit my nerves seem to be alive, I cannot concentrate, there is so much that lies ahead of us all.' William watched as she looked into the distance, what were her thoughts, he wondered, did he enter into her dreams or was it the surgeon that she could see?

'We are getting close to the end of our voyage, I hope that our friendship will continue once we are on dry land.' He said hopefully.

'We may be miles apart and therefore seldom see each other. Do you know where you will be living, will it be in Jamestown or are you going to the country?' William replied,

'I will be travelling with my companions to a plantation some forty miles from Jamestown and alas will only venture into the town on rare occasions but I am sure that when I do get the chance to come to the town, I will be able to see you and your family.' They fell into silence as they watched the river bank pass by.

Chapter 21

The coxswain steered the Neptune on the final stretch of the river before Jamestown came into view, buildings could be seen and people travelling along the river bank stopped to see what the ship was. The movement onboard was busy and those who got in the way were roughly dealt with, then at last the Neptune came to rest a little distance from the jetty. Sighs of relief could be heard amongst the prayers of thanks being said. The pastor could be seen encouraging those on deck to thank the lord for their safe arrival.

The bosun called to the captain.

'We will have to drop anchor and await our turn, there are two ships ahead of us and by their draught I would say they are fully laden.' Edward Carrick saw the two ships and knew that he might have to wait at anchor for the rest of the day and possibly overnight before he could manoeuvre the Neptune, with the aid of some small craft, to the wharf.

'So be it.' He gave the command to drop anchor and as the ship slowly came to a standstill, he looked at the distance between his ship and the wharf to see if it was safe and if so, he could rest easy. It was as dawn broke that the message reached the captain that they could move to the wharf and prepare to disembark. On deck the chief mate had all in control and with the coxswain brought the ship alongside the unloading stage.

'Good work Mr Dimmock, we should be able to start unloading shortly.' There was still a drop from the ships rail to the jetty and the passengers would have to climb down the netting on the ships side. The crew always enjoyed the spectacle there would be many uneasy passengers clambering over the side, trying to hold on for dear life.

The passengers eagerly looked towards the jetty, there was a gathering towards the side of the ship with those in better condition than others getting themselves ready to leave the place that had confined them for the past eight weeks. The crew were already lifting off the covers of the cargo on the deck below, a rope and pulley system had been rigged up which would help them lift the heavier items to the shore. Edward Carrick looked in his mirror, he had dressed in his better clothes, a clean white blouse, his waistcoat had some embroidery but not too much, his black breeches met his fresh stockings at the knee. With his frock coat he looked like a respectable member of society and one of some importance. Taking hold of his portfolio which held his log book and any other relevant papers relating to the voyage, he made his way from his cabin. He passed many who were waiting anxiously to leave the ship as he reached the rope ladder the chief mate made way for him to pass and as he did, he told the captain that there were four passengers who did not have the necessary papers to allow them to disembark.

'Keep them onboard Mr Dimmock, I will see to them on my return and if you have any problems with other passengers refuse to let them leave the ship.' He climbed down the rope ladder clutching his precious case tightly. As he stepped onto land for the first time in what seemed an age he stumbled slightly, it would take a few steps for him to get his land legs back. The Governor's house was about half a mile from the wharf, as long as it had not been burnt down or the governor had not moved his office. As he started to walk away from the jetty, he could hear a sound that he had missed while on ship, that was the sound of people going about their daily chores, he could see different colours on the faces of many, their clothes indicating their position in life. Some were in their finery, treading carefully so as not to dirty their shoes or stockings, others got on with life. The working men and women hustled and bustled, helping to sort the cargo as it was lowered onto the side of the wharf.

As he walked, he thought of how he would approach the conversation with the Governor regarding the death of Spilsby, it would, he thought be enough to explain the man's liking for alcohol and the way in which he had kept himself to himself during the voyage.

William, Alec and Robert watched the captains back as it disappeared through the throng of people who were milling about on the quayside,

'I shall go first.' Alec said as he mounted the ships rail. He was holding a bag containing the necessary paperwork which would enable him to take his cargo from the wharf and get it into the warehouse. As he began to climb down the rope ladder, he looked up and said to Robert.

'Don't let the boy get into any trouble and make sure he is kept busy.' Robert nodded and smiling he told Alec that he would keep William fully occupied. Alec lowered himself down as William and Robert looked on, they would be next. Robert had clearly marked their cargo and would be able to identify it as soon as it hit the landing. He could see items being made ready, things were progressing well he needed to hurry to make sure he was in a good position to check off the cargo against his manifest. William stood back to allow his friend to swing his legs over the side of the ship, as Robert lowered himself William felt a sense of excitement course through his body. 'What awaited him? Would he be able to fit in with those who he could see milling around below him.' Robert called to him to get ready and William eased himself over the side and on to the rope ladder. It was a lot steeper than he expected and for a moment his legs trembled and a pain shot through his shoulders. Managing to position himself on the ladder he descended slowly making sure each foot was secure before lowering himself. He let out a sigh of relief and success when his feet hit the firm surface of the jetty.

'Come on William we have no time to spare.' Robert caught hold of his shoulder and steadied him. The feeling of solid ground beneath him made him a little unsure on his feet,

'I am ready, I am ready.' He called and both men walked away from the side of the ship with a little trepidation their legs not going in the exact direction that they wanted them to go. William watched as both the men on shore and the sailors rigged up a block and tackle system to assist in lowering the cargo. It would be used for the heavier items including some of the livestock.

'What will happen to the cattle and sheep?' William asked

'They will be penned until they can be claimed.' As he spoke, he saw the face of the surgeon appear at the top of the ladder. 'It looks like your friends will be following us.' William could see the head of the surgeon appear over the ships side, he reached over clutching the ladder, over his shoulder he had slung a satchel containing his more valuable possessions. Robert tugged on William's arm,

'No time for idle chatter, come on we have work to do.' William kept his eyes on the ladder expecting to see Adel but it was her father that came next and although he wanted to wait for her, he knew that Robert would not let him delay matters.

Richard Hinds had spoken to Martin Saurin as they neared the side of the ship,

'Please make sure that your family stay close to me, I am as ignorant as you are about what will happen on shore. I am being met by my relation, who, I am relying on, it was luck and good fortune that placed me in his hands. Martin successfully made it to the jetty, he was closely followed by Francois and then Adele appeared looking over the side of the ship with a look of terror on her face. To her it was such a long way down and the rope ladder swung as those before her descended.

'Don't be afraid.' Her father called. 'Keep looking at the side of the ship and take one step at a time, do not hurry.' The three men watched anxiously as she tried to place her foot on the first rung of the ladder. She missed and almost fell. Richard took hold of the ladder and gently began to climb back up. He reached a point where he could take hold of Adele's foot and place it on the next rung.

'I will guide you down, now slowly lift your foot, that's it one step at a time.' Those waiting to get off the ship were getting a little tetchy and began to ask what the delay was. Richard ignored them and concentrated on getting Adele to the bottom of the ladder. She eventually made it and as she stood on the jetty her legs failed her and she fell into Richards arms. He held her close to him saying words of comfort.

'You are here now, you are safe.' Her whole body shook and her grasp tightened on his jacket.

'Please don't let me go.' Her cry was one of the lost.'

'I will never let you go.' He whispered.

*

Robert had taken William to inspect their cargo, there were many items and William was mystified how much could be stored in the ships hold.

He watched as Robert called out the goods and checked them off his list. Everything was then taken to their warehouse where it would stay until they were ready to move. William kept looking back to try to see Adele but he only caught one glimpse of her in the distance as she walked with her father away from the ship, he wondered if he would ever hear her tell him the rest of her family's story.

Alec returned with a smile on his face,

'All is well, I have seen the authorities and we are cleared to leave whenever we are ready.'

*

Whitmore finished packing his master's belongings into a large trunk, he couldn't quite believe that the young lord was dead, he had been in service for as long as he could remember and now what was to happen to him. He made his way to the deck with the aim of finding Norris hopefully he would have some idea of what to do next. They met by the hold where the livestock were being lifted with block and tackle, the noise that the animals made did not display any degree of comfort or confidence as they rose into the air.

'Will they be hurt or damaged?' Whitmore asked.'

'No, as long as they do not take fright and kick out all should be well.' Norris watched as the next beast was fitted into the sling which would carry them from the ship to the quayside.

'What are we to do, are we to be met by some body from the estate?' Norris watched as the individual standing next to him anxiously rubbed his hands together.

'There should be a person from his lordships plantation who will take over responsibility for the livestock and I should be able to identify him when he starts to inspect the animals.' This only raised questions in Whitmore's mind,

'What will happen to us?' Norris said with a certain amount of certainty,

'I will probably become a member of the staff looking after the livestock on the plantation.'

'But what about me?' Whitmore was beside himself, would there be a need for another servant on the plantation?

'I am sure you will be absorbed into the household.'

'But what as, will there be a need for somebody such as myself?'

'If there is no room for you in the house then I am sure I could find you a place in the stables or the field.' That did not exactly please Whitmore but as long as he was not left without anywhere to go, he would be satisfied. Norris tapped him on the arm,

'We should get ourselves off the ship, come on.' Whitmore trailed behind him and they both managed to get to the jetty without breaking anything.

The chief mate stood at the entrance to the area where the passengers had lived, they were eager to get off the ship but Dimmock had to be satisfied that they had a place to go or a person to meet them. In his hand he held a list containing the names of those indentured servants and that of the freemen. He called for the freemen first, they had paid for their passage and were at liberty to leave the ship. They would have letters detailing who they were and what they did. Most were tradesmen, skilled in carpentry, masonry, ironwork or had a knowledge of some other industry. They were not many in number and were quickly dealt with. Then came the indentured servants, this was the part that the chief mate was not looking forward too. They were mainly young men from eighteen to twenty-two or three. They had with them their indenture paper, few of them could read what was written and if they could they would not fully understand what they had committed themselves to. There were several earmarked for specific owners and a representative would collect them and take them to their new homes.

There would be individuals who may have to wait on the ship until someone arrived to collect them. As they passed him, he wondered if they had any thought of who they would be working for and what that work would entail. They would be the property of the person they were indentured to and that person had the right to treat them as he felt fit. Some would no doubt be under the roof of reasonable men who would feed, house and work them in a reasonable manner but there were many that would work them till they dropped and think nothing of selling them on. Their lives for the next four or seven years would not be their own, the one good thing is that they could look forward to the end of their term and dream of owning a small plot of land and becoming something a little more substantial than they would have done in England.

The day drew on, the noise of the wharf increased as men, women and children tried to find out where they were to be taken. Captain Carrick had found his way to the Governors house and with a little difficulty had made it clear to the staff that he had important matters to discuss with the Governor. Eventually he managed to present himself, the Governor was matter of fact until Carrick told him the purpose of his visit. The meeting was not the best that Carrick had ever attended, the Governor summoned his clerk, it would not go well for Carrick having the son of a lord dying on his ship. It transpired that Spilsby was a distant relation of the Governor's but one he had no real contact with, he informed Carrick that he would send word to Lord Spilsby but before he did so he would like to speak to the man's servant and those close bye when the young man fell overboard. Carrick thought this to be a waste of time but if that is what was needed then so be it. He left the Governor's office with the understanding that he would return within the hour together with those the Governor had requested to see. The clerk had taken note of the details in the log and that had been entered against Spilsby's name in the passenger list. He would need to make haste and make sure that the servant and the members of the crew did not leave the area around the ship.

Fortunately for Carrick those that he needed were still in the vicinity of the ship. He managed to get them together and tell them of what was required. The chief mate with the bosun were deeply involved with dealing with the passengers, Carrick managed to get Dimmock's attention,

'I have to return to the Governor's house to conclude the business of the young lord's death and I shall be taking the two men and the servant to the governor who wants to question them and hopefully that will end the matter if it is I shall be pleased.' The chief mate asked.

'Is there to be no inquest?' Carrick thought for a moment, hopefully the governors questioning of those involved would negate the need for a formal inquest and as there was no body the cause of death could not be ascertained. 'Follow me.' He shouted to the three men and they dutifully followed him back to the Governor's house.

Chapter 22

William stood at the entrance to the warehouse and watched those rushing by. They were not much different to the people he had seen on the Bristol docks before they departed. The men were mostly in stout jackets with breeches reaching to just below the knee, some were tied others hung loose. The hats ranged from woollen skull caps to wide brimmed felt hats, the working men either were bare headed or wore caps that kept their hair out of their face. The women he could see were wearing multilayered skirts that billowed out as they walked, they had blouses of linen and capes of wool most of their heads were covered by bonnets of white some trimmed with lace others plain. He noticed that the shoes worn bore a resemblance to those worn in England, some of the men had sturdy boots others shoes with thick stockings. William could see that the dirt and grime from the quayside coloured the once white stockings of the men, some were falling around their ankles others were held up with ties.

'William.' It was Alec calling for him to return his attention to what was happening to the cargo. It was being stored in the warehouse set aside for them, he answered.

'Yes, what would you like me to do?'

'Help Robert to get some of the items in place as there are several customers who will collect their goods directly from here.' He walked over to Robert.

'I thought these goods were to go to the plantation?'

'We do not go to England only for ourselves, we have to make as much money as we can so we take orders for goods and materials some we dispatched from England whilst we were there other things were brought back with us together with certain goods that we know there is a market for here.'

'You speak as though you are traders and merchants, not tobacco planters.'

'We are both and more, in this land it pays to be a jack of many trades.' William was discovering that all was not straight forward in his new country. As he turned back to the warehouse, he briefly saw the captain and three men hurrying away from the ship, what their business was he had no idea and felt easy not knowing.

Carrick kept up a fast pace which Whitmore found difficult to keep up with. At last, they reached a large house which was a lot grander than most. They were ushered into the Governor's office and were formerly greeted by the Governor's clerk. The three men were told to sit but jumped to their feet as the governor entered the room. The governor motioned them to sit and then began to question each of them.

The interrogation of the men lasted just over the hour and at the end the governor appeared content. Carrick asked if there would be any need for an inquest to which the governor said that in his opinion a record of the accident at sea would suffice. It would be noted in the records to that effect and as far as he was concerned that was the end of the matter. It was with a sense of relief that Edward Carrick left the Governor's house he could now get on with his own life. He needed to hand over the ship to the owners ready for his successor and then see to his own affairs. He had left his land in the capable hands of his plantation manager. His land was not as vast as some but he had managed to acquire over a thousand acres, his crop was, as many, tobacco but during his latest voyage he could see the price drop considerably and he wanted to try to move away from the mainstay crop of the area. During his recent stay in Bristol, he had spoken to many dealers and merchants who had seen a decline in the requests for fabric from the colonies and had told him that it appeared that more linen, cotton, wool and hemp were being grown which was taking the trade away from them. His idea was to try to grow flax instead of tobacco although he had heard that it was not an easy crop to grow and that to process it would take some skilled hands. He would not give over all his land to flax and would maintain a large proportion of it in the growing of tobacco. He had paid for several indentured servants who were onboard the Neptune, although he had never spoken to them, they had been selected as they knew the process of converting flax into linen. His overseer would collect them and take them to his plantation where they would be housed, fed and worked. They were young men who had worked with the flax crop since they were children so were well versed in the manufacture of linen. He needed to organise the change as soon as he could as it would be a further year before he would see any plausible results from a different crop.

The walk back to the ship seemed shorter and as they got closer Whitmore could see Norris talking to somebody and thought that he might be someone connected to the plantation and asking if the captain had any objection first, he made his way to where the two men stood.

Richard Hinds had not seen his cousin since they were children and then it was only on high days and holidays, as he walked away from the Neptune, he looked around trying to identify the man who had been charged with the task of securing him a place to live.

'Do you know your cousin well.' Asked Martin Saurin.

'Not really the last time we met he was a mere twelve years old and I was a child of seven, so that is some twenty years ago.'

'How on earth did you arrange for him to help finding a house?'

'We corresponded regularly over the last two years, which is how long I have been planning to change my life and come to the colonies.' Just as he finished speaking a figure emerged from the myriad of workers carrying and fetching and approached them.

'Are you Richard Hinds?' His voice was strong and full of confidence.

'Yes, is it Simon?' The two men initially held out a hand to shake but then embraced as only men meeting for the first time for many years do. Adele looked from one to the other, there was a marked resemblance although a different shade to their hair the firm jawline and blue eyes matched.

'I thought it was a good guess, you're one of the very few with a cleanly shaved chin and only a surgeon would have that after such a journey.' Smiling he turned to look at the Saurin family. 'And pray tell who are these fine-looking people?' Richard paused for a moment, Simon would not have expected anyone other than himself.

'May I present Mr Saurin, his daughter Adele and his son Francois, they have agreed to assist me in setting up a practice here, Mr Saurin is an apothecary.' Simon looked a little bemused, his cousin had arrived with a family, not his but a family non the less.

'Are you all to share the property?'

'Yes, is what you have for us large enough or do I need to make alternative arrangements?' Simon looked at the four eager looking individuals before him.

'I am sure that there is plenty of room for you all providing you are not expecting a palace because here we live a relatively modest existence compared with that of England.' Richard could see a little concern appear on his cousin's face,

'After the voyage we have just completed we would be grateful for firm ground and a little space of our own nothing more.' There was a little relief in Simon's voice when he asked where their baggage was.

'It is over there.' Richard pointed to his trunk together with various items laying beside it Saurin's possessions were neatly arranged, including his precious seeds.

'Good, wait here for a moment and I will fetch the wagon so that we can get away from this stench as quickly as possible. As Simon walked away Martin asked what Simon was. Was he a surgeon like Richard or was he a planter?

'He is a merchant and some would call him a trader. He performs various duties mainly buying and selling, some of the goods onboard the Neptune are probably his.'

'Does he have a family?' It was Adele who asked.

'Yes, from his letters he is married and has two children, a boy, Joseph and a girl by the name of Elizabeth, but enough questions let's prepare our belongings and ready ourselves to move.

Simon returned with a wagon that seemed too big for their possessions. Richard looked quizzically at Simon,

'It may seem a little large but I had no idea of how much you were bringing with you so I erred on the side of caution.'

The four men quickly loaded the wagon and Martin, Adele with Francois climbed onto the back with their baggage. As they moved slowly away from the dockside, they could see houses in shapes not too unfamiliar to them but they were on a smaller scale and very much alike. The timber frames and the faded plaster could have been seen in many Cambridgeshire villages, the warehouses of the quayside disappeared as they turned into what seemed to be a main street. There were some shops but not many, their goods were on display outside and people were busily bargaining for what was on offer.

'Tell me about the house you have secured for me?'

'Well, you are fortunate, a member of your profession had decided to return to England following some tragic events of which I will tell you about later. He has arranged the house in such a way that he could deal with whatever the people were suffering from. There are in total ten rooms which should be ample for you and your party, if you require any further space there are two outhouses which can be adapted to your needs.' Richard leaned back a little with a sense of arrival he then asked about the people and if they were accustomed to consulting a surgeon or did they prefer to speak to a physician.

'That really should not worry you as I seem to remember that in one of your letters you said that you had studied to become a physician.'

'Yes, I have but I still refer to myself as a surgeon although I combine the two.'

'You are too modest you should let them know you are a physician and be proud of it.'

'You may be right and I will take heed of what I find out in the coming days.'

The wagon came to a halt in front of a long building, like those they had seen on their way, it was timber framed and had two stories. The windows were small and evenly spaced, looking at the main door Richard could see that it was sturdy and well made. The roof seemed to be tiled but not in the conventional sense that he had been use to in England,

'What is the roof made of?' Simon looked up at the roof.

'Oh, you are not use to seeing wooden tiles are you. It is a common practice in the colony to use wood as masons and brick makers are not in abundance, what we do have is carpenters who are fully employed on construction and repair of houses, although as we speak there are more houses being constructed in brick however that comes at a high cost and I am afraid that you would not be in a position to afford such a grand house.

On entering the house Richard found himself in a hall which had various pieces of furniture against the walls. He could see a table with three chairs and a bench neatly stored to one side. In what Richard thought was the main room of the house he found a bed with curtains and valances, he could see some chests, presumably for storage of linen,

'There is enough furniture to satisfy any family, why so much and how much is it going to cost me?' Simon walked towards the window and looked out,

'This place has problems that would normally be experienced in somewhere twice its size. The owner of this house was one of the many unfortunates who suffered greatly.'

'Please tell what became of him.'

'As I have told you the previous occupant was, like you a surgeon. He cared for a great many of the folk hereabouts. His family consisted of him, a wife and two children, girls, both of a tender age. The youngest, a sweet thing, left her mother's side by the river and fell from the bank, she could not swim and within a few moments had drowned. The mother and father were distraught and it took them some time to recover from their misery.'

'A sad tale, I can see no sign of anyone living here so what became of them?'

'Their fate was more than one man could tolerate. It was three months ago that the mother and daughter were taken with malaria and although the surgeon tried everything, he could he could not save them. He was smitten with the same disease but recovered only to lose his mind when he eventually regained his strength.'

'This is something I do not wish to experience, this malaria is it common in this place?

'Like many other illnesses that we suffer from it takes its toll. Our numbers are never stable, people die then they are replaced with the arrival of the next ship.'

'What happened to the father?'

'He could not face life in this town it held too many tortuous memories for him to bear, his decision was to return to England where he had family. He had no wish to take anything from the house so he put it up for sale and included all furniture and accessories.' Richard looked around the room and tried to imagine the anguish the man must have gone through.

'So, is all that we see included with the property?'

'Yes, you will see that the kitchen has a full range of wares, there are three beds, which alas is one less than you require. There are four servants whose time has also been purchased, I will introduce you to them shortly.'

Behind Richard, Martin, his son and daughter listened intently, they heard the story and a shiver ran down Adele's spine, the thought of sleeping in a house with such bad memories did not fill her with joy.

'Wait here and I will fetch the servants.' Simon left Richard and the Saurin family and disappeared through a door, which from the smell could only be the kitchen. Richard could see the uncertainty in Adele's face.

'Come Adele let's see what other rooms there are.' He led the way into a room which had a large table and upon it he could see a series of bottles and jars next to which was a rather large pestle and mortar. Shelves lined the walls and on them were books and papers, opening the first book he could see a list of names together with ailments and the treatment given. He placed the book back from where he had found it,

'This is the room in which people would be seen and treatment given.' Simon's voice called from the hall,

'Richard, I have the servants for you to meet.' Richard moved passed Adele and as he did, he felt her closeness and again realised that there was something about her that he could not live without. There were four servants, one female and three men, their state of dress was clean and tidy the woman's bonnet shone brightly in the light that fell across the hall. The men were in familiar clothing, breeches tied at the knee, clean blouses beneath what looked like woollen jackets their heads were bare but, in their hand's, they held their woollen caps. Simon continued,

'This is Margaret, she is the most important person in the house, the cook, I know of no one else who can conjure up a meal from next to nothing and make it flavoursome and hearty.' He then went on to the first of the men. 'This is John, he will care for your horses, ensuring that they are fed and groomed. This is Ian who is the best man to have in any garden. He will provide you with the best of what can be grown to eat and finally this is Nathan, who will help to keep the house from falling to pieces, he is a carpenter by trade but can turn his hand to most things.' Richard stepped forward,

'I am Richard Hinds and like your previous master I am a surgeon and as such I require a high standard of cleanliness in all areas of the house. He turned to Martin Saurin, 'This is Mr Saurin, who is an apothecary, he will be assisting me to carry out treatment and care for all those who need my services and this is his daughter Mistress Adele, who will be your first point of contact if and when you need to discuss any matter regarding your duties and finally this is Mr Saurin's son, Francois, who will be assisting his father. We will have a great deal to do before we can rest.' He turned to Margaret,

'Please take Mistress Adele and show her the remainder of the house and Ian please show Mr Saurin the garden and any land that surrounds the house.' At this point Simon entered the conversation.

'I need to explain that there is a two-acre plot that runs adjacent to the house which I believe is large enough to grow any medicinal plants you may require and that two horses also are included with the property.' Richard stopped for a moment, this house would cost a great deal and he did not know if he could afford to purchase such a property.

'Simon, before we go any further can I speak privately?' Simon looked a little curious,

'Certainly, John, can you show Master Francois the stables and the horses?' John nodded then asked Francois to follow him. 'Now Richard if we go in here, we may be able to speak openly.' He opened the door to the room that contained the surgeon's paraphernalia. As Richard closed the door, he looked at his cousin,

'This is all well and good.' He gestured with a sweep of his arm, 'But what is the cost of this house. It is no doubt the sort of property that I need to establish myself but the expense may be hard to cover and as for an outright purchase I am sorry to say my finances may not cover such a transaction.' Simon had anticipated this, he took a breath,

'Richard, I am aware that you will need all the money you have to get yourself established and therefore my proposal is that for the short term you rent the house from me until you find yourself in a position to buy. I was very fortunate to acquire this house at a price that would normally not be within my resources but due to the circumstances the price was very reasonable. So, we can agree a rental amount, which I am sure you will find acceptable and then start your new life in Jamestown.' Richard knew he had a lot to learn about his new surroundings and the advice of his cousin would be most helpful.

'Thank you for your invaluable assistance, there is so much I need to understand about the community here, where and how I will get my name known I don't know.'

'Have no fear on that score, your presence is known and has been since the departure of your predecessor, I have made sure of that. There will be many a man or woman seeking you out in the coming days, if not hours so prepare yourself for a busy time.'

'I will need your help and that of those in this house, there is a language used hereabouts that I know nothing of and as for payment, are those here trustworthy, is credit given?' Richard's hand went to his brow, there was so much to find out. Simon could see that the situation that had dawned on his cousin and the size of the task ahead of him was becoming clearer.

'For the rest of this day I suggest that you and Martin familiarize yourselves with the house and its surroundings and I shall return in the morning with my wife and then we can make a start on getting you to a position where you can ply your profession amongst the good people of Jamestown and its surrounds.'

'I cannot thank you enough for what you have already done for me and I look forward to meeting your wife and family.' The two cousins shook hands and Simon made his way out of the house. Martin Saurin was feeling a little unsure of how he would best fit into the business that Richard had in mind but first he needed to make sure his children were settled in. It was Francois who came to him first,

'Father there are only three rooms with beds and two of those are small and if you and Adele are to take the two smallest and Mr Hinds the largest, where am I to sleep?'

'There may be outbuildings where you could sleep, we shall ask John failing that there is a settle in the hall and I am sure that after the conditions we have had to suffer during the past eight weeks anywhere with a soft mattress and a warm blanket would be paradise.' Francois was not pleased with the answer his father gave, he knew that Adele would take priority over him and that he would have to put up with any discomfort that may exist in the house. 'If you can put up with that for tonight, I am sure that tomorrow we will be able to arrange something a little better for you.' Francois knew that he would have to do a lot of persuading before he could rest in a bed and get a decent night's sleep.

After they had seen enough for the time being Richard found the cook in the kitchen,

'Can you prepare something for us to eat Margaret?' The portly cook wiped her hands,

'Yes, sir. We have meat and some bread but it may not be what you are used to, the way things are made here are not the same as in England.'

'I am sure that whatever is set before us will be welcome, and do you have something to drink?'

'Yes, we have ale and cider, I would not suggest the water it may do you more harm than good. I will have a full table in an hours' time and will call when it is ready.' This was music to Richards ears after the state of the food on the ship he looked forward to whatever was set before him.

Adele had been shown most of the house by Margaret and was impressed by what she saw. It was a well-kept dwelling with enough space for them to live comfortably. It was in a good state of repair, the rooms were small but gave enough light and space to carry out what was needed. She had earmarked a room for herself and could not wait to gain some privacy even though it would not be enough for her liking.

Following their meal of meat and bread they talked of the day and how they had been so fortunate to have Simon to help them. As the darkness fell, they went to their beds to sleep as they had not done in many weeks.

Chapter 23

Norris waited anxiously for someone from the Spilsby plantation to meet him, it would be a tricky situation explaining that Lord David had died. The livestock had been unloaded and they were now safely in their respective pens. He saw a sturdy looking individual making his way towards him and from the way he was looking from the stock and then to him he thought that this may be the man he needs to speak to.

'Are you from the Spilsby estate in England?' His voice matched his stance it was one that told all who met him that he stood no nonsense.

'Yes, I am Norris.'

'Well, go and tell your master that I have arrived to show him and the livestock to the plantation.'

'And pray tell what is your name?' The man's face formed a scowl, he was not used to such questions as all on the plantation knew him well.

'My name is Hughes and you will call me sir, is that understood?'

'Err, yes Mr Hughes, sorry I mean sir.'

'Well, where is your master he should be waiting here.' Norris took the bull by the horns.

'There has been a tragic accident onboard the Neptune and I am afraid to tell you that our master died.' This took the wind out of Hughes' sails.

'Dead, you mean he is dead?'

'Yes, he died at sea, he fell overboard and drowned.'

'Is there a body?' Norris could see that Hughes was totally taken aback by the news.

'A body was not recovered from the ocean, it was taken under and lost.'

'I was told that Lord David was travelling with a servant, where is he?' It was at that moment that Whitmore appeared.

'Here he is, he has had to give his account of the tragedy to the governor.' Whitmore came close to Norris and wiped his brow,

'Is there anywhere I can get a drink?' Hughes then turned on Whitmore with a vicious tongue,

'Drink, you have no time to drink.' Whitmore looked from Hughes to Norris who spoke,

'This is Mr Hughes, who you will refer to as sir, he is from the plantation and I have informed him of the accident.'

'That is correct, now get your master's possessions together and prepare to leave. You see that cart over there.' He pointed at a well-made cart with what appeared to be a black man holding the reins,

'Yes, I see it.'

'Everything is to be loaded onto it and as soon as all has been accounted for, we will leave for the plantation. Norris you will drive the livestock and anything that can be fitted onto the cart will be, be quick about it I need to get this news back to the main house as soon as possible.' As they tried to get everything ready to move Whitmore asked Norris,

'Has he told you anything about what we are to do other than get things ready to move?' Norris shook his head,

'No, nothing and I don't think he is the sort of man to talk to I have a feeling he is used to people just listening and obeying so be about your task and try not to get on the wrong side of Mr Hughes.

Once everything was loaded Hughes mounted his horse and instructed the driver to pull away. Whitmore ran alongside Hughes' horse,

'Can we not ride in the cart?' It was then that Whitmore felt the sting of Hughes' riding crop as it flashed down and struck him on the back of his neck.

'You will walk and care for the animals, I do not want to see any of the beasts stray, is that clear?' Whitmore felt his neck, there was no blood but there would be a bruise later.

'Yes sir.' He said subserviently and walked with Norris and together they tried to control the animals. Whitmore glanced back at the Neptune, he had hoped that after his master's death he would be in a better position but that was not to be, a servant he started and a servant he will end.

*

Edward Carrick, together with the two crewmen returned to the ship. He had more to do before he would be in a position to hand over the vessel. In his cabin he took out the log and entered the details of their arrival and that of his meeting with the Governor. He would need to contact the agent dealing with the next voyage of the Neptune. He knew the person well and that things could move quickly once he had ensured that all was well aboard. It took him a little over two hours before he had everything in order. He would spend the night onboard then in the morning would take his time in handing over the ship, he would then be free to see about his own business. Before completing his various tasks, he went on deck and looked at the scene around the ship. He could see the parson, Geoffrey Peters and watched him, as he went about his business. Carrick saw that the parson appeared to be having some difficulty in making himself understood by various individuals and it wasn't until the bosun joined him that things started to become clearer.

'Just what are you after.' The bosun asked the confused parson.

'I cannot get through to these people that I am a parson and looking for the church. They keep asking 'what church?' How many churches are there in this town, I thought there could only be one in a place such as this.'

'Parson there are many that have left not only England, but many other places and they have brought with them their god and their church. If I am right, you are looking for the Church of England, or perhaps you would call it 'The Anglican Church.' The parson nodded,

'That is exactly what I am looking for, can you assist me in finding it?' The bosun was aware of where the church was and slowly explained to the parson the best route to take.

'I have not been here for nearly eight months so things could have changed. You will probably find the current minister in the small house sitting not too far from the church. I will warn you now that the church is possibly not the size and style that you are used to so prepare yourself for something a little less grand than those churches of England.'

'Do I need to pass through the quayside before I reach the road on which the church is located?'

'As I said that is the quickest way. You may come across sights you have not seen before but that is something you will have to get used to.' The parson thanked him and made his way along the side of the quay. He had been walking for only a few minutes when turning alongside a warehouse he came into a square where there was a great deal of activity which was centred around a group of men looking at a crowd of what seemed to be a number of black men and women. When he looked closer, he could see several white men inspecting the physical state of those who had been lined up. Geoffrey Peters believed in the right of all men to be free but he was realistic enough to know that freedom come in various forms but what he was witnessing appeared to be a market for human beings.

'Excuse me, could you tell me what is happening here?' He asked one of the men standing watching as the line of black men moved slowly forward.

'These are for sale and nobody wants damaged merchandise.'

'What do you mean 'for sale?'

'These,' he pointed to the line of wavering black bodies. 'Are to be sold, there were some whites earlier on but they have gone, so if you were after one you are too late.' Horrified Geoffrey staggard back, he could not believe what he was seeing.

'Who buys these poor creatures?'

'They are for work in the tobacco fields.'

'But there are men and women here.'

'You are right and if the buyers are lucky then the women could produce offspring and any child would become his property as well.'

It was all too much for the parson to comprehend, he turned back onto the path he was taking to the church and quickened his pace. He could see a tower looming up before him and then the church itself became clear. The tower was of brick and stood over forty feet in height and was well constructed, most impressive he thought as he gazed up at the tower. Geoffery went to the door of what he assumed was the house of the incumbent minister. The door opened revealing a rather thin woman who looked Geoffery up and down,

'Yes, and who are you and what do you want.' This was not the greeting that Geoffery had expected.

'I am Parson Geoffery Peters and I think I am expected although a little late in arriving.'

'You had better come in.' The woman's tone did not put him at ease as he picked up his bag and followed her into the hall of the house. 'Reverand Michael is not at home at this moment but he is due back within the hour so you had better be seated.' He dropped his bag and then sat down his body was tired and his mind was in a whirl. He had thought that what he had experienced on the ship was enough to test his strength and belief but what he had seen and heard as he had made his way to the church had shocked and frightened him.

'Have you eaten?' The woman's voice brought him back to the present.

'No, not since yesterday.'

'So, you would like something no doubt?'

'If you have anything to spare, I would be more than grateful.' The woman disappeared, she returned moments later with a plate on which he could see some type of bread alongside what looked like meat, possibly beef. She held the plate out to him,

'This is all I have at this time, perhaps later you will eat with the Reverand.' Geoffery took the bread and bit into it, it tasted like manner he thought, after the taste of salt in everything on the ship, he enjoyed something fresh and clean in flavour.

'Were you expecting me?' He asked after wiping his mouth.

'I was aware that a new parson was onboard the Neptune and we had word that it was anchored in the bay so yes, we did expect you, any questions you have would be better presented to the Reverand not me. He and his wife will be returning shortly the one thing I do know is that they expected you to stay overnight before going to your parish so if you will follow me, I will show you the room I have prepared.' Geoffrey picked up his bag and obediently followed the housekeeper. It was over the hour until the Reverend Michael Hood and his wife Anna returned from their visits, they had been to see several of those who had children to christen and two who were arranging weddings for their eldest children. They brought with them a blast of fresh air as they opened the door.

'Reverand, you have a visitor.' Was the cry from the housekeeper.

'And who can that be Mrs Chandler?' He hung his coat up and then took his wife's and placed it on the hook next to his.

'It is Mr Peters, the new parson.' Geoffrey Peters rose from his chair and made ready to greet the Hoods. In Geoffrey's eyes they appeared a pair of healthy and robust individuals. Michael Hood approached him, hand outstretched, Geoffrey took it and shook it firmly.

'So good to make your acquaintance.' He smiled, he felt Michael's grip which surprised him in its strength.

'Your Christian name is?'

'Oh, I'm sorry, I am Geoffrey, Geoffrey Peters.'

'Well, I am Michael and this is my wife Anna, welcome to our world which you no doubt have found confusing in the short time you have been here.'

'Yes, very confusing.'

'I am afraid that the confusion will not become clearer in fact it will leave you mystified but that can wait until later, Mrs Chandler when can we eat? We have been on our travels all day and are in need of sustenance.'

'Your meal will be ready in an hour which will give you and your lady time to freshen up.'

'Good, good, Geoffrey perhaps you would like a glass of something while you wait?'

'That would be gratefully received, a glass of beer or cider would be most welcome.' Mrs Chandler left the room in a hurried fashion muttering something which only she could understand.

As they sat around the main table in the hall of the house Michael Hood began to explain to Geoffrey the situation that had created a vacancy in the area. He told him of the previous Clergyman who was very politically minded and an extremely good orator who had left to take up a position with the Assembly where he will, as an excellent speaker together with his knowledge of the land and peoples, serve us well.

'And what of his parish, who will introduce me to his parishioners?'

'Have no fear, I shall take you to your church and it is there that you will meet the members of the Vestry.'

'What is that?' Geoffrey asked.

'The vestry is something like a parish council, it is made up of laymen who are the more prominent members of the community so you will need to get them on your side in whatever venture you may take up.'

'And the church?'

'Ah, the church, it is in a good state of repair, it may not be the size of those you left behind in England but it is well attended.'

'How will I support myself, I have no idea of how the church is funded and by who.' Michael Hood could see the uncertainty in Geoffrey's eyes, he had to build the young man's confidence up before he took him to his new parish.

'You will be supported by the parish, money will be given through the county court to the Vestry and they will provide you with 200 acres of land, a house and one or two cows with possibly a pig or two. It will also pay you the princely sum of sixteen thousand pounds of tobacco per annum as well as £1 for every wedding and funeral. Whatever you can

337

make from the land to improve your life is up to you. If you manage things well you may be able to live not well but comfortably.' Everything was spinning around in Geoffrey's head, he was not a farmer and had no idea of how to cultivate tobacco but if that was what god had ordained for him, he would rise to the challenge.

'I did see something that distressed me as I walked from the quayside.'

'Oh yes, and what was that?'

'It was many men, black men being made ready to be sold and I was told that several white men had been offered for sale before them. Is this something that the church condones?' Michael looked at his wife they both knew that this was an area that many a churchman had to come to terms with.

'You must understand that in this land there is a great need for labour, without it the colony would cease to exist. It has been necessary to bring to the colony extra hands to deal with the growing of not only tobacco but other crops and to this end there have been many indentured servants that have been shipped from England but that was not enough and at this present time there is a need for many so when the Portuguese brought negroes from the coast of Africa to work for them, those in the colonies, especially those reliant on large crops, began to use black labour and today there is a growing number of them in Virginia and other parts of the colony.

'On the ship there were indentured servants who I was told would be working in the fields, so are the black men indentured?'

'It is a very delicate situation, many see the black man as something that was born to serve and as such are looked upon in the same way as cattle, sheep, pigs or anything else that is required to ensure a good crop is achieved.'

'But are they not freed once they have served their time?'

'You must realise that a servant is different to a slave and that is what the black man is, a slave, unlike the white indentured servants who can achieve freedom once they have served their time.'

'But what I don't understand is that they are both god's creatures and should they not be treated as equals?'

'Is an eagle treated the same as a rabbit, is a cow treated the same way as fish in the sea? We all have our place on this earth we are born into a life that may not be to our liking but one that we must live. It is a common debate that goes on between many, however as we speak the situation is, as I have explained, maybe in years to come things will alter and the lives of these wretches will change for the better. Now eat and drink, we have a hard day tomorrow and we will need our wits about us.'

Chapter 24

Adele awoke and for a moment had no idea where she was. Her night had been one of peace and silence something that she had not experienced for many weeks, there was no more creaking of the ship's hull, no more constant chattering of passengers. It was a peace that she welcomed to her heart. On a small table there was a bowl together with a jug of water, she scooped up handfuls and splashed them onto her face, the relief was beyond words. Her day began with Margaret the cook who was busy in the kitchen preparing something to eat, she watched as the woman gathered together what appeared to be some cereal. Adele could see oats and some beans being added to a sort of porridge which was warm and smelt a little odd but Adele was willing to try anything as long as it was not salted meat or fish. She sat on a stool and watched the cook mixing together a thick mass, she hoped it tasted better than it looked, she would soon find out. Richard and Martin met in the hall they were preparing themselves for a busy day and felt in need of something to set them off. As they sat Margaret brought a large bowl to the table and as she did Francois appeared a little sleepy eyed, he did not have a good night's sleep like the other members of his family. His bed had been the settle which was solid oak, the straw mattress only softened the hard surface a little but it was better than the ship.

As promised Simon arrived at the house together with his wife,

'Good morning.' Simon's greeting was full of energy which did not sit well with Francois. 'There are many things we need to discuss and I have a proposition for your son.' His look settled on Francois who woke up to the sound of his name, 'but first I think some basic information you might find useful.' The faces of those around the table looked up with anticipation. You will find that money is not as it is in England, the coinage varies a great deal, some transactions are made in Spanish gold coin others in English pounds but most are made in pounds of tobacco together with promissory notes. So, Richard when you are offered payment in tobacco be sure you know it's worth and Adele when you purchase something whether it be food or drink, ask Margaret for advice, don't be afraid to ask and that means all of you. There is a common currency which is Jettons that are used for trade, I will explain those in more detail later.' They sat and talked of many things ranging from the price of land to the cost of corn. Francois listened patiently remembering what Simon had said when he first arrived,

'And now to your son.' He looked from Martin to Francois. 'Can you read?' Francois was a little taken aback,

'Yes, I can read well.' At this point his father chipped in,

'He reads English, French and Latin.' Simon's response was,

'Very good, but what about figures, are you capable of keeping a tally of prices and sales?' With a certain air of confidence Francois answered,

'Yes, of course I can, my father has taught me well.' Simon looked pleased.

'In that case I would like to offer you a position which could be classed as an apprenticeship for a period of let us say for a length of time to be determined once you have seen what is required of you. My thoughts are that you would live with my family and work closely with me. This would give more space to your father and sister and you would receive board and lodging with a small wage.' For Francois this was the answer to his dream he looked eagerly at his father who, after pausing, said that he would be delighted if such an arrangement could be made. Simon continued,

'There is the matter of 'Headright.' This was something new to Richard and Martin.

'Headright is a grant of fifty acres to any person who pays their way to Virginia, that is any man woman or child, so you will be able to claim one hundred and fifty acres and Richard you too can claim fifty acres. There is a process to go through which I will help you with.'

*

Richard, Martin and his family sat with looks of a certain amount of disbelief on their faces, it all seemed too good to be true. 'I must warn you of the pitfalls you may encounter which may place a dampener on your initial surprise on what is available to you. There are many diseases that afflict the community, they range from the pox to poisoning by bad food and water. We have had some incidents were the Indians have killed some who have tried to subjugate them, they are not slaves or servants and we trade with them. There is a great deal that can be learnt from their use of all that grows in this new world so be patient if and when you deal with them.

It was a different story for Edward Carrick, he had finalised all that needed to be done for the handover of the Neptune, he had received all the monies that were due to him, which enabled him to pay off the crew, his own payment was substantial not only was he paid for getting the ship safely to harbour but he also received a percentage of the worth of the cargo. He would buy a horse and make his way to his land. He had been fortunate in that the land grants that had come his way were of good quality and not a problem with the native Indians. He had employed good men and together with a series of indentured servants they had turned the land into a profitable venture. What caused him concern was the fluctuating price of tobacco and the idea of changing his crop still lingered in his mind. The weight of his possessions surprised him, he needed more than a horse to get everything to his house. There was a reliable horse trader, which was a rare thing, that he knew would strike him a good bargain so he made his way through the various groups of bodies milling around the waterfront to the stables where he hoped to buy a horse and a mule or maybe even a small cart. A deal was completed in short time, money changed hands and Carrick could now leave the town for his own land.

The small cart he had purchased was slower than if he had been on horseback but it meant he could safely transport his possessions to his home. He thought to himself that this may be the last time he would be leaving a ship for a permanent life on shore. His land was in Henrico County, it was nine hundred and eighty acres of productive soil which he had purchased in stages, some from the government, some from his earnings and some from those who had returned to England. The Verina Parish, where his house was sighted, had all he wanted at the time. He had become a member of the vestry and now that he would be able to attend all the meetings, he would try to advance his ambition of becoming involved in the political hierarchy of the colony. As the cart wound its way through the rutted lanes, he started to formulate a path that would take him to the heights he wanted to reach. His first step would be to make himself a useful and respected member of the parish then he would put himself forward as a candidate for Justice of the Peace. When, not if, he reached that stage he would seek election to the House of Burgesses. This would take persuasion and cudgelling of his fellow plantation owners but again his land holdings and knowledge of what was happening on both sides of the ocean would stand him in good stead. He would also need luck and a great deal of it.

It took longer than he imagined to reach his home, he had no option but to seek shelter for the night at the plantation of a distant neighbour. He was welcomed with open arms as most wanted any news they could get regarding the situation in England. Edward spent a pleasant night and refreshed set out on the last part of his journey home. As he crossed the boundary of his land he had a sense of achievement, he had spent a large part of his life at sea and now he hoped to start a life that would give him success and a certain amount of wealth. As he drove the cart closer to his house, he could see that it had been well maintained, the clapperboard frontage was clean and in a good state, the land surrounding it had various plants growing and he could see a plot with several pigs grunting and burrowing their snouts into the soil. Milk cows were evident which pleased him, it would mean milk, cream and butter and it would be fresh for once. As he brought the cart to a standstill he was met by his overseer and his wife. They had news of his stop over and were ready for him.

'Welcome home, captain.' It seemed strange to be called captain on land but if that was how they saw him then he would let it continue.

'Thank you.' The couple moved towards the cart. 'Alan, I need your help in getting everything unloaded.' His overseer moved to the rear of the cart and lowered the tail board.

'I brought back the two servants from the ship and they have been quartered with the others.'

'Do they look as if I have spent my money well?' He looked enquiringly at his trusted employee.

'On first inspection they seem healthy enough but we shall have to see how they take to our way of life.' He turned to his wife. 'Woman, go and prepare something for the captain to eat and drink.' It was not an order just a request, the woman went through the open door and made her way to the kitchen.

As they finished carrying the goods into the house there conversation was non-stop, there was so much Alan had to tell the captain and at one stage Carrick halted him in mid-sentence,

'You will run out of breath if you keep on, so hold your breath and eat with me tonight when you can take your time and give me the full details of how the land has performed.' Alan was grateful, he may well have missed something crucial if he had carried on the way he did.

That evening when the meal was over Edward Carrick sat in a comfortable chair and sipped a glass of good brandy, Alan had given him a good account of what had been happening not only on his own property but news of other plantations in the area. What had interested him most was the debt transactions that had taken place. Carrick was still in the market for more land and although he would claim another hundred acres under the headright system for the two men he had brought to the colony, he needed more and if he could acquire land from those who could not pay their debts then so be it. The matter of servants and slaves also interested him, it seemed as if the number of black African slaves was increasing and he would need to be alert to what was available. He called out to Alan, who was moving some of the captain's new possessions,

'Yes, captain.'

'Alan, what of the Indians, have there been many incursions?' Alan came into the room wiping his hands.

'There have been no serious confrontations in the parish but there has been some talk of taking more land, which I am sure will not be welcomed by the tribes and there have been those that want to rid the land of all Indians, which will not end well, I think.' Edward mulled over what Alan had said, there were those who, like him wanted more land and would, unlike him go to any lengths to gain it.

'Have you heard anything regarding the Vestry?'

'There has been word that they await your return for news of what is happening on the other side of the ocean. There is also talk of a new Justice being appointed, would that be you captain?' This made Edward put down his glass and sit up,

'Tell me more.'

'There is not much more to tell, I believe that you will receive a visit from the Vestry which may be to your benefit.'

'And where did you hear this?'

'It was in the ordinary when sipping a glass of cider with those from other plantations after church. I don't think it was idle gossip but time will tell.'

'That is very interesting and I shall wait with baited breath to see if the rumours you hear lead to anything.' Alan could see that the captain was getting tired, 'your bed is ready and it has been warmed.'

'Thank you, Alan.' He stretched, took the last sip of brandy and made his way to his chamber.

Chapter 25

Alec had settled everything he could, the goods they had brought from England had been loaded on to a wagon and they were ready to leave. The excitement rose in William's chest as they left the quayside behind.

'Get used to the hardness of the seat, you will be sitting on it for some time.' William could feel the slats of the seat against his buttocks, he tried to get in the most comfortable position without getting in the way. Robert was to travel in the back of the cart making sure that the more treasured items did not get damaged. Jamestown thinned out and William could see countryside on both sides of the road. It was in some ways not that much different from England. There were open spaces where he could see various crops being grown but not the large expanse of tobacco he had expected.

'Where exactly are we heading for?' Williams questions started again and Alec looked round at Robert, smiled and shrugged his shoulders.

'Our first port of call will be to the Baxter Plantation where we will hopefully spend the night.

The Baxter family are well known to us and it is their precious cargo that Robert is taking great care of.'

'What of the land, is it much the same as this?'

'You will see, there are many rivers and streams running through this area and the woodlands can stretch for miles.'

'Will we see Indians?'

'It is almost a certainty that some will approach us mainly out of curiosity and hopefully they will not create any trouble for us.'

William stopped his questions and just looked at the countryside surrounding them. He had seen people milling around the quayside and had listened to the voices that seemed to come from many countries not only England. He had seen faces with features he had not seen before and in some cases felt a little intimidated by the way he was stared at. There was so much to see and learn, he asked himself what the morrow would bring.

Alec brought the cart to a halt just as the sun was passing its highest point.

'We need a drink and something to eat and to get off this seat for a moment.' The three travellers got down from the cart, Robert had a bundle which he opened to reveal some bread and cheese together with several slices of meat. They sat and started to eat, the bread was not what William expected its taste differed from what he was use to but he managed to force it down. Alec pulled a flagon from under the seat of the cart and pulled the cork from its neck,

'Good cider and fine cheese this should see us through until we reach the Baxter's house.' The October air was kind to them, there was no rain in the air and the ground was dry.

'Well young William what do you think of your new world?'

'I think it holds many interesting prospects for me and it has plenty of mysteries for me to solve.'

'What mysteries are they?'

'Oh, where shall I be laying my head in days to come, who shall I meet, what will they be like and will I be able to start a new life for myself in this land.'

As they approached the Baxter house Alec looked around and he saw Robert making sure that everything was in order in the back of the cart,

'Is all well?' He asked. Robert was tugging on the ropes that held everything together.

'Yes, it seems to have travelled safely. What do you think Baxter will make of his new possession?'

'I am sure that he will think he is cock of the hoop and will be unbearable when he tells all of his recent acquisition.'

William saw the main door of the house open and from it came a man of about forty years, his build was that of somebody who had worked hard all his life, broad in the beam with a firm jaw. When Alec saw Baxter, he was a little surprised, Baxter had never been one for holding back when it came to his precious furnishings,

'Hello, I have something that you will be telling all about for years to come.' Again, Alec was surprised at Baxter's lack of excitement,

'Alec, I need to speak to you, please get down and come into the house.' A worried look spread across Baxter's face, Alec climbed down from the cart and followed Baxter into the house. As they reached the hall Baxter turned to face Alec.

'There is bad news from your family.' Baxter's words hit Alec like a kick from a mule.

'What news, tell me, what has happened?' Baxter tried to keep his eyes fixed on Alec as he told him of what had happened.

'Your wife's father passed away.'

'How, when, why?' Alec felt a shiver run down his spine, how was his wife and children and had her brother been with her. He needed to get to the plantation.

'Have you a horse I could borrow?' Baxter laid a hand on Alec's shoulder,

'It is getting late and you would be foolish to try to get to your home in the dark, why don't you rest here for the night and leave at first light, Robert and the young man can follow on later.' Alec's mind raced, his wife was a strong and determined woman but she was very close to her father and it would have affected her a great deal. He knew that Baxter was talking sense but his heart fought with his head until Robert, who had heard the conversation said that Baxter was right, there was no point in risking an accident in the dark or being attacked on his way to the plantation, which was not unheard of. Alec looked at his hands, they were trembling, he managed to calm down and agreed to stay the night.

The Baxter family stood and watched as the servants, guided by Robert, took hold of the long case clock that had travelled safely across the ocean. There were murmurs of wonderment as the clock was raised and placed in a position in the hall where it could be admired by all visitors and friends. Robert attached

355

the pendulum, as he had been shown in London, and set the clock in motion.

Robert explained to William what had happened and that Alec would go on ahead and they would follow. The night seemed to last forever as Alec tossed and turned, his thoughts were of his family, what would his wife be doing, how would she be managing? He slept a little but woke as the sun was appearing on the horizon. He quickly dressed and made his way to the stable. Baxter was in his nightshirt, standing at the stable door.

'She is a fine mare and will get you home at a good pace, treat her kindly and she will not let you down.' Alec thanked Baxter then climbed onto the horse's saddle and with a wave he turned the mare's head in the direction of his home and rode steadily from the Baxter's house.

Robert and William met in the hall,

'When are we to leave?' William asked.

'We shall break our fast, see that all is well with our load then be on our way.'

'How long will it take us to reach the plantation?'

'We should be there before nightfall, but Alec will be there a lot sooner and William you must understand that when we arrive there may be a feeling of sorrow so be respectful, you understand?'

'Yes, I understand what is expected.'

After getting the cart ready to move Robert sought out Baxter and thanked him for his hospitality. They spoke briefly of the loss of Alec's father-in-law then made their farewells. On the cart Robert tried to explain to William Alec's family.

'Alec's wife is Emma, a fine woman who Alec rescued from fire many years ago. They have two sons, one called Mark and the other Luke. They are younger than you but are fully aware of the running of the plantation. Alec's brother-in-law also lives close by and he will no doubt inherit the plantation from his father. He has only one child, a girl, who was the apple of her grandfather's eye and she will miss him a lot.'

'How will Alec fit in now that his father-in-law has passed?'

'Oh, I think that he and I will resume our roles in the organisation of the plantation. We will be involved in all its aspects, so you will have to keep pace with us if you want to learn anything.' William thought that he was on the verge of something that could be the foundation for the rest of his life. The cart swayed and rolled as they made their way through woods and grassland. The trees were dressed in their autumn finery, reds and golds filled the woodlands in a cascade of colour that William had not seen in England and it filled him with a sense of wonder. Robert passed William a flagon of cider, which he greedily took.

'We will only stop to rest the horse for a short while, we have rivers to cross and miles to cover so try to rest yourself as much as you can, if you feel that the seat is too hard then ride in the back of the cart for a short while.' After drinking from the flagon William climbed into the back of the cart and tried to make himself comfortable. They crossed many streams and at least two large rivers, the fords that they used were a little difficult but with some encouragement their horse managed to get across without losing the cart although at one point William had to get down and pull on the horses reins to help manoeuvre it through the rocky river bed. He was soaked from the waist down, Roberts only reaction was to laugh at Williams sorry state.

The sun was slowly sinking into the horizon as Robert guided the cart on to the lane that led to the Jackson Plantation. William noted that the fields they had passed through had a combination of white and black workers tilling the land he could not see exactly what they were doing but realised that the work they were doing was backbreaking. The tools that they had resembled the hoes that he had used on his father's farm and he knew from experience that after a day in the field bodies would ache and take time to recover. He could see the house, it was a fine-looking building. It had two stories, three chimneys reached up from a tiled roof. The front of the house was covered with clapperboard with windows evenly spaced, it appeared to have a brick base but William couldn't be sure. The land surrounding the house was laid into beds which had a variety of plants growing in them. William tried to identify what was being grown but had difficulty to see from where he was.

'How big is the estate?'

'It's a plantation, not an estate, you will have to adopt the language if you are to succeed here.'

'How big is the plantation?'

'It stretches from river to river and covers over six thousand acres.' William shook his head,

'That's large, too large for me to imagine.'

'You'll get used to it, distance is a thing that confuses most people who still think in terms of English farms and properties.'

As Robert steered the cart into a large yard at the rear of the house William saw several people fetching and carrying. He thought he recognised what looked like a dairy, and then the stables came into sight. They were large and looked as if they could accommodate about ten or twelve beasts. As they reached a point where two servants grasped the horse's reins William thought he heard Alec's voice, then he saw him walking towards them across the yard.

'Any problems?' He shouted.

'No, the journey was reasonable the only thing that suffered was William dragging himself through the river at the ford.'

'Come, get down and I will get you something to drink.' William and Robert lowered themselves with a little care as the cart had not been the most comfortable of things to ride on. 'I will need to deal with the load as soon as possible, but a little refreshment first would be more than welcome.' They followed Alec into the house and into what William thought would be one of the smaller rooms.

'Please sit.' He gestured to the table around which were six chairs, Robert and William gratefully sat and rested their arms on the table.

'How are things with your family.' Robert asked. He could see dark rings had appeared around Alec's eyes.

'It is as you would expect there is a great deal of sadness. My wife and her brother are in the process of arranging for the funeral which is to take place in two days. I have told everyone that we have a new addition to the staff and that he is to be treated as you or I Robert.' The door to the room opened and William watched as a woman in her thirties entered. She was taller than most with her fair hair showing signs of grey, although her face was on the thin side it did not detract from her fine lines and a certain beauty that her sorrow could not hide. She looked at Robert and through her grief smiled.

'I am glad to see your safe return Robert and that you appear well.'

'I am sorry for your loss Emma, your father was a fine man and looked after me well.' Emma remembered when Robert had lost both his wife and child and how he had suffered for some time.

'Yes, he will be missed by all.' She turned and looked at William. 'Is this the young man you have brought from England?'

'Yes, please let me introduce the son of a very good friend of both Alec and I, this is William Brooks who has travelled with us and overcome one or two obstacles on the way.' Emma looked at William, she saw a fine young man with good clear eyes and a fine texture to his skin. 'I am sure that when we have overcome our loss William and I will get to know each other well.' She turned and made her way from the room. Alec watched his wife leave the room then turning to William said;

'I have allocated you a room in which you will sleep and study, you will rise with the sun and work until it sets, are you prepared for that?'

'I am at your service, you have guided me to a new land and I will be eternally grateful to you and Robert, I am sure my mother and father will thank you as well.'

Robert took William by the arm, 'Come with me lad there is something you must do, something I promised your mother you would do.' William was tired and dusty but followed Robert. In a small room William could see a bed and a table, on the table were ink and quill. Robert pulled the chair out from the table and laid some paper out on its top.

'There, you will sit and write to your mother and I shall make sure it is despatched with all haste, so sit and write.' William remembered that he had not been able to complete a letter when they were aboard the Neptune, he thanked Robert and sat down at the table.

William took up the quill and looked at the paper in front of him. As he dipped the quill into the ink, he started to think of the journey he had just completed, the ship and the motion of the sea, the damage to his leg and pain that it caused, the terrible food the water and a taste that would never leave him. He saw the faces of those who he had met and heard their voices and then the face of Adele filled his mind, would he see her again? He really did not know. He then wrote of his experience but leaving out the horrors that had befallen many on the way. As he drew to the end of his letter, he tried to express his hopes and wishes for the future, he wrote that the land that had now become his home held so many opportunities, how the land was good and how everyone had a totally different attitude to those in England. It was a land that could give so much to those who chose to take up the challenge, it was a land that he would grow with and where he would reach out to all that was good and secure a future that he could never have dreamt of in England. 'I promise that I will write each fortnight with news of my life and all that happens to me and those who I have become close to.' He finished the letter, 'from your most loving son William.'

THE END